PRAISE FOR *SUNSET AND JERICHO*

Sam Wiebe is one of the most respected names in crime fiction today and with good reason. *Sunset and Jericho*, the latest entry in the Wakeland series, is a gritty, realistic urban noir that examines the problems so prevalent in cities around the world today. With pacing that doesn't let up, and a shocker of an ending, readers won't be able to put this one down.

—**ROBYN HARDING**, BESTSELLING AUTHOR OF *THE PERFECT FAMILY*

Sunset and Jericho is classic Wakeland: sardonic, cynical and in way over his head. It's also classic Wiebe: a fast-paced page-turner with a sucker punch for an ending. If you're already a fan, you know what to expect. If this is your first foray into Wakeland territory, I envy you.

—**DENNIS HEATON**, SHOWRUNNER OF *MOTIVE*, *THE ORDER*, AND *CALL ME FITZ*

Dave Wakeland is back; battered, shot, soul-sick and heartbroken, and as tenaciously single-minded as ever in the pursuit of evil... *he* might be tired of it all, but his fans will be enthralled. Wiebe is the absolute master of noir with heart. Wakeland had better not be planning to quit, because as far as I'm concerned, when you're tired of Wakeland, you're tired of life.

—**IONA WHISHAW**, BESTSELLING AUTHOR OF THE LANE WINSLOW MYSTERIES

Wiebe has an incredible ability to pull you through the page and into Wakeland's world. You find yourself walking beside the characters, sensing the tension, tightening up at each dangerous turn, and ultimately feeling every gut punch. I think this book is the best in the series, vaulting over an already high bar. It's the sharpest and the darkest. The author has said this may be the final chapter for his PI. Selfishly, I hope not.

—**BRENT BUTT**, STAR AND SHOWRUNNER OF *CORNER GAS*

Sunset and Jericho might be Sam Wiebe's best work. He's not only one of Canada's finest writers but one of the leading mystery and thriller authors working today.

—**STEVE ABERLE,** GREATMYSTERIESANDTHRILLERS.COM

A great balance between the humanistic and hard-boiled.

—**SCOTT MONTGOMERY,** CRIME FICTION COORDINATOR AT BOOKPEOPLE

Wakeland is to Vancouver what Scudder is to New York, and *Hell and Gone* cements Wiebe's place alongside Penny, Barclay, and Atwood.

—**REED FARREL COLEMAN,** *NY TIMES* BESTSELLING AUTHOR OF *SLEEPLESS CITY*

Terminal City's grittiest, most intelligent, most sensitively observed contemporary detective series.

—**CHARLES DEMERS,** AUTHOR OF THE DOCTOR ANNICK BOUDREAU MYSTERY SERIES

Some of the most engrossing material I've read in 2021.

—**BENOÎT LELIÈVRE,** *DEAD END FOLLIES*

Sam Wiebe writes larger than life, and in *Hell and Gone* he takes his PI Dave Wakeland into hell and back. A tense, taut page-turner full of surprises in the dark, dangerous corners of Vancouver.

—**IAN HAMILTON,** AUTHOR OF THE INTERNATIONALLY BESTSELLING AVA LEE SERIES

SUNSET AND JERICHO

SUNSET AND JERICHO

A Wakeland Novel

SAM WIEBE

HARBOUR

Harbour Publishing Co. Ltd.
P.O. Box 219, Madeira Park, BC, VON 2H0
www.harbourpublishing.com

Front cover photograph and background by Sam Wiebe
Edited by Derek Fairbridge
Cover design by Dwayne Dobson
Text design by Carleton Wilson
Printed and bound in Canada
Printed on paper containing 100% post-consumer fibre

 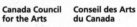

Harbour Publishing acknowledges the support of the Canada Council for the
Arts, the Government of Canada, and the Province of British Columbia through
the BC Arts Council.

LIBRARY AND ARCHIVES CANADA CATALOGUING IN PUBLICATION

Title: Sunset & Jericho / Sam Wiebe.
Other titles: Sunset and Jericho
Names: Wiebe, Sam, author.
Description: "A Wakeland novel".
Identifiers: Canadiana (print) 20220456712 | Canadiana (ebook) 20220456739 |
    ISBN 9781990776236 (softcover) | ISBN 9781990776243 (ebook)
Classification: LCC PS8645.I3236 S86 2023 | DDC C813/.6—dc23

You had such a vision of the street
As the street hardly understands
—T.S. Eliot, "Preludes"

... the very best passage in his life was the one of all the
others he would not have owned to on any account, and
the only one that made him ashamed of himself.
—Charles Dickens, *Hard Times*

ONE

FORTUNATE SON

The view from the mayor's outer office was something. Pearl-coloured clouds had flung down snow all night, piling slim white barriers atop Vancouver's roofs and awnings. A late morning rain was undoing the work, drowning Broadway in a slurry of gunmetal, platinum and ash. On Cambie Street, caution lights pulsed. An accident of some sort. It was February, and the wrong people were dying.

Beside me, Jeff Chen tilted his head back, pinching his nose through the medical mask. My partner suppressed the sneeze, dabbed at his watering eyes.

"You don't have to be here," I told him.

"Right, Dave," Jeff said. "The most powerful woman in the city asks for our help, and I'm gonna trust you to handle it alone. No thanks."

"This isn't a real consultation," I said. "It's box-checking. A way to show folks she's doing all she can. My bet, she won't even be there."

"You don't know that."

"Fifty bucks says."

Jeff snorted, wincing as he unburdened his sinuses. "An attitude like that," he said, but didn't finish the thought.

The door to the conference room opened. The woman in the doorway dressed and moved as if spring had already lighted on City Hall. A coral blouse, hair in a neat copper bob. A black knit shawl her only concession to the cold. Crooked in her arm was a tablet in a beat-to-shit leatherette slipcase.

"Mr. Chen, Mr. Wakeland. I'm Evelyn Rhee, Valerie's deputy chief of staff. Thanks for braving the weather. We're all set up for you."

No handshake or holding the door. We followed her inside. I took one last look out the window, at my reflection on the glass. I'd worn my grey suit, even shaved. It was the mayor, after all. No tie or top button. The figure I saw staring back at me looked jury-rigged but reasonably intact.

The office was narrow, panelled in blond wood, which matched the kidney-shaped table. One wall was glass, the blinds twisted three quarters shut. The windows looked down on the Cambie Bridge, beyond it the North Shore Mountains.

The man by the window gave us a tight, professional nod. He was about forty, dressed in VPD blues. His hat took up table space next to his paperwork. Evelyn Rhee introduced him as Inspector Gurcharan Gill.

"Pleased. Let's start." Gill sat down, motioning to the seats across from him. Rhee took the chair by the door.

"Val is detained, unfortunately," she said.

Jeff made a point of not looking at me.

"In the meantime, though, I'll ask you both to read and sign this waiver."

On the table in front of us was a confidentiality agreement, a pen resting by the signature line. Jeff read it over carefully and signed. I signed. Rhee collected the document.

"You've no doubt heard that Jeremy Fell is missing," Inspector Gill said. "He's the mayor's younger brother. Three days ago he and a friend went to the Alpen Club for dinner and drinks. Several drinks. The friend remembers Jeremy getting into a cab, alone, purportedly to meet a woman. Didn't say who. Cabbie confirms he dropped a fare in Gastown. That's the last time anyone saw Jeremy."

"What time?" I asked.

Gill consulted his papers. "8:20."

"Who's the friend?"

"Let's save question time till the end." Gill found his place on the sheet and continued. "Jeremy Fell is fifty-one years old. Five eight, white, brown and brown. No scars. Two Celtic-style tattoos. Guinness harp on the right forearm, tribal pattern around the left bicep."

The inspector looked at Rhee before continuing.

"The sense we got, talking to his friends, Jeremy is a nice enough guy. Not the type with a lot of problems weighing him down."

I opened my notebook, wrote the word *Dumb*.

"Arrested for drunk driving in Hawaii once. Possession of illicit substance, completion of a recovery program. No incidents since then."

Hard partying, I wrote.

Gill passed us the sheet. Jeremy Fell had never married. No kids, no significant other. Paperclipped to the sheet was a blown-up photo. A tanned handsome face grinned boyishly, eyes half obscured by a shaggy Beach Boys mop. Jeremy wore a loud dress shirt and some sort of neck jewellery, a black and gold band tucked into his open collar. A fragment of arm displayed the harp tattoo, a gold-banded TAG Heuer watch, and a bottle of Red Truck. The background showed the neon *M* and *O* of a Molson sign.

"We're getting nothing on his bank accounts, cell phone, credit cards. His car is still parked in the basement of his building. Passport still in his closet." Inspector Gill coughed and again looked in Rhee's direction. "No firearms. No previous attempts at self-harm."

"What we're hoping for from you," Evelyn Rhee said, "are places to look the authorities might not think of. We want to be thorough."

"Check every box," I said, raising my hand. "Question time now?"

"Fire away," Rhee said.

"Who thought up this so-called consultation, and why are they wasting our time?"

Gill let slip a smile, while the deputy chief of staff drew in her breath and steeled her expression. That told me whose idea it was.

"There's nothing on this sheet I couldn't glean in ten minutes," I said. "You want this guy found, we need as much info as you have."

"There are limits to what the department can share," Gill said.

"What you're willing to share."

"You want to put it that way." The inspector looked to Jeff. "He speak for you?"

"Wish he didn't sometimes." Jeff snuffled beneath his mask. "It's hard to make suggestions without more to go on. If the mayor is Jeremy's closest relative, we'd usually start with her."

"Out of the question," Rhee said. "Val's distraught, and in any case much too busy. I don't see how brainstorming hurts anything. We'll pay a consultancy fee. Whatever's fair."

Jeff looked at me, shrugged. It was their dollar.

"Did either of you know Jeremy?" I asked. "Beyond saying hi to him, or talking to his friends. Do you know what kind of person he was?"

"Never had the pleasure," Inspector Gill said.

Rhee nodded at my question. "I know Jeremy."

"Who is he, then? His best and worst qualities. We won't repeat them to Her Worship."

Rhee folded her hands and frowned. "Friendly and easygoing," she said.

"And his worst qualities?"

"Those are them," she said. "And his best. He could get along with anybody—which is sometimes a problem in the political realm. The type of person you're glad to see, but wouldn't want to rely on."

Flake, I printed. "What about drugs?"

Evelyn Rhee didn't flinch from the question. I was starting to like her.

"Jeremy partied. Cocaine and E. I never personally saw him use. Val told me he'd left that behind. Smoked a little weed to relax, but it's Vancouver, who doesn't?"

"Any financial worries?"

"None," Rhee said. "The family has money, and Jeremy never cared about amounts."

"Lucky him. Love life?"

"If he had one, I didn't know."

"My guess," I said, "and that's all this is—Jeremy's still in town, or within a day's drive. Whistler, maybe, or Harrison Hot Springs, or the Sunshine Coast. Staying with a friend, getting high or laid or both."

Rhee tapped something into her iPad. Gill made a few hasty notes.

"If you want something concrete," I said, "something that might actually help find him, give us more detail."

"Our task force has a procedure to follow," Inspector Gill said. "But thank you."

"Right." I turned to Jeff. "They're not ready for us. Let's go."

In the hallway, I told my partner he owed me fifty bucks. "What were you saying before about my attitude?"

"That it's no wonder she left you," Jeff said.

Outside City Hall, the rain had turned back into snow. Flakes of it lay pasted along the walkway. Jeff paused on the steps to swill from a bottle of expired Benylin. Vancouver's answer to Hunter S. Thompson.

I checked my phone. A text from Ryan Martz, a former cop, possibly former friend. *Sending some business your way.*

Ryan had been shot in the spine almost two years ago. He'd been told that with surgery and rehabilitation, he'd likely walk again. So far that hadn't proved the case. An abrasive sonofabitch before his injury, during his convalescence Ryan had pushed his friends away, including me. I'd let him.

What business? I texted.

I didn't receive an answer.

"Mr. Wakeland?"

Evelyn Rhee had followed us out of the building. She stood on the top step, hugging her shawl.

"Talking to you was my suggestion," she said.

"Sorry it didn't pan out."

Jeff waited at the curb. I lingered, hoping to leave things on a better note.

"Most of the time, people like Jeremy turn up in a couple of days. A fishing trip, romantic getaway. Something like that. I wouldn't worry too much."

Rhee shook her head. "Jeremy Fell is a rich, dumb, overgrown man-child, as you seem to have guessed. But he doesn't deserve what's happened. And something *has* happened. I'm sure."

She was worried for him. Not for political gain, or even out of friendship, I'd wager. One person noticing the absence of another. Evelyn Rhee's sincerity stung me, and I felt like a heel for brushing her off.

"When I mentioned hiring a private investigator, the task force officers said not to waste my time. But if I had to, it should be you. Wakeland & Chen are supposed to be the best at finding missing people."

"We can't help you," I said. "Not under these circumstances."

"You won't even try?" The deputy chief of staff shivered. "Can I ask why you don't think Jeremy is worthy of your time?"

"It's not a question of worthy," I said.

"Then why?"

Because I'm thirty-eight and heartbroken, Ms. Rhee. Because I'm the only person in our office not stricken with the flu. Because I have fragile metacarpals, a twice repaired jaw and a line of scar tissue down my rib cage from being stabbed. Because there are parts missing now, and what's left is worn down and nothing is easy anymore. Because this morning I'm finding it particularly hard to carry on with business as usual.

More than that, Ms. Rhee. Maybe it's the season, or my empty bed, or maybe I'm coming down with what Jeff has. Maybe it's old-fashioned self-pity. A missing person case demands a quantity of empathy, and I simply can't muster any for a fiftysomething rich kid like Jeremy Fell.

As I stepped off the curb, immersing my shoes in the run-off, I held up my phone, showing her Ryan's message.

"Sorry," I said. "Tell the mayor I'll keep an eye out for her brother. But I already have another case."

TWO

A CUP OF COFFEE

The business Ryan promised was waiting in our reception area. Had been waiting for some time. The business wasn't all that happy about the wait. She scowled at me with her good eye.

"I've been listening to your receptionist blow her nose for half an hour," the business said. "If the young lady is under the weather, shouldn't she be at home?"

The young lady was my half-sister Kay, who squinted at us from behind the sneeze guard on the desk. "Can I go home now?" she asked. It came out *Kai go hobe dow?*

"Go ahead," I told her. Turning back to the business, I said, "My sister is an investigator here. Our office manager called in sick."

"They must be near death, if this is your idea of healthy."

The business was in her late fifties, had the build and bearing of a cop. Her white hair was in a ponytail, a few loose tendrils obscuring the square of gauze that covered her eye. The skin around the gauze was scabrous and pink.

"Rhonda Bryce," the business said. "Ryan Martz told me you'd make time."

Jeff took over the reception desk while I escorted Bryce to my office. Wakeland & Chen occupies the twelfth floor of the Royal Bank Building on West Hastings. Most of that is the Security Division, which oversees a cadre of rent-a-cops, runs background checks and offers corporate consultations. The Investigations Division is smaller.

I explained as much to Bryce.

"My partner runs the Security side of things," I said. "I pretty much *am* the Investigations side."

We sat across from one another at my desk. Bryce craned her neck to examine the commendations and clippings on the wall. Jeff's idea. My contributions to the office decor were on the table: a box of teabags, a Russian novel's worth of unfiled reports and a battered aluminum police flashlight.

"I sure recognize that," Bryce said when she spotted the Maglite. "Your father's?"

"It was."

"Matt was on the job when I was starting out. Back in the late Cretaceous. Knew he had a son, but never know he had a daughter as well."

"He didn't," I said. "Long story. The bullet point version: he and his wife adopted me. Her troubled sister's kid. They raised me."

"And the young lady at reception?" Bryce asked. "I like to know the people I'm hiring."

I got the sense Rhonda Bryce was working herself up to sharing her problem. The question was meant to buy time. So, okay, let her buy it. The client is always right.

"My birth mother cleaned up, nine years after having me. Found Christ, remarried, and settled down in Medicine Hat. My half-sister River is the result. River Jordan, you believe it. When she fled the Prairies, she changed her name to Kay."

I opened my notebook, struck a line through the page on Jeremy Fell and held my pen at the ready.

But Bryce wasn't prepared to explain herself yet. "Ryan said you'd handle this personally. No offense to your sis. Ryan says you owe him one."

"I do, more or less."

"He also says you were on the job."

"For a cup of coffee."

Rhonda Bryce pointed at herself. "Twenty years," she said. "Another seven and change working Transit. All that time, I never lost a single piece of my gear."

The tape holding the gauze was beginning to peel from her cheek.

"Five days ago, I'm working evenings, Broadway–Commercial station. A Tuesday, pretty slow. I see a burly guy in a hoodie, and he's giving this young lady a hard time."

I made notes.

"They're standing way over the yellow line, right near the platform edge. Train's due in two minutes. I step forward, tell them to cut out the horseplay. The guy's yelling, but he backs off. I turn to the woman, make sure she's not hurt. I notice she's holding a coffee. What *looked* like coffee, anyway."

Bryce ripped up the bandage and gave a fervent scratch to the red cratered tissue around the swollen eyelid. The iris was a milky green.

"Itches like the blue blazes," she said. "Sugar water heated to high hell. Prison napalm, they call it. A few degrees hotter and I'd be permanently blind. The eye will heal, another few weeks, though I won't be in the running for Miss Universe."

She chuckled, reaffixed the gauze. Her attitude was cavalier but meant to be seen through. *This hurt me. I'm pissed about it. You can't begin to understand.*

"I'm here because of the gun," Bryce said. "The stocky fellow took it from me when I went down. The cops'll find them, or they won't, but I can't abide my service weapon being on the street."

"And a PI might have better luck asking about it, depending on the street."

"You'll do it then?"

I took down the model, a SIG P226. Rhonda Bryce recited the serial number. Her supervisor would let me view the footage of the attack.

"Just get it back for me, please," Bryce said. "Whatever it costs. I'd sleep a whole heck of a lot better."

Before I left for Transit Police HQ, I told Jeff about our new client. My partner looked over the contract Rhonda Bryce had signed. He noted the absence of a cheque.

"So you blew off the mayor, a paying consultation, and signed on to look for a gun? This another Dave Wakeland charity case?"

"A favour for Ryan Martz," I said.

Jeff coughed and moved the gravel around in his throat. "Case you don't realize, Dave, businesses don't run on favours. How we ended up behind in the first place."

I couldn't pretend to grasp our finances perfectly, but Jeff had communicated the gist. One corporate client was in bankruptcy, while another was behind on payment. The net result, Wakeland & Chen was owed money we might never see. How much money I didn't know, but for Jeff to be this anxious, it would have to be a significant sum.

"Cash in hand next time and every time, unless you want to run searches by candlelight. And Dave?" Jeff softened his tone, just a bit. "You're not at fault for Ryan's injury."

"I haven't been much of a friend to him."

"Much of anything, since Sonia left."

He wasn't wrong.

Around the time of our engagement, Sonia Drego had been promoted. It had almost ruined her. She'd gone from a patrol officer being groomed for Major Crimes, to being shunted upward into Public Relations. As a brown-skinned woman, and as a cop, she resented being forced to represent the department rather than redefine how it worked.

At first she found enjoyment in the position. Talking with kids. Coming home at regular hours. Sonia was too smart not to do well. But something was lacking. On patrol, there was risk to her work, just as with mine. That had been our agreement: a shared trust not to second guess each other. We told ourselves we accepted the chance, however slight, that the other wouldn't make it home. Without that, the danger was one-sided.

I told Sonia she could come work with me. Or put in with the Mounties and work in one of the suburbs. Or any place else. Whatever she needed to feel good about her job.

Sonia had made the worst possible choice and listened to me.

A position had opened up on a cross-border task force based in Montreal. She could parachute in at her same salary and rank. The fast track to being a detective.

She told me she needed this. I could come with her, leave Jeff to run Wakeland & Chen, maybe start up anew in Montreal.

Sonia knew as she laid out the scenario that I wouldn't go for it. I was, am, tied to Vancouver in ways I can't articulate. More than being born here, having family and a thriving business in town, or a fondness for sushi and the Pacific Northwest climate. Who was I if I wasn't here?

She knew I'd say no, just as I knew she'd already said yes.

As I rode the SkyTrain past Broadway and Commercial, the East Van cross looking grimy and yellowed above the snow, I thought how neatly I'd trapped myself. I'd never leave this place. And I'd never understand it, either. Cold and unaffordable, but now mean in a way it hadn't been. Hostile. Rents skyrocketing, people dispossessed, City Hall and the police so mired in enmity nothing was getting done. Heatwaves and floods and now a prolonged and bitter winter chill.

Two days after Bryce's attack, Jeremy Fell had disappeared. Coincidence, most likely. Or maybe, like the flu, mean was going around this season.

THREE

A BURNING CAUSE

TransLink, Vancouver's transit authority, was headquartered in the Sapperton area of New Westminster, uphill from an industrial slice of the Fraser River. Once home to a prison and the Royal College of Engineers, the area was now an admixture of century-old brick warehouses and glassy prefab office cubes. The Transit Police inhabited the latter.

Darlene Chang was Rhonda Bryce's supervisor. She met me in the lobby and I followed her down the corridor until the public service posters became bulletin boards and card-swipe entryways. Chang wore a staff sergeant's uniform, thick glasses, an affable smile.

"Rhonda is good people," Chang said. "I feel sorry as hell for what happened to her. I have to say, though, I'm not thrilled with this plan of hers."

"Plan?"

"Hiring you," Chang said.

In a conference room that could have seated thirty, she turned on the projector and dimmed the lights.

"We're actively investigating the robbery and assault. Naturally there are things I can't tell you."

"Second time I've heard that today," I said. "If there's no point in me being here—"

Staff Sergeant Chang put up a conciliating hand. "I told Rhonda I'd cooperate, so I will. She's worried sick about that gun. Driven to desperate lengths."

"Is she a good officer?" I asked.

"One of the best. What happened to her was appalling."

"Any complaints against her?"

"Of course," Chang said without hesitation. "But nothing serious. We serve an overcrowded transit line growing busier by the day. Our authority is always questioned. Complaints are an occupational hazard."

"No use of force or harassment?"

The staff sergeant shook her head.

"Any beefs with other officers? Supervisors?"

"None."

Chang called up the footage on her laptop, speeding through hours of station footage. The camera was in the rafters above the Expo Line platform. Trains streaked by, pausing only to belch out people and suck them in.

Natural light faded. The station lights cast shadows. Chang paused at the sight of Rhonda Bryce on all fours, medical attendants surrounding her. The timestamp read 21:42. Chang wound back to an empty platform, seven minutes before.

Bryce strolled in an arc across the right corner of the screen, from the bank of escalators, toward the walkway that bridged the two Sky-Train lines. Nothing for forty seconds. The westbound train came in.

A slender woman stepped off the second car from last. A toque sat on top of a mound of blond hair, the red tendrils of yarn hanging down her shoulders. A dark peacoat, rainboots, large mirrored shades. She was wearing red mittens and cupping a travel mug.

"No ID on her yet," Chang said. "The cup is full of sugar dissolved in boiling water. The solution loses its temperature less rapidly than straight H2O, resulting in a longer, more continuous burn."

A man trudged from the direction of the walkway. Slightly left and above centre frame. Jeans and a dark blue hoodie, black and white Vans. Broad in the shoulders and well below six feet. Hunched slightly forward, hands not visible till he approached the woman. Blue latex below the cuffs.

"Cleaning gloves," Chang indicated. "No fingerprints from either of them."

The man and woman were talking. She took a step away from him. He closed the distance quickly, causing her to inch back closer to the platform. Shaking her head at him. Yelling.

Enter Bryce from stage right, half a foot taller than the man. What's the problem here, son? Miss, is this fellow bothering you?

The woman's mouth opened, forming an O. The lid to the mug went into her pocket. Bryce ordered the man back, and he went. Bryce spun and the woman flicked her hands up and the cup's contents flew at Bryce's face.

Bryce reeled back, sank to her knees. Her hands pawed at her face. She wobbled on the ground, then skidded back from the edge of the platform.

Darlene Chang sucked air between her teeth. "Thankfully Rhonda had the presence of mind to avoid the tracks," she said.

As soon as Bryce was down, the man in the hoodie began struggling with the Transit cop's belt. He freed the pistol, a black automatic, and shoved it into the centre pocket of his hoodie. He bolted out of frame the same direction he'd come.

We watched Rhonda Bryce writhe for a moment. It was unpleasant. I hadn't eaten in hours and I was glad of it. Eventually a train brought onlookers and another Transit cop. Soon after, the medics. Darlene Chang hit pause.

"Want to see it again?" the staff sergeant asked. "I have other angles."

This time we followed the woman's trajectory, onto the platform, driven back by the man. Once Bryce was on the ground, she beat a swift retreat down the elevator and onto Broadway.

Chang called up a still from the video footage, the clearest possible shot of the blond woman. Beneath the hair and toque and sunglasses, the face was still obscured.

"Cold as ice," Chang said. "Doesn't look back once she throws the stuff. And notice she takes the cup with her."

"Which station did she start from?" I asked.

"She boarded at Metrotown at 9:22. Already had her ticket. The guy in the hoodie boarded from Waterfront at 9:28, paid cash for a one zone. Opposite ends, different payment methods."

Chang flipped to a similarly nondescript still of the man in the hoodie.

"That's the best we have on them," the staff sergeant said. "No clue how Blondie and Hoodie are connected—*if* they're connected—or why they targeted Bryce. Our best guess, they're fiends, and the gun will show up in a pawnshop, or the backroom of some dealer. Which I guess is where you come in."

"Very disciplined for fiends," I said.

"Takes all kinds."

"How structured is the route Bryce takes? Is she always posted around Broadway–Commercial?"

"It's shiftwork, and depends where we're needed."

"Could someone have clocked her schedule?"

"Hard to imagine, but it's possible, I guess. To what purpose, though?"

No answer came to mind. The pair had arrived separately on the platform, staged a row that attracted Bryce, ambushed her, and made off clean. As chaotic as the attack had looked, it had been carried out with precision and without hesitation.

And now they had a gun.

FOUR

THE DRIVE

There were a handful of pawnshops along Commercial Drive within walking distance of the station. I decided to start there. The Drive is the eccentric heart of the city, a hodgepodge of sushi and shawarma joints, Black hair salons, third-generation Italian cafés. Croatia, Portugal, Vietnam and Somalia have all left some stamp on the neighbourhood. There is nowhere like it, and it's home.

But it's a home in danger of repossession, bedeviled by big money. Rezoning had led to sites projected for towers in the next few years. Plus something called an "Entertainment District," which seemed to be developer-speak for "Fuck you, get out." This wasn't simply my nostalgia for The Way the City Was. This was survival economics. Only millionaires need apply.

You don't walk into a pawnshop and ask for a gun. The buying and selling of munitions is regulated, and most pawnbrokers won't touch them. The cops had doubtless already asked, papering the streets with the make and serial number of Rhonda Bryce's weapon.

What you do, instead, is wait for a lull, which on a snowy afternoon isn't difficult. Stamp your feet on the mat and make some remark about the cold. Browse, and let the owner sidle up and ask if they can show you anything.

You have to take the measure of the person you're talking with. An honest pawnbroker wants money with a minimum of trouble. You explain that you're trying to recover an item, that there's a reward, and no questions will be asked. The item itself would be worth a couple grand. A lead on the item, a few hundred.

Now obviously such an item isn't in stock, being illegal and wanted by the authorities. But inventory changes, and a person hears things, or knows people who hear them. You leave your card and bid the owner good day.

With a less reputable shop, or the street merchants who lay out their wares beneath the elevated tracks of the SkyTrain, a more naked appeal to avarice usually works. Buy something cheap—a Playstation game, a bootleg DVD of *A League of Their Own*, or a copy of *The Bluest Eye* stamped by the library it was stolen from. Let them know what you're *really* in the market for, and what price you're willing to pay. When they accuse you of police affiliation, point to your purchase. How many cops read Toni Morrison? You're just a customer talking shop.

After three hours I'd covered most of The Drive, and Broadway between Nanaimo and Fraser. Six pawnshops, two military-surplus outfitters, three thrift stores and two street merchants enterprising enough to set up amid the slush. I had a cappuccino at Abruzzo and another at Joe's, overheard talk about the new towers going in, how the neighbourhood was going to hell and how the mayor was in bed with the developers.

"Valerie Fell's as crooked as a bucket of triangles," one patron said. Old, Italian, eyes on the soccer game playing on the café's TV. "Now this nonsense with the brother."

"They gonna pick him up in Costa Rica any day now, some place like that," his twin at the next table said.

"With how much of my taxes, what I wanna know."

"City Hall ain't been honest since Sullivan."

"Can't blame her for being in Adam Colville's pocket. Developers got deep fuckin' pockets."

"Must be nice."

I wandered back up The Drive in the direction of home, thinking that Jeremy Fell wouldn't find much in the way of sympathy among the citizens on The Drive.

My apartment was close by the station, but first, I wanted to walk the platform where the attack had occurred. It was crowded and the station always seemed in a state of perpetual renovation. The passageway to the Millennium Line was a tunnel of plywood, the pulse of jackhammers and industrial drills hidden from view.

I followed the route the man in the hoodie had taken, up the escalator on the north side of Broadway, across the covered walkway to the platform. It was crowded and I didn't learn anything.

There was a drugstore to the right of the station, fast food and flower carts to the left. The bus line out to UBC started in front, the pavement marked with red to denote where the line should snake and fold. A fat man sang basso profundo to the commuters. No hat on the ground or panhandling sign. Singing because that's what he did.

A security guard stood just inside the drugstore entrance, at the beginning of the cosmetics aisle. A thin dark-skinned woman in a ribbed black vest over navy blue shirt and slacks. The uniform from one of Wakeland & Chen's competitors.

I asked if she'd been working the night of the attack.

"The cops already ask me. That man and woman, they didn't come in the store."

I shrugged, worth a try. "Anyone weird come in the last few weeks?"

The guard smiled like that was the dumbest of questions. "Always weirdos. Nine, ten o'clock, we get all the ones on drugs. They steal toilet paper, baby food."

"Violence?" I asked.

"Not so much. They run, most times. It's the women that fight."

I sidestepped so three teenagers could gain access to the celebrity perfumes. "But nothing unusually violent?"

"No," the guard said. "A paint fight, but it was nothing."

"You mean someone with a paintball gun?"

"No, a tube, to write. You know." She mimed shaking a spray-paint cannister, made a low *shush*. "A man sprayed me. Got silver in my eyes."

"When was this?"

"Two weeks ago, I think."

"You tell the police?"

"I tell them when it happened but they do nothing. So much graffiti, they say."

"What did he look like?"

"White, not too tall. Dark clothing. I didn't look close, and then I couldn't see."

"This guy sprayed you intentionally in the eye?"

A pattern of eye attacks would be something to go on. But the guard frowned and shook her head.

"He was putting a tag on the outside. I tell him to stop. He sprayed me so I can't chase."

Outside I circled the building, looking for silver. Initials of bored commuters had been scratched into the glass storefront. Pen marks in blue and black.

Behind the station, in silver paint, someone had scrawled a *D* and *K* on the brick.

Initials? A gang tag? I took a photo of the letters, for no other reason than to prove to Rhonda Bryce that I'd made a solid effort. Chased down every possible lead. So sorry it had come to nothing.

I was cutting up Tenth, on my way home, when I got into a fight.

FIVE

NEIGHBOURHOOD WATCH

"Our women deserve safe conduct through the community," the shorter one called out to passersby.

"Government sure as shit ain't gonna do it," his taller buddy added.

Both white, the taller one six-three or -four, with a jutting Adam's apple and an Amish beard the colour of pulled taffy. The shorter one had a shaved head and acne scars and carried a rubber-handled cane. They wore matching denim vests with white lightning bolts sewn on the backs, above the words WODEN'S BASTARDS and PROSPECT.

I'd heard of the group. They'd disrupted an anti-racism rally a year ago, stomping through the crowd using shock canes on the protestors. The canes gave out an electrical charge somewhere between a hornet sting and a punch. The prospects looked like homeschooled kids from the suburbs who hadn't dressed for the cold. The type who'd join a half-assed neighbourhood watch named after a one-eyed Norse deity. You laugh at these people, I do at least, with their heads full of vape juice and comic book violence. You laugh, and then months later they kill somebody.

They'd positioned themselves at the mouth of an alley between an Ethiopian restaurant and a cheque-cashing place. Offering to escort East Vancouver's white maidens home through the barbarian hordes.

The maidens weren't having it. One told them to go fuck themselves. Another hurled a bottle of Kokanee at them. Brown glass and suds decorated the shorter man's boots.

"Out of here, mongrel," he told her, brandishing the cane.

It's rare when your urges align with the right thing to do. Yes, they were trash, their ideas despicable and hitting them was justified if not downright noble. The saviour of the community, good whites policing bad. But I rushed across the street because at bottom I wanted to hit someone. I like it. I was spoiling for a fight.

"Afternoon, kids," I said to them. "Either of you know anything about a graffiti tag, silver, the letters D and K?"

"Why the fuck are you asking us?" the tall one said.

"You seem civic-minded."

"We're here to help our community," the one with the cane said. "The parts worth helping, anyway."

"There's a Ukrainian church two blocks west that runs a soup kitchen. Always looking for volunteers."

"Fuck on out of here," the tall one said. "Think I'm fuckin' kidding with you, guy?"

"I think you saw a TV show about bikers and traded in your DMX albums."

"Our community is under siege." The short one transferred the cane to his left hand, bringing out a wad of pamphlets rubber banded together. "What's happening to old-stock Canadians is a type of genocide."

"How many types can you name? Top of your head, no looking at your phone."

"You just came over here to waste our time?"

"I came over here to hit you," I said.

The taller man sneered and began saying something like, "You don't want none of this." I struck him with a right fist that had been forged two months ago, travelling since then, looking for a suitable target. It knocked him into the side of the building and he slipped, and I scored a good left on his way down. Unsportsmanlike. I tried to forgive myself.

The shorter man looked stunned and dropped the pamphlets. He shook the shock cane at me, like scolding a dog.

"Get fuckin' back, less you want a million volts."

I hit his friend again, smiled and stepped into it.

There was a click and an involuntary snap of my shoulder as the cane sparked. I took another step and he prodded again, but this time I was ready and grabbed hold of the cane, ripping it out of his hands.

The shorter man considered his options, turned and darted up the block. The taller prospect was staggering up the alley, a hand cupped under his nose.

In the scuffle I'd bitten the inside of my mouth. I tossed the cane onto the roof of the restaurant, spat, watched the blood surf the grey run-off on its way to the drain. My good deed for the day.

The TV was on inside my apartment, murmurs of French conversation and Miles Davis. *Ascenseur pour l'échafaud.*

On the couch, my sister emerged from beneath a Hudson's Bay blanket and sniffled.

"Good movie," Kay said, "but I guess I fell asleep."

There was chicken soup left on the stove. Half a package of Stoned Wheat Thins. I heated the pot, crushed crackers into mugs that said GOOD MORNING, HANDSOME and DON'T TALK TO ME TILL I'VE HAD MY COFFEE. Sonia's sincere-yet-kitschy furnishing touches. I missed her. I ran my skinned knuckles under the water.

"Feeling better?" I asked.

"Meh. Not really." Kay's voice was still husky with the flu. "You get in a fight?"

"Not really."

When the soup was hot, I filled the mugs and joined Kay on the couch.

"Forgot to ask about your meeting with the mayor," she said.

It already seemed days ago. "Her Worship no-showed," I said. "Her assistant wanted advice about the missing brother, but without giving us anything to go on."

Kay swirled the spoon around the mug, making irritating scrapes and clangs. "What was with the eye-patch lady in the office today?"

I told her about Rhonda Bryce and her missing gun. Kay seemed less enthusiastic about this than the prospect of working for the mayor.

"Isn't it impossible to find stolen property?" she said.

"Unlikely, yeah."

"So why do it?"

I pinned the spoon to the side of the mug with my thumb so I could sip without getting an eyeful of cutlery. The salt stung the cut. The strips of cracker melted on the tongue.

"She'd been referred by Ryan Martz," I said.

Kay frowned. "Doesn't he hate you?"

"Guess I should find out."

We watched some of the movie. The characters drifted through Paris on that elegant Davis score. We'd been watching old Criterion films from the library. *My Beautiful Launderette, Picnic at Hanging Rock*. The movies a person always means to see.

For a while I didn't think about Sonia.

"You don't have to, Dave," Kay said, when the movie was over, and I'd smoothed the couch back into her bed. "The gun thing, I mean. You don't have to chase after it. You don't owe Ryan. It could wait till I'm better, if you have something else."

My instinct was to go for the glib and obvious. Even a hero requires the odd break from the glamor of library films and leftovers. But it wouldn't come. Nor did the straightforward appeal to the credo of work. It's my job, it's what I do.

"I don't have anything else," I said, looking down at my knuckles. Maybe it was just that simple. "Work tends to keep me out of trouble."

SIX

JUST A JOB TO DO

The stench of burning plastic filled the back of the bus. A woman half-way up the aisle, seated on a sideways bench, held a tub of protein powder upside down on her lap. She was using a lighter to melt off the expiration date.

I pried open the window, letting morning air sweep through the bus. Someone protested, preferring the fumes.

East Van. You had to love it.

Hastings Street scrolled by. First flat and industrial, then older, more derelict. The tiki-themed Waldorf, the Astoria Hotel, where I'd boxed as a teen in the long-gone basement gym, the Grand Union country bar. In between the landmarks now were smart, clean shopfronts and the odd block of pristine apartment towers. An artisan donut shop next to the Aboriginal Friendship Centre. Pockets of smokers, panhandlers. Communities on top of each other, pretending the others didn't exist. Like the passengers crammed next to each other on the bus, staring straight ahead or at their phones.

I got off early and walked past Victory Square to the Wakeland & Chen offices. The pawnshops weren't open yet. It was a clear morning, cold but dry. Puddles of slush lingered here and there. The sidewalks had been cleared, the roads heavily salted.

Inside, Jeff Chen and his wife Marie were standing over the reception desk, their coats still on, in the middle of one of their famous rows.

"Sick is no excuse," Marie said. Her hair was circled by a fur-trimmed headwarmer, and she nodded perfunctorily as I entered. Marie Chen wasn't a fan of the Wakeland School of Business Management.

"When you're in your seventies, sick's a big deal," Jeff said. He seemed clear-headed today, his congestion not as bad.

"Then the man shouldn't be working here, honey. You can't go on without an office manager. It's not done. What if a client comes in and there's no one to greet them?"

I casually slipped around them and checked the phone and computer. No messages.

Jeff said, "It's only the fourth day. Ralph's usually good."

"You need someone else."

My partner appealed to me, but I shook my head.

"Y'see?" Marie said, taking my abstention as siding with her.

She was right, I was. Jeff had staffed the reception desk with retirees, which cut costs and worked reasonably well. But the job couldn't be abandoned during flu season. Before Jeff's cousin Shuzhen had gone to law school, she'd been a first-rate office manager. We needed someone that committed, that industrious. And that healthy.

Two thoughts knitted together. "I know someone," I said.

"Really?" Marie's skepticism was mildly insulting. "Who do you know that's reliable?"

"Leave it to me," I said. "Might just have the perfect candidate."

I left the office, carrying my mug of Twinings with me to the parking garage. Street parking around my apartment was scarce, so I usually left my Cadillac at work. The car had 246,000 klicks on it, most of them ugly and uphill. I could relate. The Caddy needed a cleaning and a tune-up, and the all-weather tires were starting to lose their tread. It skidded slightly as I changed lanes, heading up Hastings into Burnaby.

Red Hill Gold & Pawn was near Boundary, but before I reached it, I pulled off into a residential area just past the PNE fairgrounds.

A cluster of townhouses sided with light blue vinyl. I parked in the visitor's space and sought out Ryan Martz's unit.

He'd been transferred to a first-floor suite, with a ramp leading down to the front entrance. I pressed the buzzer and heard a cheery tinkle of chimes from inside, followed by cursing, wheels traversing wood.

Ryan opened the door.

"Fuck do you want?" he said.

He'd lost some weight and muscle and had a sallow look to his face, but he was groomed like always, his head still shaved clean. Dressed in sweats and a Pantera T-shirt, his phone on a lanyard around his neck. The chair itself was electric but Ryan shoved it back to let me in.

"I was in the neighbourhood," I said. "How are things?"

"Peachy fucking keen," he said.

"How's Nikki?"

The sarcasm mellowed at the mention of his wife. Nikki Fraser was still on the job, a firing-range instructor when she wasn't on patrol. "She's doing good. At work today. Made the sergeant's list."

"Good to hear."

"Speaking of good news, I heard Sonia left you."

"Career reasons," I said. "She's in Montreal."

"Probably fucking some French guy right now."

"Her life."

"And that doesn't bother you?"

"It's really good to see you, Ryan," I said.

The hallway was cluttered but clean. The coat rack had been lowered, the bedroom door rigged to remain open. It was the apartment of any couple.

"I'd've tidied up if I knew you were coming," Ryan said. "Why did you come, anyway?"

"Say thanks for referring Rhonda Bryce to me."

"Waste of time looking for that gun," he said. "But Rhonda was my supervisor at one point. And nobody likes a good hopeless case like my buddy Dave Wakeland."

"Some truth to that," I said.

"And that's why you're here now?"

"How're you fixed financially?" I asked.

"I don't want shit from you."

I nodded. Ryan Martz had been shot, paralyzed. Our friendship had faded in the months after. Yes, he'd become more caustic, his sarcasm more cutting. But I'd taken that at face value, instead of the desperate flailing of someone who needed friends most at that moment. I'd failed him.

"I'm still your friend," I finally said. "Not a great friend, maybe."

"Or a good one, even."

"Or a good one. Which is why it's only now I'm coming to you with this offer."

"What offer's that?" Ryan said.

"Jeff and Marie think you'd be perfect. I told them I'd ask, but that you probably weren't up to it."

"What offer, Dave?"

"We're hiring an office manager. Full-time, starting tomorrow. Benefits and everything."

Any stray hope that had escaped into his expression now evaporated. Ryan Martz scowled.

"I am nobody's goddamn secretary," he said.

"What I expected from you, and why I didn't ask until now."

"The fuck out of here with your charity, Dave."

"It's nothing like charity," I said. "You think it's answering phones? It's running the office of the number one security company in the city. You'd have to bust your ass to get up to speed, and you'd have to smile. You'd have to eat shit and learn to like the taste. Frankly, I don't think you could do it, even if you wanted to."

"Fuck you," he said. "I got a nice settlement. I don't need money."

"Good. I told Jeff this would be a waste. Typical Ryan, he'll say it's beneath him, and come up with a hundred and one excuses not to do it."

"This is you trying to reverse-psychologize me," he said.

"That's right, chum. Now excuse me while I get back to my job."

I walked to the door, paused, my pose the very image of The Detective at Wit's End.

"Look," I said, appearing as if fighting against my better judgment. "You want to give this a try, come in tomorrow at eight. Maybe we can figure out a way not to kill each other."

"Hey Dave?"

I looked at Ryan Martz, whose eyes were shining.

"Go fuck yourself," he said.

SEVEN

A BREAK

Outside the pawnshop, I phoned Jeff and told him that I'd invoked his name in the hiring of Ryan Martz. He sounded less than thrilled with my solution.

"There's no way he'll actually come in tomorrow," Jeff said. "Is there?"

"Worth a shot."

Jeff sneezed into the phone. Sniffled. "How's Ryan doing?"

"His usual pain-in-the-ass self. More so, maybe."

"But he's in shape to work?"

"Think so. We're all a little more banged up than we used to be."

"A receptionist has to be good with people, Dave. Ryan strike you as a people person?"

"He strikes me as a person who needs a job," I said.

"And polite, too. Good with people *and* polite."

"So there are a few skills he'll have to pick up."

Red Hill Gold & Pawn had bars on the outside of the windows, a vestibule you had to be buzzed through to enter. The shop floor was concrete, hardware shelving holding a snare drum, mitre saw, compound bow and vertical stacks of DVDs. Jewellery, video games and electronics were under glass near the till.

If I was in a hurry to pawn a gun, this was where I'd take it. For one thing it was beyond city limits, in the suburb of Burnaby. For another, the stickers on the door—EVERY CHILD MATTERS, IDLE NO MORE, DEFUND THE POLICE—implied the owner wasn't favourably disposed toward the authorities.

The man behind the counter was about my age, Indigenous, with a thick braid down his back. His black T-shirt said COLONIZE THIS. He nodded at me. We were the only two people in the store.

"Help you with something?" he said.

I looked up at the bow. "Sell a lot of these?"

"A few, mostly thanks to Green Arrow and Hawkeye. Lotta folks think they're superheroes."

"Got anything in the way of firearms?"

His gaze became more scrutinizing, and he shuffled sideways, closer to the till. "Not sure I can help you, bud."

"Sake of argument, let's say you could. Say I was looking for a gun that was stolen from a Transit cop six days ago."

"That would be a SIG nine-millimetre or forty cal," he said. "In theory, at least."

"A nine. In theory."

The owner crossed his arms. "Who's theoretically asking about this?"

I showed him my security licence.

"Wakeland," he said. "Luke Red Hill. And you want to get hold of this theoretical blunderbuss why?"

"The public good."

He smiled. "I don't have it, haven't seen it."

"Theoretically?"

"Actual fact. However."

The door chimed and Luke Red Hill buzzed a customer in. She dithered over guitar pedals, picked out a Super Fuzz and then left after hearing the price. When she was gone, Red Hill came out from behind the counter and locked the door. He twirled the OPEN sign to CLOSED and leaned against the bars.

"You working for the Transit cop?" he asked.

"No comment, but one would imagine she'd be grateful to have it back. Or at least out of general circulation."

Red Hill nodded, debating something. "I don't like cops. Even Transit cops. Puts me in a bind."

I waited, letting him decide.

"But I like handguns even less. They're a settler tool, no different than blankets with smallpox."

I nodded.

"A guy came in asking for a gun like that. Said specifically he wanted a gun like a cop or a Transit cop carries."

Or a Transit cop. "When was this?" I asked.

"Two weeks ago. Thereabouts."

"You don't have security footage of this person, do you?"

Red Hill pointed at the black plastic bubble on the ceiling. "Camera stores a week's worth of footage. And this guy was off, but he didn't strike me as *that* off."

"Even though he was looking for an unlicensed gun."

"The things I get asked for in here, you wouldn't believe."

"I believe I wouldn't."

"More than that," Red Hill said. "I've known killers. From the stone-cold type, to the pushed-to-my-limit type. This guy was neither. When I asked why he needed that model gun specifically, he said it would help him out with something."

"What kind of something?" I asked.

"Way he talked, I figured it was some, I dunno, bullshit art project. Demonstration, maybe. Set a cop's gun on fire. I wasn't gonna sell him a real weapon, understand. But we do get in the odd replica."

I showed him the photo of the man in the hoodie. Red Hill glanced at it and shook his head.

"Nah, this guy was average height, on the scrawny side."

"He give a name?"

"Left me his number, too. Case I heard of any guns like he was looking for. Told me to ask for Kyle."

I wrote it down and thanked him. The question of payment hadn't come up. I opened with two hundred dollars.

"It's better this dude doesn't have a handgun," Red Hill said. "But if you find it, and you want to do some *real* good? Pitch the damn thing into the river."

EIGHT

ON THE TRAIL OF THE GUN

The phone number was assigned to the Van Ness Hotel on Carrall Street. A narrow gilt-painted door in between an Irish snug and a cigar store, the SRO took up the second and third floors. I'd responded to calls from there as a cop. The eventful kind.

In my car, I dialed the number and asked a tubercular-sounding desk clerk for Kyle.

"Not here just now," the clerk said. "Can leave a message if you must." Her tone made that seem like a massive imposition.

"Any idea when he'll be home?"

"Not his keeper, sir."

"All right. No message for you. Question, though."

"What." The word accompanied by a sigh.

"I was gonna give him this cheque, but I guess I'll just mail it. How do you spell his last name? My nephew's a nice kid, but handwriting's not his strong suit."

"'Cause they don't teach them cursive anymore," the clerk said. "Standards aren't what they used to be. Too much on their phones."

"Those damn phones," I said. Mr. Agreeable talking to Mrs. End of the World. "Anyway, I can't make hide nor hair of this surname. Not without an Enigma machine."

The clerk's laughter was the creaking hinge of a cemetery gate followed by the gasp of a strangulating horse. She coughed and begged pardon. I heard the shuffle of papers.

"Here we are," she said. "Spelled—you got a pen?—*H-A-L-L-I-D-A-Y.*"

"And which unit was that? I think I can make out the rest of the address. Carrall Street, right?"

She recited the address and postal code. Kyle Halliday occupied unit 312.

"Thanks a bunch," I said. "Has Kyle lived there a while?"

The clerk didn't know, but told me Halliday's papers were near the top of her stack. I could imagine a cluttered, disorganized registration office where the top meant a recent arrival.

Now that we're properly acquainted, Mr. Halliday, let's figure out who you are, and why you're asking around town for a Transit cop's firearm.

Locked in my office with a pot of Earl Grey, I ran my new friend's name through every database we had, searched news articles, social media. I made calls. In a new document, I bullet-pointed Kyle Halliday's life.

- 24 years old, born Surrey Memorial Hospital
- parents both deceased, father a dockworker, mother a medical transcriptionist
- last employer, Bertin Sugar, general labourer, quit two years ago
- the same time he gave his notice, he enrolled at Langara College, took student loans, entered the Business program
- awarded for academic achievement in his second semester, dropped out in his third
- rented a two-bedroom apartment on Oak and 21st, sharing with Naima Yassin, 34, nursing student from Aleppo, Syria
- married Naima eight months ago
- rented a room at the Van Ness
- two weeks ago, approximately, asked Luke Red Hill for a gun

There were gaps in this timeline large enough to tug a garbage scow through. But it sketched a picture of a young working-class guy who'd been trying to better himself. Taking classes, getting married. And then within a year he'd moved into an SRO and started hunting for a weapon.

Kyle Halliday had claimed his name on social media, but hadn't posted anything. Not publicly, anyway. The photo he'd uploaded showed a reedy, fair-haired white man with a serious expression, hands shoved in his pockets. His beard was patchy, the moustache barely more than peach fuzz. Over his shoulder I recognized the corner of a large beige factory abutting the train tracks. The sugar refinery where Halliday had worked.

His wife, or ex, I couldn't tell, still occupied the apartment on Oak. Naima Halliday had graduated a year ago and was currently employed at Vancouver General.

I grabbed my jacket, passing Jeff's door. I could hear him on the phone with a client. His voice was friendly, boisterous, energetic. No trace of the plague.

"…Not acceptable at all," Jeff was saying. "We've had a good relationship, minus a few hiccups, but waiting till next quarter is pushing it. We can't keep staffing your work sites if you're not making good on last year's invoices…"

Kay stood behind the reception desk, showing Tim Blatchford how to work the intercom. Sitting down, Blatchford was about the same height as her standing. A former pro wrestler, Tim dwarfed the desk, knees banging on the underside. He stabbed the intercom and looked to Kay to see if he'd done good.

"That was incoming," Kay said.

A second later, Jeff opened his door and shouted "Tim, what the hell?"

"Sorry," Blatchford said. "You want me to dial 'em back?"

"Just stay off the lines." Jeff noticed me and said, "Where are you headed?"

"Find that gun," I told him.

Saying it made real the possibility of danger. Kyle Halliday could be armed. I decided to bring the Maglite. It wouldn't deflect any bullets, but it was innocuous and had proven itself as a cudgel.

Blatchford pushed the chair away and stood up. "So much for us rotating office duties, I guess."

"No way," my sister said. "You're not getting out of office duty just 'cause you suck at it. That's unfair."

Duly chastened, Blatchford sat back down.

Despite their differences, the two got along well and usually partnered together. Blatchford had been in and out of the PI business for a decade, while Kay was smart, dedicated and computer savvy. It was a mentorship that ran both ways.

"How're you feeling?" I asked my sister.

"Tired, a bit foggy, but Jeff said he needs someone to cover night shifts this week."

The thought of Kay patrolling an empty office building in the snow gave me a pang of fraternal concern. "You both don't need to work it," I said.

Kay sneezed and said, "I can't take another night on your couch."

Their shift didn't start for two hours. I showed them my write-up on Kyle Halliday.

"You could check out the college for me," I said. "Maybe he and his wife were popular." As an afterthought I showed them both the photo of the silver *D* and *K*. "Mean anything to either of you?"

Kay squinted, shook her head.

"Donna Karan?" Blatchford guessed. "Duke Kahanamoku?"

"Probably one of them," I said. "Congrats, Tim, you cracked the case."

I grabbed the flashlight. When I passed reception for the second time, Kay was on the college website. Tim had a poker game open in his browser.

NINE

THE BATTLE

The address on Oak Street was a clay-coloured low-rise with a recessed front entrance, shielded from the street by square-hewn hedges of laurel. The name Halliday was in the digital directory attached to the buzzer. Apartment 314. I rang, to no avail.

Night was dropping in. I watched the doorway for about an hour, standing by the bus stop across the street. Once upon a time, a standing watch would have been my prime smoking hours. I'd chain Rooftops or Parliaments beneath an awning, knowing the ciga-rette justified my presence. I'd quit for the same reason I made most attempts at self-betterment. For Sonia. Without her, I wasn't sure why I didn't light up again. Inertia, perhaps. There wasn't a convenience store within sight of the door.

Sonia. I wondered what she was doing right now. Probably some-thing a damn sight better than freezing.

At 4:40 a cab pulled up and dropped off a woman in a leather jacket over hospital scrubs. I crossed the street to intercept her as she was digging out her key.

"Mrs. Halliday?" I asked.

She started at my voice, hand jammed in her bag. I held my palms out facing her, *I come in peace.*

"I'm a private investigator," I said. "Hoping to speak to you about your husband Kyle."

"A private investigator. That's like a researcher?" She spoke with an accent I wasn't knowledgeable enough to place, pausing between each sentence as if to inspect the words one last time before sharing them.

"Similar to a researcher," I said. "Depending on the case, sometimes very similar."

"But not police."

"No, I'm unaffiliated."

"Does a private investigator carry some ID?"

I produced my security licence, then handed her a card. "The Wakeland in Wakeland & Chen," I said. "Dave or David is fine. Could we talk inside?"

I followed her into the elevator. She held her fob to the scanner and tapped in the third floor. Naima Halliday was striking, her black hair shot with grey, eyes dark and roving, mouth drawn taut and gnawing its bottom lip. The arms of her jacket hung over her wrists. She smelled of disinfectant and long hours on her feet.

Inside her apartment, Naima hung our coats on a nail driven into the bathroom door. The den was crowded with a love seat and sofa, bookshelves holding medical textbooks. A small TV on a metallic stand, a coffee table heaped with journals and Arabic newspapers.

"Do you take tea?" Naima Halliday asked.

"Please."

Water drummed metallically into the kettle. I told her I was trying to get in touch with Kyle. "Do you have any idea where he is?"

She futzed with the teapot and bags, making no reply.

I tried a more roundabout approach. "You and Kyle met at school, right?"

"In the cafeteria." Naima smiled. "He had nowhere to sit, and he was so grateful."

"Love at first sight?"

The smile faded. "I have soy milk," she said, gesturing as she poured the tea.

"I take it on its own. Are you two separated?"

"No."

"But Kyle doesn't live here anymore."

No answer. Naima set the teapot and cups on the coffee table.

There was a battle going on I wasn't privy to. Worry and distrust vied for influence over a disposition that was inclined to reach out, for whatever reason. I'm not a charmless lug. I say please and thanks and I put the toilet seat down and I know how to hold a teacup. And I liked her, the mature and easy way Naima Halliday inhabited her apartment. She was concerned for Kyle, and for herself. Maybe I was the first person who'd asked.

"Laying my cards on the table, Mrs. Halliday, I know Kyle was trying to get hold of a firearm."

The news seemed to shock her. Naima poured the tea and gripped her mug in both hands. The battle continued in silence.

"I'm not the police," I continued. "I don't want to bring Kyle any trouble. Or you. All I want is take that gun out of the picture."

"He's a good young man," Naima said.

I didn't argue the point, though the way she said it was more parental than romantic. Not even a year of marriage. I wondered if Kyle and Naima had slept separately by the end, and if so, what had gone wrong. I wondered what had drawn her to Kyle in the first place. I could imagine pretty well what had attracted him. In any case, he'd married well.

"Why are you smiling?" she said.

I hadn't realized I was. Mentally I'd been reproaching myself for appreciating someone's company while mourning the absence of my fiancée. The head and heart, or the heart and loins, at odds.

"I was thinking of how we don't get a choice of who we care about," I said.

"That's true."

"When did you last see your husband?"

On the wall was a dry erase calendar with her shifts written in red, days off and reminders in purple. She scrutinized it for a moment.

"He borrowed my car," Naima said. "January 28th."

Two weeks ago. About the same time he'd contacted Red Hill Gold & Pawn. And the silver graffiti had gone up.

"Did Kyle bring the car back?"

"No, not yet. I don't know why."

She sprang up, still carrying her mug, and slopping tea across the floor. I watched her take a pile of envelopes from atop the fridge, free one and hold it in front of me.

"This came last week," she said.

It was a strip of paper with a barcode on it. CITY OF VANCOUVER BY-LAW NOTICE at the top.

"Parking ticket," I said, looking it over.

The location given was in Stanley Park, a lot near English Bay. Five days ago, 7:08 p.m. Naima's car was a brown Celica. I memorized the plate numbers.

"Do you know anyone who lives around there?" I asked. "Anyone Kyle would visit?"

"No."

"Why do you think Kyle borrowed your car?"

Here the battle seemed to shift, and she wouldn't say more.

I showed her the photos of the SkyTrain attackers. She shook her head at the man in the hoodie, barely looking at the blond woman.

"What about this?" I held up the photo of the graffiti tag.

Naima couldn't suppress the rush of breath. Recognition and fear and more. She put two fingers to her mouth, stifled an answer, and pointed her other hand at the door.

"Leave now, please," Naima said.

So I left, knowing I'd come back and knowing I wanted to.

TEN

A DEATH IN SUNSET

Kyle and the gun. Kyle and Naima. Kyle in a brown Toyota.

Snow was falling as I drove through Stanley Park on a fool's errand. If he'd been ticketed there once before, my thinking ran, maybe Kyle had returned. Maybe I'd find him, strolling the beach with the gun. Maybe as straightforward as that.

Once, as a cop, I'd interrupted a woman who'd set out walking from the West End. Barefoot, in cutoffs and a T-shirt. I'd taken an old revolver away from her. The woman's plan, she told me on the drive to the hospital, had been to walk until she found the right spot.

What would that spot look like? I'd asked.

"The heart will know it when it finds it," she'd replied.

Was that Kyle Halliday? Parked at the beach, watching the waves, the gun on the passenger seat?

Even with the roads obscured by snow, a nighttime drive around Stanley Park was pleasant. I stuck close to the Seawall, rounding the five-and-a-half-mile perimeter of the park. The Cadillac's stereo played Oliver Nelson, *The Blues and the Abstract Truth*.

My headlights lit up the roads and walkways, snow-dusted sand, water like black velvet. Occasionally a car would shoot down the causeway. I spotted a pair of raccoons, a surly, slinking coyote. You were never alone in the park, though it could feel that way when the only lights were your own.

I rounded Prospect Point, passed Third Beach, Second. When it came to names, the people who'd stolen the park from the Squamish People hadn't been blessed with creativity.

Rolling past Sunset Beach, I almost missed the car. A brown Celica, parked flush against the trash bin occupying the leftmost space in the lot. The licence plate matched.

I parked next to it and peered inside. The driver-side door was unlocked.

Sand glittered on the floor under the beam of my flashlight. On the back bench was a dark blue hoodie, slightly damp and smelling of sweat and ozone.

The Burrard Bridge loomed to the left of the beach, headlights streaking along its surface. A snack bar and restroom to the right. Ahead was the breakwater, a mound of rubble shaped something like a pinball paddle.

Tracks in the snow, overlapping footsteps heading out to the rocks. One set large and narrow, the other smaller. Both faint and fading as more flakes accumulated.

I splashed across the asphalt, skidded over the mucky grass. The tracks ended on the rubble. I picked my way to the top and stood, king of the mountain, observing the slow beat of the tide.

Something seesawed in the water below. A pale arm, snagged in the rocks. The flashlight revealed a torso in a blue and yellow checked shirt. A wave lifted the form, knocking it gently against the breakwater.

Call it in, then rescue, or rescue, then call? *Rescue* wasn't even the proper term. The man was facedown in the water, the only movement courtesy of the waves.

But the waves were picking up. The next one might unmoor the arm, carry the body into the bay, or worse, drag it under.

Decision made, I tucked the flashlight and phone into my coat, folded it, and piled it on the stone, then clambered down the broken staircase toward the water.

"Have you out in a sec," I told the dead man, just to break the silence.

Deadlifting him without secure footing wouldn't work. Jumping in was a last resort. Instead, I sat, letting my legs dangle into the water. A chill shot up to my chest. I untrapped the wrist, scooped the torso under the arms, then braced my feet and leaned back as I stood, heaving the body up onto the rocks.

The man's hair hung in my face, lank as kelp. I half dragged, half carried him up the pile. Shivering, I draped my coat around my shoulders, catching my breath before rolling him over.

He'd been in the water only a short while. What had put him there was a coin-sized depression in his skull. A trickle of watery blood still seeped out.

Hoping for the miraculous, I pressed two cold fingers into his neck, checking for a pulse. There was nothing. Jeremy Fell was dead.

ELEVEN

SHOCKS

A deep-tissue chill gripped me. My pants were heavy with water and my shoes squelched. Bringing Jeremy Fell's body off the rock pile would mean dragging him over the tracks left by his assailants. So I left him there, stretched out like a Viking prince.

His pockets had yielded nothing. The clothes were off-the-rack, no wear to the jeans, an XL sticker still attached to the lapel of the shirt. In the photo the mayor's brother had been wearing loud club clothes, neck jewellery, a watch worth more than my Cadillac. Nothing added up.

Running back to the car, I saw, steepled on the lip of the dumpster, a brown wallet. Snow had gathered on the spine. I took it, slapped it on the dashboard before popping the trunk and grabbing my gym strip.

I changed standing in the parking lot, bare-assing to slip on sweats and a dry T-shirt. A little exhibitionism to round out the evening.

Inside the car, with the heater cranked, I dialed the police and asked for Inspector Gill of the Jeremy Fell task force.

"In the field, for the present," the dispatcher said.

"He'll want to hear this."

"Can you stay on the line?"

The heater roared like an exasperated St. Bernard. My limbs began to thaw, but the chill had wrapped itself around my chest. Outside, the wipers beat time and the running lights lit up the rocks. The body was cast in silhouette, just another part of the rubble.

I opened the wallet. No money in the billfold. Kyle Halliday's earnest face looked up at me from his driver's licence.

Had Kyle done this? Kidnapped the mayor's brother, walked him out to the water's edge and knocked a hole in his skull? If so, why the desperation to get hold of a firearm? And what exactly was the murder weapon?

I was hunched close to the vents, drawing imaginary lines connecting Kyle Halliday and Jeremy Fell, when the inspector came on the line. Gill said a brusque "What is it, Mr. Wakeland?"

"Jeremy Fell is at Sunset Beach," I said. "He's dead."

"Is that so?"

"I just fished him out of False Creek."

"That was decent of you," Gill said. "I'm a bit preoccupied at the moment—"

"I'm staring at him right now," I said, trying not to stutter from the chill at work in my chest. "The tracks of whoever killed him, and it looks like there were two of them, are fading pretty fast."

"Wakeland, if this is a joke," Gill said.

"Why would I fuh-fucking joke about that?"

"I'm not given to understand PIs." Gill paused. "You're a hundred percent certain the body belongs to Jeremy?"

"Un-luh-less he's got a twin."

Gill muttered something I couldn't follow.

"I'll send someone down immediately," he said. "Stay there, if you don't mind. Even if you do. I'll be along once I've explained to my boss we have a second scene."

"Suh-second?"

"I'm in Vanier Park right now," Gill said, "staring at a body with no face. Whom I thought till now was Jeremy. Life isn't short on surprises, is it, Mr. Wakeland?"

TWELVE

A WARNING

The heat crept up until the car's interior was hovering around the Mojave at midday. I was sweating. And still there was a pellet of cold lodged in my chest, like a bullet too close to the heart to remove.

Gill said to wait. So I waited.

I wondered if Evelyn Rhee knew that Jeremy was dead. How would the deputy chief of staff react? I was glad I wouldn't have to tell her.

And the other body—faceless and either similar in shape or dress to Jeremy Fell. Was Kyle Halliday connected to that body as well? Who would inform Naima that her estranged husband was linked to at least one homicide?

The bloody depression in Jeremy's skull. Without a pulse or muscles working beneath it, his skin had felt like wet rubber. What a way to die.

Snow melted as it lighted on the windshield, but the glass had fogged up. I rummaged a napkin out of the glove box and wiped it, restoring my vision of Jeremy Fell and the breakwater.

Someone was standing over him.

I activated the high beams, lighting up the beach. The tide was rolling frantically now, the spray leaping at the rocks. A woman in dark clothing and a baseball cap crouched down and aimed something at the body. The illumination of a screen, followed by a camera flash.

Out of the car, the cold now enveloping me. How had the officer, if that's what she was, reached the body if not through the parking lot?

And where were the patrol cars? The flashing red and blues? Where was Gill to take down my statement and tell me to go home?

I waved to the woman. "Over here."

"You're good where you are, mate."

The voice was male and came from behind me. I turned but a hand seized the collar of my jacket. I felt something brush my neck, warm and metallic.

"Stand still," the voice said, and called to his partner. "You almost done?"

The woman nodded and moved down the pile with an athlete's confidence, jogging first toward us, then breaking left to skirt the building. I couldn't guarantee it was the blond woman from the Sky-Train attack. The distance was too great, the snow too thick, and her cap sat low over her eyes. Her hair was darker, too. But the mouth and jaw bore a resemblance.

My shadow in the snow from the car's high beams was drawn out and enormous. The shadow behind me stretched even longer. From the tilt of the barrel pressing down above my ear, he'd be six-four, six-five. Much too tall to be the accomplice in the hoodie.

We stood there until the woman was out of sight, our breath turning to smoke in the night air. I felt absurd, freezing sockless in wet shoes, snow pattering my hair.

"We know who you are, mate," the man said. "We know all about you. Your partner, too. You want to leave us alone. You want to sit this one out."

"I don't disagree," I said.

"We're not after working folks like you, but you won't stop us, either."

"Stop who?"

The blow had plenty of force behind the unforgiving steel of the gun. I found myself sprawled in the wash of freezing water. Not unconscious but dizzy, bleeding, and with a stampeding headache.

By the time I stood up, they were gone, and a patrol car was nosing into the lot. Just in the nick of time.

THIRTEEN

D K

There was a nervous, skittering buzz to the Cambie Street police station. Officers and support staff moved through the halls efficiently, as if each were in danger of a reprimand. The mayor's brother had been murdered. This was not a night to fuck up.

A plainclothes officer escorted me to an interview room and brought me a mug of tea with a handful of creamer thimbles. I'd skinned my knee, and the dried blood had pasted the sweats to my leg. I thought of asking for disinfectant, but having to take my pants off or roll up the leg seemed too childishly shameful for the surroundings. I paced the room, drank tea, tried not to be cold.

All I knew about the second scene was that a body had been found bearing some resemblance to Jeremy Fell. Was it Kyle Halliday, and if so, why him? And why Jeremy, for that matter? Were these separate crimes, a series, or one the result of the other?

When the tea was gone, I held the mug in both hands, absorbing the last of its warmth. Weariness was working through my muscles.

Someone had begun to scratch a chessboard into the top of the interview room table. They hadn't coloured in the alternating squares. I was helping them out, using the tongue of my jacket's zipper, when the door opened.

Sergeant Ray Dudgeon regarded me for a second, before breaking into a humourless grin. In English flavoured with Québécois vowels, Dudgeon said, "Don't you get all the damn luck."

We shook hands. I knew Dudgeon a little. A friend of Sonia's, and a somewhat friendly acquaintance of mine. The Black sergeant wore a suit beneath a nylon windbreaker. The cuffs of his pants bore salt stains.

"Busy night tonight," Dudgeon said. "Gurcharan Gill tells me you know our second vic."

"You're part of the task force?" I asked.

"Me and everyone else got a uniform and half a brain. Top priority around here. At least the chief wants to be able to *say* it's top priority, if City Hall asks. Get you another coffee?"

I didn't correct Dudgeon on the beverage, and it didn't taste much different than what passed for tea. We went over my story twice, up to the point I was knocked on the head. Dudgeon read it back to me for editorial approval, then dug a cellphone out of his pocket.

"Gonna show you a couple of pictures," he said. "You supply the commentary."

"Before I do," I said, "do you have a line on the couple who hit me?"

"I wish. He called you 'mate,' huh? Sound Australian?"

"No discernable accent," I said.

"Which means what? He spoke like any white guy from Vancouver?"

"Pretty much. Except for the 'mate.'"

"Maybe he's a chess player," Dudgeon said. "Ready to look at some pics?"

Dudgeon placed his phone on the table, screen facing me. The first photo was of the body. I saw why identification had been hard. The bullet had exited through the face, shifting around what remained substantially. What was left at the centre looked like the entrance to a red cavern. Morbid humour hit me—a Picasso face—and I suppressed a tired, stupid grin.

"Know this fellow?" Dudgeon asked.

"If that part is a beard, it's probably Kyle Halliday. His wallet is in my car."

"How'd you two meet?"

"We didn't," I said. "Halliday was looking for a Transit cop's gun."

"Which you know how?"

To keep Luke Red Hill's confidence, I told the sergeant it was just something I'd heard.

"We'll come back to that," Dudgeon said. "Photo number two."

The body at remove. Kyle Halliday was propped against a short set of stairs, his head lolling away from the camera. Small mercies, I thought. I recognized the wardrobe. Club shirt, watch, leather necklace lashed around an oval of carved jade. His feet jutted out in suede loafers.

"Jeremy's clothing," I said.

"You can see why we thought it was him. Jeremy's wallet was in his pocket, too. Still had the receipt from the Alpen Club."

"Any witnesses?"

"Couple dogwalkers say they saw a man and woman. Vague stuff. Ready for the last picture?"

Dudgeon swiped and held up a picture of the *Gate to the Northwest Passage*, a square arch of rusted steel about sixteen feet tall. One of the rare pieces of Vancouver public art with something close to a soul.

You stand on the park side of the *Gate*, look through it at the mountains, Stanley Park and the bay. Weathered metal frames your view, a reminder of the ugly cost of seizing all that beauty.

Only now Kyle Halliday's body was laid at the base of the *Gate*, on its steps. Lettered neatly on the arch, in silver paint:

ONLY THE RICH FEAR THE DEATH OF KINGS

"Like something outta Dante, isn't it?" Dudgeon said. "Abandon hope all you fuckos who enter."

"Or a labour camp."

I stared at it for a moment, blowing on my hands, feeling more confused than ever. Then I told Dudgeon I had a picture of my own to show him.

FOURTEEN

TRESPASS

My car was corralled by the crime scene now, which covered both parking lot and beach. Retrieving it tonight was out of the question. Dudgeon drove me home. On the way he asked which neighbourhood I was moving to.

"I don't understand," I said, thinking of how many topics that statement could be applied to.

My nostrils were still filled with the smell of saltwater and copper. The crown of my skull throbbed from where the tall man had struck me. Why did they go back to the crime scene? Just for a photograph?

No, I didn't understand.

"The Point is pretty okay," Dudgeon was saying. "Or was when I left. My wife, she grew up in NDG, which is nice for an Anglo neighbourhood."

"NDG?" I asked.

"Notre-Dame-de-Grâce. Montreal." Dudgeon took his eyes from the road to glance at me. "You're moving there, aren't you?"

"Hadn't thought of it."

"No? You and Sonia done, then?"

A question I couldn't answer. Between Halliday and Fell, the bruise on my head and the chill that suggested I was coming down with something, I wasn't in a frame of mind to discuss my love life.

But I missed her.

"When my wife got a job at a hospital out here, we moved," Dudgeon said. "First year is tough, then you figure a new place out. Make new friends. How's your French?"

"Marginally better than my Uzbek."

"West Coast thinks it's part of Oregon," Dudgeon said.

I didn't ask him to elaborate.

My apartment was empty, Kay's blanket folded neatly on the couch. At work, I remembered. She and Blatchford patrolling a job site on Annacis Island.

I soaked under a hot shower, trying to burn out the chill. Drying off, I spotted a coarse black hair still wound around the cap of a shampoo bottle. Sonia's. I remembered long post-coital showers, rubbing the citrus-smelling gunk into her scalp.

The loss was everywhere.

At eight I woke up with grey sunlight pouring through the blinds. Kay was asleep on the couch, still in her work clothes. There was a text from Nikki Fraser, Ryan Martz's significant other. *He'll be there 9 a.m.*

I'd forgotten this was Ryan's first day.

The muscles in my shoulders felt tenderized and heavy, my head clotted, stomach unsettled. My sinuses were clear, though, which meant I was still the healthiest employee at Wakeland & Chen.

On the SkyTrain ride downtown I read the VPD's press release on the deaths. Jeremy Fell's took up the bulk of the paragraphs. The department expressed its deepest condolences to Her Worship, and a renewed commitment to find the persons responsible. Near the end it made mention of "a second deceased person who may or may not be linked to the death of Mr. Fell."

News coverage was already substantial. No word from City Hall, but "a source close to the task force" had been quoted about the "strong likelihood" that the second deceased was either Fell's killer or an accomplice. No mention of the man and woman at the beach, or Rhonda Bryce's firearm.

In death, Kyle Halliday would be convicted without trial. Doubly true if the others weren't found. The murder of the mayor's brother would be closed, even if Halliday's stayed open. Politically smart. And in the long game, maybe good strategy.

As I left the station, I wondered why that didn't sit well with me. After all, Kyle had been looking for a gun. He was somehow in league with the pair from the beach, familiar with them at the least. It was very likely they'd either killed him, or knew who did. If Kyle wasn't the person who'd broken Jeremy Fell's skull, then he had likely been on a first name basis with the killer.

So why wasn't that good enough?

Coffee on. Tea to steep. All the morning motions that made up the ritual of opening for business.

Jeff had left a voicemail saying his kid was sick and Marie had a meeting, so he'd be in two hours late. His voice was still nasal from the cold. Pretending to be healthy was wearing on him.

A second message, also from Jeff: "Just had a thought, Dave. You maybe want to shift the printer table back against the wall, make more space for the wheelchair. Other than that, I think the office is pretty accessible. But doublecheck."

Jeff had been right about the printer table. I moved it flush against the wall, creating an avenue behind the desk that was easier to negotiate.

The project with Ryan was tenuous, delicate. I was unsure if the job would help him. I only knew what work had meant to me at my low points. What it meant now. Something to occupy the mind, to get good at. Sometimes what got you out of the pit was pretending you were already out.

And sometimes we never get out.

There were still two chairs behind the reception desk, from when Kay and Blatchford had been working. I rolled one out and down the hall. Opened the door of my private office. And saw on the glass, spelled out in silver paint:

DON'T ASK FOR US
DON'T LOOK FOR US
DON'T SAY ANYTHING
WE CAN FIND YOU
STAY OUT OF OUR WAY

FIFTEEN
OPEN DOOR POLICY

The building's security system included cameras at every entrance, one in the foyer, two in the parking garage and one by the elevator on every floor. It was theoretically impossible to break into the Wakeland & Chen office without being seen. "Theoretically," of course, is worth four-fifths of fuck-all when you're staring at evidence to the contrary.

Once my nerves had unstrung, I examined the lock. It was a serrated-pin Yale, not easy to pick. The keyhole and plate had only the normal scratches you'd expect. Which meant it had either been left open by someone, Blatchford most likely, or picked by an expert, or opened with a key.

Since Wakeland & Chen handled security for the building, we had a set of master keys. They were on a ring in Jeff's desk, seemingly undisturbed.

Calling up the security footage was another dead end. The server wasn't responding.

In the basement near the garage, I opened the door to the electrical room—it was also unlocked—and saw the grey shell of the ancient computer lying on the ground. The hard drives had been torn out. The security footage was gone.

It had happened something like this. They'd either picked the building's front door lock, or gained entrance through the parking garage gate. Broken into the office and written on my window. Then taken care to remove evidence of their visit. That meant studying the building's layout, or guessing that the server was in the electrical room.

Standing in the parking garage, I phoned Blatchford. When he didn't answer for the third time, I tried his live-in boyfriend, Paul Royce.

"How pressing is this, Dave?" Paul asked. "Tim only knocked off a couple hours ago."

"It's an all-hands-on-deck situation."

"Give me five minutes to pour some coffee in him."

As I waited, I looked at the parking garage gate. No dents or pry marks. No sign of tampering to the entryway. It was fob-activated, its radio signal changing after every use, but anyone with a code-grabber and an RFID writer had an even shot at hacking it.

Stay out of our way. More than one person, connected somehow with Halliday and Fell. Capable of breaking into the office of a security company without leaving a digital trace.

Worrisome.

"Dave?" Blatchford sounded like he'd caught whatever Kay had.

"There any chance, Tim, you left the doors unlocked last night?" I asked.

"Don't think so."

"Any chance."

"Why?"

"Why do you think?"

Silence over the line as Blatchford considered it. "Kay and I finished our shift, came back, filled out our sheets, and went home."

"You didn't see anyone?"

"Nope."

"Which of you locked up?"

"Me. And I'm ninety-nine percent sure I locked the office."

"Ninety-nine."

"And a half, Dave. It was late, and I don't feel so good."

"A security company can't afford to make mistakes," I said. "Reflects poorly on us."

Blatchford answered with a series of hacking coughs. I let him go back to sleep.

Basement to office to server. That was how I would have done it. All this to send a message. Well, it had been received.

What to do about it, though?

It would be easiest to do nothing. I didn't owe Kyle Halliday or Jeremy Fell. I wasn't investigating their deaths. I'd been hired to find a gun, which would either be found by the police and logged as evidence or had been tossed away by Kyle's shooter. Either way, I'd failed. Job over. Can't win 'em all.

The problem with that was I'm hardwired for defiance. Not in a rebellious-punk sort of way, though that's probably part of it. I hate bullies, hate cruelty that goes unanswered, and I'm haunted by the times I said nothing.

When I was fifteen, I spent weekends training at the Astoria Gym. Depending on his mood and how the week had gone, my father would sometimes drive me. Matt Wakeland had boxed in the military, done well for himself, and would sometimes stay to watch or give direction. He was proud of me.

One Sunday I was up at seven. Finished my roadwork and tossed back my breakfast. He'd promised to drive me that morning. He was late coming down the stairs, said nothing as he had his coffee and Crown, a drink he treated himself to on weekends.

I knew something was up but I was thinking only of getting down to the gym, seeing my friends. Of fighting someone.

We were late leaving by twenty minutes. I said I could catch the bus if he really didn't want to. He only grimaced and told me to bring him his shoes.

It wasn't a long drive, but it was snowing. The car slalomed across Laurel Street. He pulled up in front of the gym and left the motor idling. My father drove a '78 Malibu with timing issues, and the engine would make a puckering sound if it was cold out and the gas was low.

I told him thanks, and began to leave, grabbing my bag from the back seat. As I leaned out of the car, he brought his hand down at the point where my neck met my shoulders.

I fell forward, out of the car, into the street. My father, adoptive father, drove off.

It wasn't the first time I'd ever been hit. Or the hardest. But it was inexplicable. I never asked him for an answer. Or another ride.

He was killed in an on-duty collision two years later.

Teenage cowardice, maybe, or the mistaken belief that brushing it off was more of a fuck you than asking for apology. He wasn't a regularly abusive person, or a particularly bad drunk. We both acted like it hadn't happened. And the fact that I couldn't forget about it decades later, that it still caused me a flush of anger and shame, meant I'd handled it wrong. You can't prevent being threatened, and you can't indeed win them all. But you can hold them to account.

There's no forgetting with matters of violence.

SIXTEEN

FIRST DAYS

Ryan Martz was late. At nine I phoned Inspector Gill, letting the task force know there was evidence at the office. With two murders on their hands, the attitude toward the threat in my office seemed to be, No Great Rush.

Kay and Blatchford came in at ten. Both were shocked when they saw the message scrawled on my office window.

"Swear to God, Dave," Blatchford said.

I waved off the apology. "Even if you'd left the door unlocked, or forgot to set the alarm. They wanted in badly enough, they'd've got in somehow."

"But why?" Kay asked.

No answer came to mind. There was only a window of a few hours' time when the office was guaranteed to be empty. Which meant they knew our schedule. Had targeted us. Me.

"Find out anything about Halliday at the college?" I asked Kay.

"Not really. His wife is one of the nursing program's success stories. I don't think Kyle stuck around there very long."

At 10:40, Inspector Gill and Sergeant Dudgeon showed up, a pair of forensic techs in tow. None of them looked well rested, and none looked happy to be there.

"Any late-breaking news?" I asked.

"Prints ID our Vanier Park vic as Kyle Eric Halliday," Dudgeon said. "Single shot up close, nine-millimetre most likely. Hole through his face like the Marianas Trench."

"Sergeant," Gill said, shutting up his subordinate. "Where is it, Wakeland?" No 'Mr.' anymore.

I showed them into my office. The techs began taking photos.

"Wait outside, please," Gill said.

I had tea and checked with the others, finding Kay on her laptop and Blatchford snoring in the conference room.

"Weird to think this place is like a crime scene," Kay said. "Spooky, know what I mean?"

I nodded. The office felt less secure, and somehow less familiar.

"You didn't see anything last night?" I asked. "Anyone waiting around?"

"Nuh-uh."

"Tim told you he locked up?"

"He's usually really good about that stuff," my sister said. If Tim wasn't, she wouldn't break confidence. I felt pride at that.

The door of my inner office opened and Gill stepped out. Ignoring me, he moved to Jeff's door and entered. I found him going through my partner's desk.

"We keep the loose change in a box at reception," I said.

"Very funny." Gill held up a permanent marker.

"The dry erase ones are better to sniff."

He removed the cap, turned to the window and made a quick slash across the pane.

"Silver," Gill said. "We'll see if it matches. These offices aren't locked separately?"

"No."

Gill nodded. "Keep out of the hall for now, please. The technicians will be finished by this afternoon."

"No terrible rush," I said.

"No, there isn't," the inspector said, bristling at my tone. "We do have the small matter of Jeremy Fell's murder."

"Which this might be connected to."

"Might," Gill admitted. "Along with a million other mights. We're doing what we can. Do you want the techs to string up some cordon tape, or can your people remember to stay out of there for a few hours?"

I looked to Dudgeon, but the sergeant's expression was deliberately neutral. I took them down to view the electrical room.

"This door's usually locked?" Dudgeon asked me.

"Always."

"But the key is just lying around your office."

"It's in a drawer in a locked office, under video surveillance. Was I supposed to have an Indiana Jones boulder to protect it from being stolen?"

"You're the security expert," Gill said.

"We keep our weapons locked up in a safe and our files double encrypted," I said. "There's nothing worth stealing in the office."

Realizing I was making excuses, I shut up.

I walked with Gill and Dudgeon out of the garage to their unmarked Charger, parked at the curb.

"Are you treating Kyle Halliday as a separate case?" I asked.

"Looking at every possibility," Gill said. "We'd love to know how you learned he was looking for a gun."

"Confidential," I said.

"We'll see."

A Chrysler minivan pulled up behind the car. Nikki Fraser was at the wheel. She nodded at Dudgeon and Gill as she climbed out.

"Dave," she said, giving me a harried smile and a hug. Nikki was in uniform, blond hair ponytailed and sunglasses resting on her forehead. "My fault we're late. Big time apologies. Hope it didn't put you out."

The back side panel slid open. Ryan Martz was belted in. He struggled free of the straps while Nikki worked the hydraulic lift that set his chair on the ground.

Ryan scowled at me. Nodded when his wife said she'd pick him up at three. Smiled wolfishly when he saw Dudgeon.

"Old Fuckface Ray, how's it going?"

Dudgeon nodded. "Hey, Ryan. No complaints."

"Still married to that fat-ass nurse?"

Dudgeon wasn't offended by the banter, but neither did he respond like a colleague of Ryan's. He nodded again, cordially. There was distance there, discomfort.

Gill said, "Hello, Ryan," with professional good humour.

"Hey, Inspector." Acknowledging me, Ryan asked, "You arresting this mope?"

Gill looked at me and smiled. "Not at present. Good seeing you."

After the van and patrol car had left, Ryan and I took the elevator up.

I was late to realize that what I'd just seen was every interaction Ryan Martz had with his former friends and colleagues. Pity and discomfort hiding behind formal politeness. He'd been a shithead, but a shithead on equal footing.

"What'd they want?" Ryan asked me.

"Someone broke in, left a threatening message."

"Can't imagine why. Nice guy like you. Helps his gimp friends out."

"Not if they're late," I said.

His face darkened. "Nik said it was her fault."

"She did."

"It wasn't."

"I know."

"I didn't want to come. Nik said if I didn't give it a chance, she'd leave. Fucking believe that?"

"Can't imagine why," I said. "Nice guy like you."

"Don't break my balls, Dave. I'm just explaining."

His eyes were downcast. It was as much of an apology as I'd get.

"We start here on time," I said.

Ryan nodded. "Won't happen again."

SEVENTEEN
HEAVY DEBTS

I spent the morning and early afternoon showing Ryan the ropes. The filing and messaging was all straightforward. Billing was more complex, and Jeff would have to explain that, deficient as I was at all things financial.

When it came to answering the phone, I told Ryan I'd handle it for now. He could work his way up to the cheerful professionalism required of a receptionist.

The techs worked swiftly. Two sleep-deprived women efficiently documented the scene, bagged the silver marker, scraped paint flakes off the window for analysis. I gave them elimination prints. The techs were thorough, but there wasn't much to do. The office was returned to us at noon.

Jeff brought lunch, hot and sour soup and a bag of Chinese doughnuts. Nikki had packed Ryan a sandwich. I wasn't up to eating just yet, so I read the news.

Headline space was given to Jeremy Fell and the political implications of his slaying. City councillors and Hollywood North celebrities paid social-media tribute to Jeremy's "good heart" and "zest for life." In contrast, Kyle Halliday's name hadn't yet been released. I didn't know if that was tactical, to lull whomever killed him into thinking the police weren't following up on the connection. Even if it was, I didn't feel good about the disparity of column inches. One death shouldn't mean so much more.

"What are you going to do about the message?" Jeff asked.

"Don't know yet." I turned to Ryan. "What would you do?"

He stared at the writing. As a cop, Ryan Martz never possessed a keen investigative mind. Inexplicably he'd been assigned to Missing Persons, where he'd seemed beleaguered and overwhelmed. The plodding, methodical side of casework wasn't for him. Neither was he adept at consoling the relatives of the missing, assuring them that everything was being done.

But I remembered back to our training at the Justice Institute. Whatever deficiencies he had as an investigator, that role appealed to him, and it brought out his best. Despite the risk to his career, Ryan had always found ways to help me when I needed info on a missing person. Doing the right thing wasn't foreign to him.

He stared. For a second something keen and engaged flitted across his face. A hunter's instinct. Then it died down and disappeared.

"Fuck if I know," Ryan said. "I'm only the secretary."

At three, Nikki Fraser came to pick up Ryan. She was all smiles in the reception area as her husband did up his coat. "How'd it go?" she asked me.

"First days are first days," I said. "But we got some work done." To Ryan I said, "Tomorrow at nine?"

He moved past us to the door, and out. Nikki followed.

Kay and Blatchford donned their jackets for another night of corporate sentry work. Better them than me. I wished them luck, and told Kay to make sure Blatchford locked the doors.

Jeff and I were the only ones left. We swapped the locks, replaced the broken server with an outdated MacBook that had been in our closet.

"Hope this doesn't get out," he said. "Last thing we need is word getting around that we can't protect our own office building."

"Are we really in that bad shape?" I asked.

"Do you really want to know?"

"Well don't bore me."

We hiked to the top floor and went down level by level, checking windows, the doors to the fire exit stairs. Everything was working as it should.

"Short answer is, we're overextended," Jeff said. "Dijkstra, our third biggest client, went into receivership, owing us north of a hundred grand. We'll be lucky to get pennies on the dollar from whoever buys them, and we won't see that any time soon."

On the fourth floor, one of the counsellors had wedged open a window. Too small for a human to fit through. We closed and locked it, adjusted the thermostat.

"Companies fold all the time," Jeff continued. "We can carry that amount. But Solis, our top client, they're four months behind on our invoices. Last month they said it was a switch to a new system. Now they're saying it's a bank thing."

"All of a sudden they don't need corporate security?" I asked.

"Those four months, they're making the interest off our money instead of us. Counting on us not wanting them to take their business somewhere else."

"There's no one else as good," I said.

Jeff smiled as if I'd made a reasonably funny quip. "Not as good, maybe, but cheaper. Always get cheaper."

"So how long can we carry them?"

"Another month or two, maybe."

"I didn't know," I said.

Again, the grin. "Of course you didn't. You think looking for guns and missing people pays the rent."

When we finished, Jeff drove me to Sunset Beach to collect my car. The afternoon sky was clear and the snow on the grass had been trampled into patches of ice. Cordon tape roped off the breakwater. On the Seawall, bike riders and joggers passed us, not even bothering to rubberneck at the crime scene.

"I won't ask what you're planning to do," Jeff said.

"Good, because I have no idea."

"There's multiple people out there who want to hurt you if you get involved."

"True enough."

"Sure be stupid to do it, then. Wouldn't it?"

I pointed at the breakwater, lit up by the descending sun. A black mass below orange flame.

"A man died there last night. If I hadn't seen him in the water—hadn't been looking for Rhonda Bryce's gun—"

"What do you want, Dave? A medal?"

"I want to understand."

Jeff wiped his nose and sniffed. "Sometimes you forget I know you."

"Meaning what?"

"Everything you do comes from two places," my partner said. "Guilt and anger."

Before I could argue the truth of that, Jeff's phone rang. He answered and said, "Okay" and "probably fifteen minutes." When he hung up, I asked who it was.

"Evelyn Rhee," he said. "Asking can we come out to the house."

"Whose house? Hers?"

"Valerie Fell's."

EIGHTEEN

HER WORSHIP OF WOLFE AVENUE

The mayor of Vancouver resided in Shaughnessy Heights, a neighbourhood where a million dollars gets you closer to a vagrancy charge than to owning a home. Valerie Fell's two-story craftsman would have been described as "modest" fifty years ago. Now modesty was dead, and the house was a symbol, both of status and of How Folks Used to Live.

There was no street parking outside the house. Three blocks over I slid the Cadillac in behind Jeff's Prelude. Together we trudged back along the curve of Wolfe Avenue, passing the gates of three-storey houses, driveways full of Beemers and Mercs. When Wakeland & Chen started turning a profit, we'd each bought the car of our dreams. Ten years out, those dreams looked shabby and provincial compared to the respectable money of Shaughnessy.

"We may have the only cars on the block not made by Germans," I said.

"I think I saw a Tesla back there." Jeff didn't say anything else until we reached the door of the house. Then he whispered the words, "Best behaviour."

"Scout's honour," I said.

We were prepared for butlers and maids. For high-ceilinged foyers and drawing rooms and palace guards. Valerie Fell opened the door herself, holding a half-smoked cigar. She appraised us with a glance and said, in perfect deadpan, "Apparently I *am* ready for you."

Inside we took seats in the living room. The blinds were drawn. Evelyn Rhee poured cognac and handed the snifters to us.

"Good to see you again," I said. "Wish the circumstances were better."

Rhee nodded, her look saying, *go along with this.*

Seated in the living room was a white-haired man I recognized as Ferguson MacLeish, the deputy chief constable of operations. MacLeish didn't much like me. I wasn't exactly subscribing to his newsletter, either. Seeing me in the mayor's home, sharing a sectional with him, made the city's second-highest-ranking police officer blanch.

I smiled and raised my glass to him.

The mayor wasn't sitting. Valerie Fell stood with her back to the fireplace, dropping ash on the floor. Behind her, on the mantel, was a tryptych of photographs showing her brother in childhood, adolescence and middle age. Jeremy Fell smiled in every one of them. Even younger, he had that same wastrel look. A grown-up kid having too much fun to mature.

"Fergie, I need a second with these boys," Fell said.

The deputy chief stood awkwardly, shaking his head. "I really should be here, Val, if you're going to make some sort of secret deal."

"If you were," the mayor said, "then it wouldn't be very secret, would it?"

MacLeish set down his snifter and replaced his cap. He made a dignified exit, nodding to everyone but me.

"Hope you enjoyed your Christmas cake," I called after him.

It put a hitch in his step.

When he was gone, Fell said, "You two aren't popular with VPD brass."

"Jeff is slightly more popular," I said.

"Hard to be less."

"MacLeish loused up a case I worked once," I explained. "Since then, I like to send him cards around the holidays. The occasional baked good. As Seneca says, wherever there's a human being, there's an opportunity to be kind."

Valerie Fell drew on her cigar, exhaled and smiled.

"Cut the shit," she said.

A portrait of power. Fell was sixty but looked mid-forties. About six feet tall, trim, hair a shade more metallic than honey blond and cut to the jawline. Black suit, smudges of ash on the knees. Eyes red from tears but nothing in her carriage that hinted at her grief.

The mayor spoke fast, gesticulated with the cigar. Evelyn Rhee took note of her and tried to anticipate what she'd want.

"I asked you here for two reasons, one of which was a wee bit disingenuous. I wanted Fergie to see you come in. Hopefully it'll light a fire under his ass, get Jeremy's murderer behind bars. Sooner that happens, the better."

"Our condolences," Jeff said.

"Yeah," Fell said, acknowledging with a wave. "Second reason is to put you to work finding out about Jeremy. Who killed him, yes, that's priority one, but anything sensitive he was involved in, anything he might have done. I want to tie a bow on this as neatly as I can."

"Dave and I aren't homicide investigators," Jeff said.

"I'm not hiring you boys for your acumen with a magnifying glass," Fell said. "I'm hiring you because I *can* hire you. Because what you turn up while in my employ is confidential, mine to give to the police if it'll help them find his killer, mine to sit on if I feel that's best. Understand me?"

"Not totally," I said.

"I chair the police board. My relationship with the department is contentious, when there's any relationship at all. I want them to do the best job they can, for Jeremy's sake. But I also can't have them thinking that buys them anything. And any surprises from my brother's colourful history, I want to know about before they do."

The mayor opened the grate of the fireplace and tossed the butt of the cigar in. She clapped her hands. Evelyn Rhee brought her a wet wipe, took it from her when she was done. Her hand lingered on the mayor's for a second, a small gesture of intimacy.

Fell sat across from us, running her hands over the arms of her chair.

"I'm not this much of a hard-ass all the time," she said. "I loved Jeremy. Maybe I'm hurrying through this before the shock wears off and the reality hits that he's dead, that his photos are going to sit up there the rest of my life. My baby brother."

She took up MacLeish's glass and downed the cognac. Leaned back and yawned and crossed her legs.

"I'm not going to sit through a lengthy interrogation," Fell said. "Ask your questions and get the rest from Ev. And before you say it, no, I don't know of anyone who would want to harm my brother. If I did, you wouldn't be here."

I let Jeff take first crack. "What was Jeremy like when he was younger?" he asked.

"An absence," the mayor said.

"You mean he ran away from home?"

Fell clipped the end from another cigar.

"I mean," she said, "our parents gave us an infinity of options. Too many for him. I knew what I wanted pretty much from the jump. College, business, elected office. A privileged existence, but I had talent and resources behind me. I became who I wanted to be."

"And Jeremy?"

"I still don't know who he was," Fell admitted. "He didn't know either. The most damning thing I can say about a person. His dreams changed so often, had such a lack of will behind them."

She outlined a few of Jeremy Fell's brief passions. The drums. Texas hold 'em. Being a DJ at a goth night club. Raising fish and turtles, riding motorcycles, kung fu, tai chi, attempting to get a commercial pilot's licence. Either he'd suffer a setback and quit, or he'd segue into the next momentary obsession.

"For a heartbeat he was into gardening," Valerie Fell said. "He'd shadow our mother in her greenhouse, ask questions about fertilizers and organic pesticides, the whole schmear. Ma had a stroke and couldn't tend to her garden, but felt it was in good hands. And that's when Jeremy decided that online poker was his real calling. Her greenhouse ended up overgrown, infested with aphids and rats. He killed it, the negligent putz."

She blew cigar smoke at the ceiling. Still disappointed with him, even in death.

Jeremy didn't work. He'd inherited money and got a stipend from his sister to stay out of trouble. Valerie Fell had no idea about his friends, how he'd spent the last days of his life.

"Did your brother resent you?" Jeff asked.

"Of course. Deeply. And I him. When our mother kicked off, I had a heap of paperwork to do, on top of my business and political career. I answered the phone nonstop for a year. Jeremy got to be sad. He got to be distraught. When he slipped, everyone forgave him; after all, he'd been through so much. Me, I don't get to slip. Not ever."

Valerie Fell dropped her second cigar into the brandy glass. It hissed and smoked. She banged a fist on the arm of the chair.

"Come on, boys," she said. "The top PIs in the city, you must have better questions. Ask me what the police won't."

"Who did he fuck?" I said.

The mayor smiled. "That's better. No steady partner I know. He was malleable. If I lined up the guys and gals I know he had congress with, all they'd have in common was a dominant personality. Outgoing. My brother was fundamentally weak."

"He cared for you," Evelyn Rhee said, speaking softly but with conviction. "During the campaign no one worked harder. Jeremy was proud of you."

"I'll miss the wretch." Fell sighed as if irritated by her own grief. Rhee placed a glass of water in her hand, rested her palm on the mayor's neck.

"Last line of questioning, boys," Fell said. "Make it good."

I looked to Jeff but he gave me a wave, *all yours*.

"Where did Jeremy leave wreckage?" I asked.

The mayor thought it over, tapping her knuckles against the water glass.

"That deserves a better answer than I can give," she said. "Financially, here and there, but he never put the bite on too hard. Especially not with his friends. He'd let people down, though. Disappoint them. A couple years ago he felt his alcohol and pot consumption was a little too high. He registered for treatment. I was happy to see him make the effort. Three days later, Jeremy was on my doorstep, lighting himself a joint. A week after that, the doctor showed up looking for the rest of his money. Jeremy had skipped out."

"Was that the only time he tried to get clean?"

"God no," Valerie Fell said. "The court ordered him to. And he went voluntarily a couple more times."

"Why does that occasion stick out?" Jeff asked.

Her answer came quickly. "The doctor. He was on local TV at the time, this dignified gentleman with an old-hippie-gone-straight sort of look. When he showed up asking for Jeremy, he looked positively frazzled. More than that. *Ruined*. When you said *wreckage*, his face came to mind. Like he'd watched his dream of having Valerie Fell's brother as his success story get ripped to pieces in front of him."

"What was his name?"

"Van something," Fell said. "I remember the ad. What was his practice called, Ev?"

Evelyn Rhee had her phone out, already looking it up. But Fell snapped her fingers, her memory beating her assistant to it.

"The Jericho Centre," she said.

NINETEEN
THE JERICHO CURE

Mattias Van Veen had a spiel worthy of a nineteenth-century medicine show.

His website, long inactive, explained how as a young man Van Veen had left medical school seeking "a more holistic approach to wellness and self-mastery." His quest had taken him to the Far East, where he'd apprenticed with Master Chandrasekharan, a guru who'd devoted his life to perfecting the principles of *brahmacharya*. Could the benefits of pure living, the young Van Veen wondered, be attained without giving up the material comforts of the West?

It took Van Veen a year and a half to soak up the wisdom he needed. He opened his own clinic the next year, advocating wellness, positivity, self-discipline and peace.

The Jericho Cure, so named because the clinic was spitting distance from Jericho Beach, was a hazy nebula of yoga, abstinence, organic nutrition and talk therapy. You could attend a free info session, or book a stay at the clinic. The stays could last a few hours or as long as a month. There were take-home programs, a set of DVDs, and audio lectures for download. If you were in the market for spiritual betterment, the good doctor would meet you halfway.

The Cure claimed to heal the following ailments:

- depression
- addiction

- obesity
- mood swings
- eros
- chronic pain
- fatigue

It could also "stem the growth of carcinogens and toxins in the self."

The Jericho Centre was in vogue for a couple of years among Vancouver's elite. Hockey executives, restaurateurs, pulp and paper millionaires, actors on teen superhero shows, real estate emperors, landed gentry. Some of the names on the testimonials page I recognized from Wakeland & Chen's own client list.

It was easy to see through Van Veen, to mock him and his phony mysticism. To hate the insinuation that whatever was wrong with you, from fatigue to cancer, could be fixed with a few easy payments. My birth parents had met through an alternative religion, had given me up as a way to free themselves from encumbrances. Damn right I despise hocus pocus.

But I tried to understand what drew people like Jeremy Fell, like my parents, to that sort of thing. To call it weakness was only to pat yourself on the back.

Years ago, I'd dated a woman named Shay, an addict perpetually in and out of recovery. Our relationship had crashed on that rock. She'd stolen from me several hard-to-find Nick Cave albums, though she'd given a few of them back.

Shay and I had once been out for drinks at some horrible test kitchen downtown. Waiting for Jeff and Marie, we'd talked ourselves out on every other topic, finally swinging around to *purpose.*

I told her I didn't think much about it.

"But you have to think about it," Shay said.

"Actually, I don't."

"So you're one of those 'biological imperative' types. Mate and work and don't ask why we're here."

"No," I said. "I just think it's a bad question. An ungrateful one."

"Who 'zactly am I 'sposed to be grateful to, Dave?"

I didn't have an answer.

Shay believed there was a calling, a more perfect way to be. Her addiction kept her from reaching this. If she could conquer that, solve it, she would elevate. Be a truer version of herself.

"Disagree," I said. "You're fine how you are."

"Well, I disagree with *that*."

"What good does judging yourself do?"

"It's not *judging* myself," Shay said. "I don't even think I can explain it. What are we living for?"

She made a gesture with both hands encompassing the two of us, our watery bourbons, our uncomfortable aluminum stools. And beyond the bar, the city, the cosmos. The whole shebang.

"How is this enough for you?" she asked.

I told her I didn't realize it was an option.

A few years later I'd run into Shay. She'd gotten on methadone, got clean, stayed clean, and was working at the Union Gospel Mission. She'd married and had a son. A true success story. They're rare.

I wondered if Shay had found her *enough*—job, family, purpose— or if she'd lowered her expectations and made do.

Jeremy Fell had found the world wanting. And I suspected my birth parents felt the same. Maybe we all do. Or the good ones, at least. The ones who aren't kidding themselves. Maybe they see the lack that the rest of us try to pretend isn't there. Quacks like Van Veen feast on that kind of searching vulnerability.

I don't believe there is a purpose to the world. But I like people. They interest me. I find my purpose in them.

TWENTY

BRIGHT IDEAS

A military march beat down on my patio. I'd bought a pack of cigarettes, tore the cellophane off, but didn't smoke them.

Instead I stood with the sliding door open, listening to the rain. I stared at the construction site across the street, the crane and concrete skeleton looming over my patio fence. The future. It was ugly.

Jeremy Fell and Kyle Halliday, Rhonda Bryce, the man and woman from the SkyTrain attack. The one who'd hit me and held a gun to my head. And now Van Veen and his clinic.

None of the names coalesced into a workable theory. At least not one that could compete with the official narrative. Halliday killed Fell, was killed in turn by his accomplice. That was simple and efficient, painted Kyle Halliday as the bad man and Jeremy Fell the angelic victim. One plus one. Justice served. And why not?

I looked at the cigarettes, remembered my promise. Which only made me think of Sonia.

It would be three hours later in Montreal. The future.

Reflexively I'd picked up my phone. The number I dialed was Naima Halliday's. To my surprise she picked up.

"Yes?" Her voice sounded plaintive but steady.

"I spoke with you yesterday," I said.

"Mr. Wakeland. David."

"I'm sorry for your loss."

A long pause, her breath on the line. "Thank you."

"If you need anything."

"All right."

"I'd like to talk with you again."

"About Kyle?"

"Yes," I said, reasonably sure I was telling the truth.

"Tomorrow, maybe," Naima said. "I'm very tired. David?"

"Yes."

"Goodnight."

I threw the cigarettes over the fence, in the general direction of the future, shut the door and went to sleep.

The original Jericho Centre was gone, replaced by Kumon, cannabis and an H&R Block. Mattias Van Veen's home address was a short walk through the Point Grey neighbourhood. While Shaughnessy was a closed-off enclave of winding streets and secretive mansions, Point Grey had money that desired to be sociable. The yacht club and private academy gave the wealthy a sense of community and made the neighbourhood resistant to change. Social housing, drug treatment—those were East Van problems. Not in our beautiful backyard.

And it *was* beautiful. In the early morning, with the snow sluiced away by the rain, the houses in Point Grey looked clean, their lawns tidy and ready for spring. Van Veen's was no exception. The front staircase and cedar shakes looked new.

A woman with a scarf around the bottom half of her face opened the door. Maybe thirty, red hair. She was holding a cup of coffee in a Santa Claus mug. She'd never heard of the doctor.

"We just rented the place last year," she said. "Me and my husband and daughter, my sister and her partner and our mom."

Her posture was non-threatening, but the scarf and the mug brought to mind jailhouse napalm. I kept a hand on the railing, ready to move.

"Could you do me a favour?" I asked, raising my voice. "I'm hard of hearing and reading lips is easier for me." I mimed lowering the scarf.

"Oh, sure."

She exposed the rest of her face. An underbite and a mild upturn of the nose. Not the features of the woman from the SkyTrain. I relaxed a bit.

"These heritage homes get so cold in the morning," she said. "One of the things I need to bring up with the landlord."

"Speaking of whom. How do you get in touch?"

A wariness edged into her voice. "We signed a two-year lease," she said.

Everything in Vancouver comes back to real estate.

I smiled and tried to look harmless and well-housed. "I'm not in the market," I said. "Just looking to talk with Dr. Van Veen."

"We've never actually met the owner. A young guy picks up the rent last day of the month."

"Pay by cheque?"

"You swear you're not in the market?"

"I've lived in the same East Broadway apartment since I was twenty-one," I said. "No chance I'm giving it up."

"Stuck in a good deal, huh?" She smiled, the threat removed. "We pay in cash, which I know sounds iffy, but that's how he wants it. We pay the utes."

"What's the young guy's name?"

"Dagan Moody."

I showed her the picture of the man in the hoodie. The woman shook her head.

"Way taller than that," she said. "And he always wears a leather jacket, a funny one with zippers. Even in the heat."

"Does he ever refer to other people as 'mate'?"

"Oh, so you know him," the tenant said.

I nodded and told her we'd met.

TWENTY-ONE
THE CLINIC IN THE HILLS

Dagan Moody wasn't listed as a realtor or a property manager. He was absent from social media, had never held a job. Born in Pretoria, South Africa to low-level Canadian diplomats. Both dead now. Moody had a birth certificate, a driver's licence and a home address that matched Van Veen's.

Halliday, Moody, the woman from the beach and her stocky partner in the SkyTrain attack were all in their mid-twenties. Van Veen was double their age, Jeremy Fell about the same. Was there a generational angle to the deaths?

Naima Halliday was older than the quartet, in her mid-thirties. But thinking of her shifted my thoughts to a different track.

Both Jeff and Ryan Martz had beat me to the office. I could hear them at reception, going over time sheets and payroll. Ryan was swearing every third word, which I took as a sign that things were running as they should.

"Wrong date," Jeff said. "No. Don't delete that column."

"Whoever invented this spreadsheet shit can slobber on my column."

I shut my door and drowned them out with a Kamasi Washington album.

Van Veen had played the corporate shell game, listing the Jericho Centre as an asset of another business, which he also controlled. Not illegal, but crafty. His umbrella corporation owned a half acre in the North Vancouver hills. Satellite photos showed a house and two smaller buildings grafted onto the cliff, a winding driveway and plenty of foliage near the front gate.

The doctor wasn't in jail, and wasn't still practising. That left myriad possibilities. If Moody was collecting rent on Van Veen's behalf, maybe he had other responsibilities as well. Worth a conversation.

On my way out of the office, I told Jeff and Ryan where I was going.

"Want company?" Jeff said.

"If you can tear yourself away."

"Ryan's got a good handle on things."

A compliment from Jeff Chen was rare. It meant something. Ryan only scowled and went back to the spreadsheet.

We took a work van. Jeff drove. Down the Stanley Park Causeway, over the Lions Gate Bridge. On winter mornings, the park with its expansive swaths of evergreens was little more than a thoroughfare for commuters and a background for the cycling set. The roads were too busy for the snow to stick.

"What's with Ryan?" Jeff asked. "Tell the guy he's doing good work, he looks at me like I pissed on his shoulder."

"Think about what we're doing," I said. "And what he's doing. And which he'd rather be doing."

"I guess," Jeff said. "But if he hates the office so much, you're just forcing him to do what he hates."

"One way of looking at it."

"What other way is there? Either he's right for the job or not."

"What if the job's right for him?"

Jeff muttered something about square pegs and made the turn off the bridge.

Up in the canyon, off the highway, the houses clung to the hillside, glass and stained wood. Snowdrifts on the shoulder, roads speckled with purple salt. Another haven for millionaires. In the eighties, Lynn

Valley had been where families moved who couldn't afford the city. Before that it was called Shaketown, a collection of shacks for lumberjacks and millwrights. Mountains appropriated from the Squamish and Musqueam and Tsleil-Waututh, turned into luxury homes.

"Just dynamite it all," I said.

My partner glanced over at me. "Not a fan of lodge house style?"

"Not a fan of the rich."

"Like you'd turn one of these places down, you could get one," Jeff said. "Remember what I said about guilt and anger?"

Van Veen's property might have been a half acre, but most of it ran on a diagonal down the foot of Mount Fromme. The house was cut into the granite shelf, with the two smaller structures, duplexes, on either side. The compound was connected by pathways and staircases. No upkeep had been performed in several months, maybe longer. The red cedar had greyed. Here and there, steps were missing.

Propped up against the gate, on the inside, was a sign in black metal, gilt letters etched into it. THE JERICHO TREATMENT CENTRE AND SCHOOL OF WELLNESS.

No cars in the driveway. The gate was nine feet, secured with a bicycle lock. The buzzer didn't work, and the black paint on the bars were green with moss. An eight-digit property left to rot.

I shouted the names of Dagan Moody and Dr. Van Veen through the fence. No response.

"We could sit on it for a while," Jeff said. "See if anyone comes out."

The gate had been designed for privacy more than security. A hideaway rather than a fortress. I could reach the top, barely, but there was no foothold. I opened the back of the van.

"Or we could canvass the neighbours," Jeff said.

We'd filled the back of the van with tools to give it the illusion of a work truck. A short collapsible ladder was clipped to the side. I unclipped and extended it, then propped it up against the fence.

"I'm not breaking and entering, Dave."

"This is more in the realm of trespassing," I said. "Just a look around. I'll be quick."

It was a short drop and I landed on my feet.

"Feed the ladder through the bars so I can get out," I told Jeff. "Or you could climb over."

"Not happening."

"You're on mayoral business, Jeff. If now's not the time to flout the rules, then when?"

No cars had come along the road. We heard crows in the trees, Steller's jays, but nothing else. My partner looked each way before taking a grip on the ladder. He sighed.

"What the hell," Jeff said.

TWENTY-TWO

WELLNESS

YOU ARE HERE.

Posted at the junction of the driveway and branching footpath was a map and bulletin board, the paint eroded by years of neglect. A few sun-yellowed brochures still sat in the clear plastic tray below the map.

"Welcome to the Jericho Centre," the brochure said. "Your privacy and wellness are our topmost concern. WE are here for YOU."

The duplexes, or "privacy bungalows" as they were called on the map, were deluxe accommodations. Less well-heeled guests had to make do with the suites in the Main Lodge.

The front doors were locked, but since the walls were mostly glass, we could walk the circumference and see inside. A dingy dining room, chairs up on the tables. A trash-strewn pool and hot tub. A devotional room with the fixtures missing, the edges of the yoga mats gnawed by rodent teeth. No sign anyone lived here but squirrels.

"Why hold onto this property?" Jeff said. "Van Veen could sell it or rent it out. Waste of money."

A glass shield enclosed the cliff-facing patio. Deck chairs. Ashtrays on metal tripods, leaves and cigarette butts floating inside.

This is where we make you perfect, I thought, *for the reasonable sum of a thousand dollars a night.*

You'll become sober, attractive, slender, confident. A whole person, and a genuine one. And if you want to keep smoking, or spiking up, or getting laid with a modicum of privacy, we can accommodate you. Progress at your own pace. Rome wasn't built in a day, friend, and neither was the Jericho Centre.

"Look at this," Jeff said.

One of the ashtrays held an inch less water than the others. Cigarette butts piled up inside. The marble inset was cracked.

"It's been moved recently," Jeff said.

"And emptied out." I pointed to a shrub where, around the roots, several decaying filters had been dumped.

"So we know someone's been here, least within the month."

"And they liked to smoke," I said.

There was an overgrown garden, a gazebo at the centre with part of its roof caved in. I thought of Jeremy Fell. Why had he left Van Veen's care? Did he sense it was a scam, or was there an incident that prompted him to run?

We crossed the tennis court and doubled back. For a large piece of land, it gave the impression of being cramped, of trying to offer too much on too little ground. Tendrils of the garden snaked out onto the court, which was now puddled and uneven.

Bungalows C and D were connected by a more intact staircase. The path doubled back on itself so that the front doors were hidden from the driveway, and from each other. No glass walls here, only a few tinted windows. Solar panels in the roof.

The locks weren't engaged. I nudged open the door of Bungalow C and caught a whiff of putrefaction, heard an insect hum. I recoiled. The door swung farther open. Jeff gagged, took two steps, and threw up in the laurel bushes.

All I could see from the doorway was a bundle resting on a bed, a sleeping bag serving as a winding sheet. Tucking my nose into my shirt collar, I stepped inside and walked to the bed. Bloat had set in, the sleeping bag stuffed like a sausage casing.

I had a sense of who it was, but wanted to be sure. That meant dragging the bag's zipper down. As I did, I tried to think pleasant thoughts. Glenn Gould playing "Moonlight Sonata." Oscar Peterson with strings. Deborah Kerr in the arms of Burt Lancaster. A Maker's Mark on ice at The Narrow Lounge. I thought of waking up in the hospital to find Sonia and Kay at my bedside, feeling safe and cared for. The smell and the feel of the corpse were bad enough to pollute these thoughts. Instead, I thought of nothing.

Emptying my mind. How Zen. Van Veen would approve.

The male deceased hadn't been shot or stabbed. Other than that, I had no idea how he'd died. Liquefaction happens generally a month after death. Factoring in the cold and the sleeping bag, say four to six weeks.

My hand found the dead man's wallet. The long silver hair of the corpse matched the driver's licence photo. The mole on the right cheek in the picture corresponded to one on the body. The height was the same. Other than that, in death Mattias Van Veen was unrecognizable.

TWENTY-THREE
DANGERS OF THE TRADE

While I was examining Van Veen's corpse, Jeff had called it in. We stowed the ladder and waited outside. Soon a patrol car arrived and two uniforms from the North Vancouver RCMP took down our story. We heard what sounded like a shout, officers. Hopped the fence only to offer assistance. Found Van Veen's body. Touched nothing. Called it in right away.

Lying to the authorities sat less easily with Jeff, having never been an officer himself. After they'd taken our statements and let us go, my partner turned the van in the direction of the city, his silence loud in the van.

Eventually he said, "I shouldn't have gone over. Shouldn't encourage you."

"We did zero harm. Maybe even some good. Someone would've discovered the body."

"This way, I get these memories. That smell."

"It comes out," I said. "A little tomato juice and lemon—"

"That's not it," Jeff said. "You're a bad influence on me, Dave."

"Because I don't really care about making money?"

"Because you don't really care about staying alive."

"I'm not suicidal," I said.

"No. Just reckless."

Traffic slowed on the bridge. The open windows carried the scent away, but it was cold in the van. Jeff coughed.

"I'm almost forty," he said. "I can't be doing stuff like that."

"No one forced you to climb that ladder," I said. "Maybe you don't care, but someone broke into our office. Hit me. Killed two people, maybe three, and blinded another. I want to know who and why."

"No matter the cost?"

I didn't answer.

Jeff undid the buttons of his suit jacket. He reached into the breast.

"I've got a family," my partner said. "A career. Much as you pretend, you got these things, too. You need me for anything legal, I'll be around. Rest of the time, Dave, you better carry this."

He passed me a small black .32 automatic.

"I don't like guns," I said.

"People you're dealing with, I don't think you got much choice."

TWENTY-FOUR
WORKING LUNCH

City Hall couldn't afford to stay in mourning. The corridors were quietly abuzz with clerks, councillors, assistants and security. A guard in a yellow slicker asked who I was and what I wanted.

"David Wakeland to see Evelyn Rhee."

"Wait right here, sir. I'll call up."

I lingered between potted palms, overhearing excited talk of budgets and school board seats, and how they'd just seen Jeremy at the Christmas party, and who could've done such a thing?

At the clack of heels on terrazzo, I turned. Evelyn Rhee wore black and looked as tired as I felt.

"Val is in crisis mode today, Mr. Wakeland. Which means I can't give you much time."

"It's Dave," I said. "I owe you an apology."

"Not necessary. What do you need?"

I'd damaged something between us, lowered myself in her esteem. No helping that now. All I could be was efficient and not waste her time.

"The murder books for Jeremy and Kyle Halliday, for a start."

"Police files aren't something I can just ask for," Rhee said.

"But the task force briefs your office on the investigation, don't they? You have a sense of where they're at?"

One of the elevators was broken, and we stepped to the side as the lineup for the other grew. A pushy swarm of suits tried to enter.

A mechanic in blue work coveralls and a black turban pried open the doors of the malfunctioning car.

"You've got a vehicle?" Rhee said, making her decision.

"Parked across the street, a van." I'd aired it out and added a new air freshener.

Rhee looked at her phone. "It's 1:20 now. At two sharp pick me up at the intersection of Cambie and Tenth. Northwest corner. I can spare half an hour for lunch."

"Will do."

"And bring food with you."

"Any requests?"

"Don't skimp on the heat."

I timed the corner pickup exactly, earning only one chorus of honks as I paused long enough for Evelyn Rhee to climb in.

She sighed and wound up her window. Used the mirror on the sun visor to smooth her hair. "What an absolute shit-mess of a week," she said. "Mind if I turn the heat up?"

I drove toward Little Mountain. Lanes wound up through Queen Elizabeth Park, to the tallest point within city limits. Plates of ice floated on the duck ponds. A wet snow was falling.

"We used to play there, my sister and I," Rhee said, pointing at the pond. "We'd get these Pirate Packs from White Spot, the meals that come in the little cardboard galleon. After lunch we'd sail our My Little Ponies on the pond. If the boat sank, our dad would wade in and rescue them. Soon he was bringing hip waders and a pool net with him to lunch."

"It's one of the last good places in the city," I said. "Every once in a while I think I should start keeping a list. Remind me that Vancouver's not only for the rich."

She nodded.

"About the task force," I said.

"Food first. What'd you bring?"

"Tacofino." I handed her the white paper bag from the back seat. "Crispy chicken burrito. Extra garlic and ancho sauce."

Rhee peeled back the foil and bit into her burrito. "Christ, that's good." She set to work on it with what could only be described as "efficient gusto."

"Did they find the murder weapon?" I asked. "No judgments for talking with your mouth full."

"They still don't know what was used on Jeremy," she said. "Blunt object of some sort. But they recovered some bullet fragments from the other guy."

"Kyle Halliday."

"Right. No prints. Nine-millimetre, which matches the gun stolen from the Transit officer."

That all but confirmed it. I'd have to tell Rhonda Bryce I'd failed, and her nightmare scenario had come true.

"No ID on the two people who stole the gun?"

Rhee shook her head, kept working on the burrito.

"How about time of death?"

"Not exact, but both the same evening, roughly between four and eight in the evening. Halliday likely killed Jeremy and then was killed himself, probably within the hour."

Rhee finished her food, packed the wrapper like you would a snowball, and tossed it into the bag. "Thanks for that," she said. "When I get home I barely have enough energy to reheat my son's mac and cheese. Seriously, the last two months, I've had more cold noodles and rice than I've had hot."

"What's his name?"

"Seong," she said. "Sonny."

"Nice names. Did the task force talk to anyone named Dagan Moody?"

"I wouldn't know."

"No leads on who killed Kyle?"

She bent the mirror and inspected her teeth. "Inspector Gill doesn't share everything. Just says they have 'avenues of pursuit.'"

"Gill's big on avenues, isn't he?"

Rhee smiled. "He did say they'd gone through Halliday's apartment. Found something that tied him to the kidnapping."

"You have no idea what?"

"Inspector Gill wouldn't get into specifics."

"That writing on the *Gate to the Northwest Passage*," I said. "'Death of Kings.' Any leads on that?"

"Gill didn't mention it," Evelyn Rhee said. "It's almost two-thirty. I need to get back soon."

On the drive to City Hall I asked her to tell me about Jeremy.

"Val was being truthful with you. Her brother couldn't stick to anything for very long. Most people pegged him as a failure. You did."

I nodded. "You think that's unfair?"

"No, but it's not the full picture."

Rhee pressed a napkin to her mouth, wiped, then began to reapply lipstick using the mirror on the sun visor. The light around the visor had burned out long ago.

"Jeremy knew who he was," she said. "Remember, he lived his whole life in Val's shadow. That's no picnic. But he was generous and outgoing, and genuine in a way few people are."

"How so?"

A spray of breath freshener. Rhee smoothed a stocking.

"He got me this job, in a way. I was working part-time on Val's campaign, filling in around the office. Most days I had Sonny with me. Jeremy would look after him. Play cards or Connect 4. He saw this kid alone among all these busy grownups, bored out of his skull, and identified with him. You can't know what it's like, being a single mom and finding your child isn't just tolerated at work, but welcome and valued. I did my best work that fall, and when Val won, Jeremy told her she'd be a fool not to bring me on as her personal assistant."

"And you became more than that," I said, slowing as we neared the corner where she'd get off.

"A deputy chief of staff. Pretty good for a single mom with no connections."

"I mean more personally."

"We keep it quiet, but yes. I love her. I loved the both of them."

A candle-flame of intuition. "You were the last person to see him," I said. "The woman Jeremy was dining with at the Alpen Club."

Evelyn Rhee nodded. "We were talking about what to get Val for her birthday. The person who has everything, you know?" She unbuckled her seatbelt and opened the door, adding before dashing to the crosswalk, "Everything and nothing."

TWENTY-FIVE

SHADES OF RED

In the police parking lot below the Cambie Bridge, Sergeant Ray Dudgeon gave me five minutes time. "Long as it takes me to smoke this," he said. Dudgeon lit a cigarette, a Gauloises Red, and offered the pack to me.

Beware temptation. I stood in the fumes of his tobacco, feet sinking in the wet gravel.

"What did you find at Kyle Halliday's apartment?" I asked.

"Pretty conclusive evidence he kidnapped the mayor's brother. Spray-paint cans in silver lustre, which seems to match the graffiti. Some zip ties, takeout containers and a T-shirt of Jeremy's wound up like a gag. The kid was quite the reader. Some interesting books on his shelf."

"Nothing about his associates?"

"No names or addresses," Dudgeon said. "Seems Halliday was working with a group called Woden's Bastards. You know 'em?"

I shook my head. That wasn't right. The suburban idiots hassling women on street corners couldn't mastermind a B and E, let alone a kidnapping.

Dudgeon took my headshake at face value. "They're white power freaks, mostly bridge-and-tunnel types. Loose ties to a Scandinavian biker gang with the same name. Seems Halliday was a prospect. He had a bundle of their close-the-borders pamphlets in his apartment."

"His wife is Syrian," I said.

"Ex, I believe. Wouldn't be the first racist with a colourblind prick."

"There's something off about this. Did it seem like the place had been gone through already, maybe by his associates?"

Dudgeon shrugged. "I'm just telling you what we found. Sure you don't want one? Hate to get cancer all by myself."

"You mentioned books," I said.

"Yeah. Radical stuff. Anarchy, communism. Some poetry."

"Does that sound like the library of a skinhead?"

Dudgeon cocked his head. "You really asking a Black man if there's a type of white supremacist that a white guy like you don't believe exists?"

I nodded. More than a fair point. "What about Van Veen? Get anything from the Jericho Centre?"

"Looks like the good doctor is an overdose," Dudgeon said. "All the signs of a fentanyl spike. Not sure how it's connected. We'll want to question this Dagan Moody, though."

There was something askew about the line the police were taking. Odds were it was correct, but those odds weren't definitive. I hid my frustration and thanked Dudgeon. The sergeant plucked a Gauloises and pressed it into my hand.

"Case you change your mind," he said.

"You're an enabler, Ray. *Qu'est-ce qu'on dit* 'enabler' *en français?*"

Dudgeon laughed. "Not bad for the West Coast," he said. "Might make a Frenchman outta you yet."

With the cigarette rolling across the van's dashboard, I drove to Oak Street and parked in front of Naima Halliday's building. I debated how best to approach her. If I should approach at all.

Ultimately, this was what I had to work with. Hunches and conversation. It's what detective work comes down to, time and again. Someone knows something. So you ask.

Naima let me in. Like everyone else I'd interacted with lately, she looked in need of twelve hours of uninterrupted sleep. She wore a canary-yellow sweater with an oversized collar, the arms over her wrists, black leggings and sandals.

The apartment had undergone a police search, the household knickknacks and stacks of magazines all at slightly off angles. The apartment's owner retreated to the couch.

"How are you feeling?" I asked.

"Hollow," Naima said, after thinking for a moment. "I talked with the police for hours. Do you want some tea?"

"I'll make it, if you'd like."

She didn't object. I fumbled out the mugs, filled the kettle.

"I have questions, of course," I said. "But while you drink this, let me run down a theory. What the police think happened."

She took the mug and nodded. Aside from a redness to the eyes, she looked the same as before. Strong and vulnerable, a combination that worked on me in ways I wasn't entirely proud of or comfortable with. There's a beauty in resilience, a sexual charge to a person still standing after tragedy. My type and, it seems, my unavoidable weakness. I concentrated on the window and spun out the official narrative.

Kyle Halliday is young, emotionally immature. His marriage goes south. His career isn't taking off. He blames immigrants and City Hall for his failures, and turns to the comforting poison of white hate. He falls in with a group called Woden's Bastards, who hatch a plan to kidnap Jeremy Fell. To that end, Halliday goes looking for a gun. Not just any firearm, mind you, but a police service weapon.

His compatriots strike first, stealing Rhonda Bryce's pistol and blinding her. Halliday borrows his ex-wife's car and helps pick up Jeremy. He stashes the mayor's brother in his SRO for a few days.

And then … something.

The police get too close. There's a PI asking around. The time comes for action.

Jeremy Fell is hit over the head and dumped in the surf off Sunset Beach. Halliday and his partners end up across the bridge in Vanier Park, where they turn on Halliday, shoot him, dressing him first in Jeremy Fell's clothes. They arrange his body and scribble graffiti nearby. Aside from briefly returning to Sunset, and leaving a threat in my office, Halliday's accomplices are never heard from again.

"Does that make sense to you?" I asked Naima Halliday.

She held back her answer, maybe still wondering if she could trust me. I wanted her trust, very much, but she had to offer it freely. As yet another investigator, white and male, following on the heels of the police, that wouldn't be offered easily.

"Parts of it don't sound like Kyle," Naima said. "Other parts I don't know."

"I have an alternate theory," I said. "One where Kyle isn't the ringleader, but a confused participant. I didn't tell the police this, but the words he used when he was trying to buy the gun were, it would 'help him out with something.' Do you know what he meant?"

"No," Naima said. "Why would you not tell the police?"

"Because it was told to me in confidence."

"You're telling me."

"I am. The circumstance warrants it. My theory is that Kyle was trying to get hold of the gun to *prevent* the SkyTrain attack. I don't think he was comfortable with violence. I think the people he was with are more than comfortable. And I think Kyle was killed because he wouldn't go along."

Naima looked at me, evaluating something in my character.

"Kyle's mother's people were from Spain," she said. "His grandmother was in the Cafetería Rolando when it was bombed by the ETA. She dragged a woman to safety and saved her life. Kyle said I reminded him of her. Not just brave, but... strong." She pursed her mouth at the inaccuracy of the word she'd settled on. "But an inner strength. Confidence from being through something bad."

"Being tested."

"I look at you," Naima said, "and I see that kind of confidence. You know what death looks like. It's not video games. It's not glory and wonder. To some people it's small and very cheap. I learned that at a young age. Before I came here to study, I saw people killed by bombs. A child. You don't forget."

I nodded again.

"Kyle didn't know such things," she said. "He wanted to. Sometimes he'd tell me how happy he'd be to die for the right cause."

"What cause?"

She shook her head. "To change things. Make the city better. He hated the rich."

Kyle and everyone else trying to make rent here. "Tell me about the others," I said.

"I don't know very much. A small group, six of them. Most the same age as Kyle. I thought they were his friends from school."

"Was one of them tall?"

"Quite tall, yes."

"Where was it you saw them?"

"Here," Naima said. "I came home from work and they were all in the kitchen. The tall one was very excited."

"This is before you separated?"

"Months before, yes. Kyle and I, we were…" She paused. "I came here as a student, in 2013, before the refugees. When I finished, I couldn't go back to Damascus, and there was an issue with my visa. Kyle wanted to help me."

"By marrying you."

"That's right."

I took that in. It explained Naima's reluctance to tell me, and her choice of words describing Kyle. *A good young man.*

"What prompted him to move out?" I began to ask, but a fist beat on the apartment door, urgently. We quieted.

"Parcel for Halliday," a male voice called through the door.

Naima took a step but I put a hand on her shoulder. We were quiet.

"Sorry I didn't buzz, the numbers got mixed up and your neighbour down the hall let me up. Miss Halliday? Don't you want your parcel?"

I'd never heard a delivery person offer a prolonged explanation. Not to a closed door. Had he heard Naima's voice inside?

The knocks grew softer but the tempo increased. "Mi-iss, I need a signature. Please?"

The handle turned, testing the lock.

I moved to where I'd hung my coat, retrieved Jeff's pistol. The sight of it caused Naima's face to freeze with concern. My footsteps were loud on the wooden floor.

Standing to the left of the door, I hazarded a glance through the spyhole. Saw a torso in dark leather and the bearded lower half of a jaw.

"She's busy," I said. "Leave it on the step."

The voice through the door said, "Can't do that without a signature, mate."

TWENTY-SIX
A GAME OF TAG

I couldn't see a parcel through the spyhole. The arms were bent as if resting in the pockets of the jacket. If Dagan Moody was armed, he was concealing it.

"Is she in there with you?" Moody asked. "I'm speaking with Dave Wakeland, correct?"

Being named brought the cold of the beach back to me, the confusion of being knocked to my knees in the melting snow. The gun in my hand was lightweight and I pointed it at the door, wondering if a .32 slug would punch through the wood.

"It'll cost you to find out," I said.

Turning my head to Naima I mouthed the word "police," gesturing at the phone. She shook her head. I nodded insistently and at last she picked up the cell.

Moody's voice was friendly, chiding. "I told you to stay out of this."

"You also said you weren't after, what was it, 'working folks like me.' Remember?"

No answer. I wanted to risk another look, but knew he'd anticipate that. Behind me I heard Naima reciting her address, her voice betraying less anxiety than mine.

"I know your name," I said. "I know about the Jericho Centre."

"You know absolutely nothing, mate. Fat fucking zero."

"Tell me, then."

"All righty, listen close."

The door jolted inward, the frame snapping with a percussive *platt*. I spun away toward the wall. Dagan Moody had booted the door with impressive force. In the aftermath I could hear feet stamping on the carpeted staircase.

I unchained the door and pulled it inward, squeezed through. "Put a chair in front till the police come," I called to Naima.

Moody's footsteps echoed. It took valuable seconds to realize he wasn't going down but up. I reversed course, reaching the fourth floor, the fifth, hearing above me the battering of another door.

On the top turn of the stairwell the dimensions turned funhouse. The ceiling and steps met at a half door on a slant. Moody had battered his way through it to the roof.

Before I took the last few steps, I listened. Could hear nothing but the distant sounds of Oak Street traffic. I hunched down out of necessity, braced myself as much as I could and bounded through the opening.

Puddles of melted snow on tarpaper. The building had the layout of a digital *W*, all straight lines and ninety-degree angles. Moody was making his way toward the centre, scanning the edges. I loped after him, the splashes bringing his head up briefly, his focus turning back to the search for a way down.

This was the first real look I'd got at him. Dagan Moody was a presence, not just tall but imposing. Auburn hair with an old-fashioned part to the side. Beard a shade darker. The padded jacket added a round-shouldered bulk above white jeans and heavy leather boots. Hands in leather gauntlets, the overall impression a biker from a fifties film exploded to size-and-a-half proportion.

I held up the pistol and told him to touch his head.

Moody looked at the gun and grinned. "You don't carry one of those."

I wanted to ask how he'd know that, but instead took a step closer.

"Funny what you find in your winter coats," I said. "Old pack of cigarettes, ticket stub, gun."

"You're a killer now?"

"Let's not find out," I said. "Hands up and kneel."

The heel of his boot scraped the edge of the roof. Moody's arms went up half-heartedly. Bemused, as if he knew how this would play out and was indifferent to the knowledge.

"Are we really going to shoot it out up here? Cops and robbers, cowboys and whatever the proper term?"

"That what kids play in Pretoria?"

"Very good," he said. "Under different circumstances you'd be a guy to know. If the world wasn't conspiring against us."

I nodded reflexively, knowing what he meant. It was ludicrous, but if things had been different, I could imagine sitting across from Moody in some punk bar near the city limits, hashing out political differences, telling dirty jokes, discussing our romantic woes. I felt a keen lack of that sort of male friendship. The role Ryan Martz had once played.

Instead I had a borrowed pistol pointed at him. Dagan Moody was backing toward the lip of the roof.

"Face down," I said. "Keep your hands above—"

He pivoted to the edge and didn't hesitate, the leap graceless, into the arms of gravity. Like a man assured he can walk on air. Then out of sight, followed by a metallic report that shook the roof.

I ran to the edge. Ten feet below was the top cage of the fire escape. Moody was racing down it. Below him the alley.

As I debated whether to risk the drop in pursuit, the cage shook and squealed. Moody launched himself over the side, landing in mud, stumbling to his feet.

I'm no marksman. It was too late now. I watched Moody sprinting up the alley, skating over a patch of ice as if falling were an impossibility.

Behind me I heard footsteps and a voice with a police cadence. "Slowly lower the weapon, sir. Now."

I did as told.

TWENTY-SEVEN
CHARGES PENDING

A rooftop comedy of errors. Me explaining that I wasn't the intruder. Just ask Naima Halliday. Was this my personal firearm? My partner's, actually, Jefferson Chen, but registered to our office. I had a security professional's permit to carry.

"But this weapon isn't registered in your actual name, is it, sir?"

The .32 was confiscated. Jeff was called, and our lawyer, and the officer's immediate supervisor. The case would be reviewed. No charges at this time. Council would be notified if and when that changed, and I'd be expected to appear.

Disarmed and duly chastised, I returned to Naima's apartment to find her in conversation with Inspector Gill. Or more accurately, standing silent in the face of Gill's questions and persuasions.

"You didn't see this man, so how do you know there was one?"

She pointed at the door. "That's not proof?"

"Did this gentleman speak to you? And did you recognize the voice? The more cooperation we get, Mrs. Halliday." Gill broke off as he saw me. "Mr. Wakeland, circling around the proceedings yet again. You'll hear from us on the firearm."

"You might get Moody's boot print off the door," I said. "Or the one to the roof."

"Thank you for telling me my business." Gill nodded to Naima. "Ma'am, if anything comes to mind."

After he made his exit, I asked her what he wanted.

"He thinks I know Kyle's friends," she said.

"Do you?"

Her eyes burned. "I told you I saw them one time."

"All right." The door could be hammered in place, but would need to be rekeyed. "I think you shouldn't stay here, Naima. I can book you a hotel downtown for a few nights, and have someone change the locks."

She nodded. "You're afraid of these people?"

I thought of the jocular smile with which Dagan Moody had greeted the pistol. The lack of hesitation he'd shown clambering down the scaffolding.

"Utterly," I said.

Wakeland & Chen had done security work for the Hotel Vancouver. I booked Naima a suite, charging incidentals to our corporate expense account. We could afford a twenty-dollar can of Pringles if she wanted one. The north-facing room had a view of the snow on the mountains. With a telescope I might have been able to pick out the Jericho Centre.

As Naima put her things away, I asked about her husband.

"What made Kyle angry? Was he a violent man?"

"Truthfully, I don't know," she said. "Men become violent for so many reasons. Kyle felt the world was against him. When we married, he felt he'd won a victory against the government, denying them their wish to send me back to Damascus."

"Did you feel that way?"

"A bit," she said, hanging her hospital scrubs. "People here want to be thought kind. They don't want to share. My experiences made Kyle angry. Like an insult that he had to answer. I told him white privilege, systemic problems, they can't be fought like that. He grew upset."

"At you?" I asked.

"Maybe partly, yes. Angry that I didn't fight in the same way. He accused me of giving up."

Anger flashed on Naima Halliday's face.

"I told him every day is a fight. But it's a fight for more compassion, more patience. Not to hurt people."

"And Kyle didn't understand that," I said, wondering if I did.

She frowned, holding a half-folded blouse. "He wanted things to be better," she said. "School was always difficult for him. He hated not working, even though I could support him."

"How did he meet Moody and the others?"

"School, I think. For a while he seemed happy. A few days after I saw them in the kitchen, Kyle said he was moving out. All our furniture I could keep. He didn't take anything."

Naima shut the suitcase with her undergarments still inside. The room was warm. She took her toiletry kit to the washroom. I stood near the bureau, listening to her place things around the sink.

"Did he ever mention the mayor, or the mayor's brother?" I asked.

"Never by name," Naima said. "He was upset at the city, though. About housing and overdoses. Reading how Vancouver was the most expensive city, how young people had to move away. How 10,000 people have died from bad drugs. He'd say no one cares."

The noise in the washroom halted. Cognition, something falling into place. She stepped out of the washroom, stared at me with concern.

"Kyle wouldn't say what he was doing. But he acted like it would help stop those things. Make a difference. I thought maybe he was working at a needle exchange or a safe-injection site. But it could have been something else."

"Something darker?"

"Maybe, yes," Naima said. "Kyle was a dreamer. That kind of person can do terrible things."

"You recognized the graffiti when I showed it to you. *D* and *K*. Above his body was written 'Only the rich fear the death of kings.' That hold any significance for you?"

Naima moved from the doorway of the washroom to the closet. Her hand picked up the cuff of her uniform.

"When I worked in oncology, once, a woman got sick on me. I went home and put my clothes right in the wash. On the wall of the laundry room someone had written that. *D* and *K*. The paint was wet."

"Could it have been Kyle?"

"I think it was," Naima said. "He was home that day. He moved out soon after."

Whatever the group had become, the idea behind it had captivated Kyle so completely he'd rejected everything for it. His marriage. His future. Naima was paying that cost as well.

I cupped a hand on her cheek, her face cold, and kissed her. The convenience of the bed, the shared sense of survived danger, her grief, my loss—every undermining thought or justification was drowned by the urge to know her body, her history, her desires. I felt her respond. My hand travelled over a warm hip, a cold small of the back, taut bra strap and hook, shoulders that pressed into mine. Our moment of exploration and rampage.

After, she took my hand in both of hers, tracing it from the pubic thatch to her belly, to the faint teeth marks above her left breast.

"I'm warm all over now," she said. Her matter-of-fact delivery with its natural sultriness was enough to start us again.

"Sure seems like it," I said. "But I better doublecheck."

Later in the evening, sharing a single-serving coffee, I thought of Sonia and was surprised I wasn't hounded by guilt. Not much of it, anyway. What Jeff had said about my motivations wasn't so wrong. Maybe I could make it wrong.

Naima finished the coffee, smiling. The bedsheet was tucked up to her waist. "I'm going to order some food," she said. "I like to eat after."

"It was smoking for me, till I quit," I said. The cigarette in bed, acrid smell of the match cutting through sweat and deodorant.

"Kyle liked to smoke as well."

"I thought you and he." I stopped, not knowing exactly what I thought.

"For a time we tried to live like husband and wife. Our honeymoon. He was nice. A handsome man."

She spoke about him wistfully, as if he'd been dead for some time—longer than two days. The cigarette butts floating in the ashtray at the Jericho Centre—had Kyle been there?

Sitting on the edge of the bed, I watched her extend a leg to brush down my chest, hooking her heel around my hip. I knew less about Kyle Halliday than I had hours before. Whatever his motivation was, he'd given up everything for it, including his life, and a chance for something far more precious.

TWENTY-EIGHT

HIDDEN TROPHIES

In the morning I saw Naima to work, then headed to the Van Ness Hotel.

The police presence at a low-income flop like the Van Ness caused an atmospheric shift, like a summer storm. The patrol cop stationed in the lobby was the only one at ease. Behind the desk, the hotel clerk penetrated the cubbyholes with a dust-caked Swiffer, muttering along with the radio. "Chest Fever" by The Band played from old computer speakers.

I held up my licence for the pair of them. "On business for the mayor's office. Like to take a quick look at Mr. Halliday's room."

"Surprised there's anything left in there to look at," the clerk said. If she recognized my voice from our phone call three days ago, she didn't let on. "The racket they've been making, stamping up and down."

"I'll be quiet as a church mouse studying to be a mime," I said.

The officer accompanied me up. Behind us, the clerk called, "Tell Mayor Fell we need new heaters. Snowing out, and half the darn things don't work. That seem like responsible leadership to you?"

Eighty years ago, the Van Ness had been a desirable hotel in a less than desirable neighbourhood. That equation was reversed now. The red carpet showcased burns and stains, the fixtures cracked or missing. An astringent smell of mould and weed and Pine-Sol filled the hall. More valuable than the building was the space above it. If and when the Van Ness stopped housing the city's poor, its demolition could make a fortune for someone who probably already had one.

Kyle's room was on the second floor, unlocked but X'd over with red cordon tape. Ducking below it felt like skipping past a VIP line. Valerie Fell's name was proving a useful password.

"Don't take anything," the officer said.

"Just a look."

Squares of carpet had been excised. All electronics removed. What remained were the lonesome trappings of a single-male life. Dirty clothes, hot plate, socks balled up in a top drawer lined with wallpaper.

My flat was barely five hundred square feet, ground floor and nothing special. A palace compared to this. The Burj Al Arab.

I don't know what I hoped to find. Confirmation, maybe, of the choice Kyle had made. Giving up domestic life with Naima for these cramped quarters. Hermits and fanatics made such choices.

And maybe this was a way of accepting a debt. I'd slept with his wife, moved into the space he'd left vacant. I benefited from his absence, and, in turn, maybe I owed him understanding.

Pulling down the Murphy bed, I watched a family of cockroaches scurry for the crevices. In the recession above the headboard, Kyle had carved DEATH OF KINGS, tracing the linework with blue ink.

I traced a finger over the letters. More than just a phrase idly tagged above a crime scene. A group. An identity. Whatever Death of Kings stood for, Kyle had believed in it completely.

Down the back of the mattress was a small collection of hood ornaments, Jags and Mercs and Beemers and a Ferrari shield. Trophies. The officer went on tiptoe to peer over my shoulder.

School, I think, Naima had said. The linkage seemed to go like this. Jeremy Fell to Dr. Van Veen, recently deceased, to Dagan Moody, his executor, and from Moody somehow to Kyle. The last was what I couldn't grasp. Or didn't want to.

It was easier thinking of Kyle as a well-intentioned, misled fool. Easier than thinking of him as a self-deceiving killer. Easier because we had things in common. A thought as uncomfortable as anything I found in the dead man's room.

Jeff was already at the office. He'd cut a neat hole in the drywall above the reception desk, the size of a postage stamp. He was threading a small camera and battery pack through it.

"Runs off USB," he said. "Feeds into the laptop in my office. MicroSD backup for seven days. We'll have to remember to change the battery every couple weeks."

"We should've thought of this before," I said, starting to make tea.

"I did," Jeff said. "You shot it down."

"Why would I do that?'

His attention was back on his wiring. "I'd go crazy trying to guess your reasons, Dave."

"Maybe something about spying on our clientele."

"Better than them thinking we can't keep our own office secure."

His reasoning was sound. Corporate clients appreciated Jeff because he did what he said. Any problem, he solved it. If they heard about the break-in, he could assure them, truthfully, that it would never happen again. A business had to project adaptive competence. It couldn't afford to continue making the same errors—unlike people.

I helped Jeff set up another camera in the basement security room. We tested them. Both worked fine. Not the highest resolution, but good enough for a clear picture of everyone who entered or exited.

We silently agreed not to tell the other employees. Not that they weren't trustworthy, but the cameras were a response to our failure. The less attention drawn to that, the better.

The phrase "Only the rich fear the death of kings" didn't match to anything, but "death of kings" showed up in Shakespeare, in *Richard II*. Not the one with the princes and the winter of our discontent. "The usurpation of the weak but rightful King Richard by his exiled cousin Henry." I hadn't read it. The text was online, but I wanted a copy with a readable font and footnotes. The library opened at ten.

At 8:45 a.m. Ryan Martz texted that he was at the entrance. I let him up and told him what he'd be doing for the day.

"Jeff is going to show you how to file," I said.

"Christ, Dave. Shoot me now why don't you."

For the next two hours Jeff sat next to him and patiently, painstakingly, showed Ryan the system. There was a mail drop in the building, so they walked through each step, from logging the hours reported by personnel, verifying them, entering the numbers into the bookkeeping software, then printing, doublechecking, and mailing the invoices.

It was painful to watch, but I learned a few things. Ryan messed up the first three. He didn't swear, though. Teeth gritted, he allowed Jeff to point out the errors, made notes and didn't repeat his mistakes.

As they began going through the email protocol, the phone rang. Ryan picked it up, said "Yeah?" into it, and then, "Hiya, Rhonda... Working here, yeah. As an investigator. Secretary stepped out for a butt." He looked at me, covered the receiver. "Rhonda Bryce. Says she needs a word."

I took the call in my private office, with the door shut. I could hear the Transit cop clear her throat over the line.

"Gurcharan Gill told me my gun was prob'ly used to shoot this fellow Halliday," Bryce said.

"I'm sorry," I said.

"What can you do? Some white power crazies want your gun, not a whole lot could stop it."

"Does 'Death of Kings' mean anything to you?"

"Gill asked that too. No, it's gibberish to me."

"I think it's the name of a group Halliday formed with a man named Dagan Moody," I said. "The two who attacked you, also. I think the police are after the wrong people."

"Doesn't much matter," Rhonda Bryce said. "I'll never see my SIG again, unless it's in a courtroom. Invoice me and I'll pay you first of the month. And thanks for giving it your best."

For nothing, I thought, as she hung up. What does one charge for no service rendered?

I turned in my chair to look at the message on the window and at Hastings Street beyond the glass.

STAY OUT OF OUR WAY. The forensic techs had scraped the bottom of the *S*, making it look like a backwards question mark.

This was a noble exit of sorts. I could poke around Jeremy Fell's sex life a bit to satisfy the mayor. Leave the rest to the police. If I was wrong, no loss, and if right, I'd save myself time and trouble and danger. The Death of Kings, whatever it was, didn't operate by the same rules. These were fanatics, and yet I thought I understood them.

I wondered what that said about me.

TWENTY-NINE
REVOLUTION

Richard II sits on the throne, watching a duel between his cousin Henry Bolingbroke and another noble. At the last minute, before they strike, the king orders both men into exile, their lands and titles forfeit. He relents a little, telling Henry he can come back at some later time.

As a leader, Richard is a mess. Profligate, ineffectual, a sensualist, bleeding his kingdom into bankruptcy. A revolutionary force conspires to land Henry on the shores of England, depose Richard and install Henry as the new monarch.

The plan works. Richard is captured, forced to participate in Henry's sham coronation, ripping the crown from his own head and placing it on his cousin's. He laments his fallen station: "I wasted time, and now time doth waste me."

And at the point where Richard has learned exactly how much he's lost, Henry tells his followers in vague terms that their new king would sure feel happier if his cousin were dead. An ambitious man jumps on this suggestion and kills Richard. He's rewarded for this assassination by being sent to his own death by the sanctimonious Henry.

What was the point of all this—that a lazy, corrupt status quo was better than a violent revolution? Or just the opposite? A proper scholar could probably argue both sides. Online guides to the play told me *Richard II* was about "the rise of the modern Machiavellian." Nothing about Halliday's choice of inspiration led to easy interpretation.

Before his assassination, while imprisoned and meditating on his fortunes, Richard turns to speechifying, telling his loyal friend, "Of comfort no man speak:"

> Let's talk of graves, of worms, and epitaphs;
> Make dust our paper and with rainy eyes
> Write sorrow on the bosom of the earth…
> For God's sake, let us sit upon the ground
> And tell sad stories of the death of kings;
> How some have been deposed; some slain in war
> Some haunted by the ghosts they have deposed
> Some poison'd by their wives: some sleeping kill'd;
> All murder'd…

Halliday's quote came from the middle of that speech.

The notes in the edition I took from the library said, "Here Richard dispels the notion of kingly difference, accepting the mortality and humanity of monarchs."

Meditation on authority. Meditation on death. It was an interesting way to pass a few hours, but it didn't reveal Halliday's motivations—or his killer. I listened to an audio recording of Richard Burton reading the lines. He sounded weary and resigned, in need of a neat whiskey and a romp with Liz Taylor. I felt his pain.

Here was an explanation to Death of Kings, and instead of making sense it only begged other questions. Halliday and Fell weren't kings. The reference itself seemed ambivalent, even sympathetic, to Richard's deposition. No gangs I knew of regularly referenced the Bard; and if it was a political group, what exactly had it accomplished?

When Kay arrived, still exhausted from her late-night security detail, I asked if she knew who taught poetry or Shakespeare at the college. If Kyle had taken their class, maybe they could shed light on the reference.

"I can look it up," she said, stifling a sneeze with the back of her wrist.

"Find out anything else about Kyle at the school?"

"Haven't exactly had a lot of time."

"How was last night's detail? Tim behave himself?"

Kay nodded. "It's dull, Dave. And cold. We're keeping watch, though." She gestured toward the reception desk. "Is Ryan working out?"

"All right, I think. Better than I expected."

"That's nice." My sister let out a barking cough worthy of an elephant seal. "Your mom wants to speak with you."

"About what?"

"Finance stuff, I think. Aunt Bea doesn't talk to me about that."

Kay usually lived in my adoptive mother's basement suite, but to avoid spreading the plague had moved onto my couch. The two were close—closer, in fact, than I was with my mother.

Kay yawned again. I told my sister to go home, rest up. I could check out the college on my own.

Langara was located on Forty-Ninth Avenue between a collection of South Asian markets and shops and the secluded residences of Marpole. The grey stone buildings of the campus bordered a public golf course. Students funneled out the main doors, creating a percussive symphony on the heavily salted concourse.

The English department offices were quiet, most teachers in session. I asked the office manager, a bearded youngster who smelled of e-cigarette vapor, who taught Shakespeare.

"Chhaya Bansal teaches Studies in Modern Drama. At the moment she's teaching a one-hundred-level in one of the auditoriums. She finishes in twenty minutes."

I caught Bansal's class filing out of the auditorium, a couple hundred students of various ages, ethnicities and apparent levels of enthusiasm. I let the wave of backpacks and laptops wash out and down the halls, then headed inside, down the sloping theater seats to the front of the hall. Bansal lingered near the front, discussing something with a trio of students.

Chhaya Bansal was thirty or thereabouts, stout, and attired in a tailored grey suit over a plum blouse. She dealt with the students easily, sending each away smiling with understanding or relief. The last in the lineup required a thoughtful and complex answer, and by the time she finished, Bansal looked at me with the vexed expression of a marathon runner being asked mid-stride if she had a minute to spare for Jesus.

"I'm investigating the death of Kyle Halliday," I said.

"He was a student of mine," Bansal said. "If I recall correctly, Kyle frequented my office hours quite a bit. He struggled with one of the papers."

"Was Kyle frustrated, angry in some way?"

"If he was," the instructor said carefully, "that wouldn't necessarily make him unique. A lot of students struggle, especially those that don't have the luxury of being groomed for college by their families. They're not just learning in class, they're learning how to *be* in class. It's a difficult transition."

"I was hoping you might remember something specific about Kyle," I said.

"There are three or four hundred new students every year. I'm sorry to disappoint. Was there anything else?"

"*Richard II*," I said. "Does the phrase 'death of kings' have any special meaning?"

"I don't often get to teach the history plays," Bansal said. "Are you asking me for textual analysis?" Her smile was barbed with *don't waste my time*.

"Halliday graffitied the phrase several times before kidnapping Jeremy Fell. I'm a working stiff, professor, and while I appreciate a well-turned phrase as much as the next PI, this is a little out of my area."

She nodded and took my library book, briefly scanning the pages. Beside us, another instructor attempted to meld his laptop with the projection system.

"This sort of indecisive poeticizing is characteristic of Richard," Bansal said.

"Okay."

"In layperson terms, the king doesn't do much in the play, but he speaks beautifully of what's being done to him. The ironies of fortune, the impossibility of being a monarch if people don't recognize him as one."

She handed the book back.

"I could give you any number of readings of the passage, but my own take follows C.L.R. James. You know his work?"

"Not as well as I should," I said.

"Very worth reading," Bansal said. "He was criticized for his interpretations, but his insight was second to none. James said the recurring theme of Shakespeare's work was to attack the conception of monarchy. That England's greatest poet was a revolutionary. I don't know if it's true in the strictest sense, but it's a useful approach to the Bard. The idea that revolution is at the heart of Western culture. Essential in some respect."

"So the 'death of kings' means…"

"Exactly what it sounds like," the professor said.

THIRTY

SWEET DREAMS

I bummed around the cafeteria and student union, browsed the bookstore, hoping someone remembered Kyle Halliday. But no. Too many fresh faces flooded the campus each semester, and Kyle's hadn't made enough of an impression.

What about Dagan Moody? No record of him as a student. Did the Jericho Centre ever have a presence on campus? Handing out pamphlets, running an info session? No one could tell me.

My own stint as a college kid had been brief, alcohol-fueled, the solitary drinker as opposed to the partier. The first person in my family to go to college, I was defensive, ill at ease, felt perpetually a day late with my applications and fees. For years I disdained higher learning, remembering only the financial shame. Being mocked for duct-taping the spine of a used textbook or cutting my own hair. Nearly brawling with a photographer who wanted to overcharge my mother. Using a black marker to fudge the dates on my parking pass.

Now I looked around at these faces buried in phones and laptops, and felt disconnected, at a remove from the world. Was this what they'd wanted from college, or what they had to endure to get what they wanted? Naima had excelled, both in her studies and as a nurse. I didn't know her experiences, but I could appreciate her drive. A mature student. There were benefits to that.

Eventually it was clear, even to me, I was dragging this out to postpone my next stop. I left the school and drove to my mother's house on Laurel Street, parked in the alley, which was now virtually a street of its own. Laneway houses crowded the yards of almost every property. No more gardens or garages. The space too precious not to build on.

The house itself needed trim and a few shingles. Its neighbours had all been raised and expanded, blown up to accommodate entire new wings of renters. My mother's house was a silent protest, a keepsake from an era where working-class families, one-income families, could afford a house in Vancouver.

She answered the door limping. My mother had been older when she'd adopted me, and was now in her early seventies, a twist of sinew and brown hair dye in a red-and-black work shirt and paint-dappled slacks. Instead of letting me in, she moved to sit in her porch rocking chair, directing me to rest an ass cheek on a dry stretch of railing.

"How you been, Ma?" I asked.

She raised one shoulder in an offhand shrug, pairing it with a shake of the head. "Usual aches and pains."

"You're limping."

"Not much. How are you?"

Our conversations always started like this, grappling for the right to interrogate, volleying and deflecting. If she texted it was a series of questions, as if prepping me for a conversation to be had later. There was never a later.

"You told Kay you wanted to see me? Something about finances?"

"That's what I told her."

I crossed my arms, waited to hear the reason for her deception.

"I'm worried about that girl," my mother said.

"About Kay?"

"You have another sister?"

The sting went out of her voice. In fact I'd once had an older sister who'd stayed in the commune with my birth parents. She'd died of some undiagnosed medical condition, an event that prompted them to rethink their devotion to the Reverend Whoever.

"It's fine for Kay to work with you, for now," my mother said. "She needs to finish her schooling. Make something of herself." Adding, to avoid an argument, "Like you have."

"She's twenty-five and can make her own choices," I said.

"She's a Prairie twenty-five."

"Meaning what?"

"I don't want a big kerfuffle, David. Just, if you talk to her, mention it would be good to have a degree. She looks up to you."

"Debatable."

My mother lit her pipe. Soon the cold air was scented with the rich, corky tobacco. "How's Sonia?" she said.

"She left, I told you that. Montreal."

"You don't speak?"

"We haven't," I admitted. "I might have met someone."

"Oh, that's good to hear."

I didn't elaborate. She'd never taken to Sonia, both from a stick-with-your-own-kind anxiety, and a police widow's complex feelings toward anyone sharing her husband's occupation. Sonia hadn't much liked her either. I wondered how my mother would take to Naima, if that became anything. I hoped it would.

Thinking of Naima brought her husband to mind, and the Death of Kings, and the unproven ground I found myself treading.

"Did Pop ever talk to you about cases he worked on?" I asked.

"I heard my share."

"Did he ever deal with fanatics?" I asked. "People who were motivated by something, I don't know, political maybe? Spiritual? I don't understand what to do about them."

Saying it out loud made me appreciate the truth of it. I had more in common with Kyle than Jeremy Fell, with the people I was looking for than those who'd hired me. Shooting Moody on the rooftop hadn't felt right, but maybe I should have. Maybe I hadn't wanted to.

My mother stoked her pipe and thought. "You don't mean protestors," she said.

"No. Zealots."

"There was a young man who killed himself in front of your father. Jumped from the window of a hotel while he was trying to talk him down. He was on drugs, I think. Unhappy. Your father didn't say much about it." She plucked a thread out of the knee of her slacks. "Does that help you?"

I thought of my father witnessing that, bringing it home with him, bringing it back to work. I replayed Dagan Moody's leap of faith to the fire escape. Different and yet the same.

My mother stood up. "Reminds me. I found a few of his albums in the closet the other day. You like all that old country junk. I just don't have the ears for it anymore."

I followed her inside and accepted a small pile of worn LPs. Charlie Pride. Buck Owens and the Buckaroos. The newest a soundtrack from a Patsy Cline movie called *Sweet Dreams*.

I thanked her, turned down a perogy dinner and as I was leaving glimpsed a stack of mail resting on the shoe rack. A slit bank envelope, the notice inside peeking out. SECOND WARNING written across the top.

"What's this?" I asked.

"Not important. Leave it."

She'd borrowed twenty-one thousand dollars against the house, then failed to make the minimum payments. In fact she hadn't made any payments in months, not on the mortgage and not on the line of credit.

"Christ, Ma."

"Language."

"You're losing your house—how's that for language?"

She didn't offer an explanation. There were other letters in the pile, some postdated months ago. Banks and credit-card companies and two from a collection agency.

Apprehension was slow, but I got it. Asking for help wasn't Beatrice Wakeland's style. Maybe she'd lost courage, and maybe she'd left the envelopes out, planning for me to find them. It didn't matter. She was my mother and I was responsible for her.

"Any idea, ballpark, how much you owe?" I asked.

"I borrowed about twenty for the roof, but then the heater went, too. And when I took that trip to Reno with Carol and Aunt Lorraine, everything cost a little more than we budgeted for."

"Yeah, casinos tend to be like that," I said. "So the twenty-one grand plus is just the start."

"If I don't get it, they won't let me renew my mortgage."

"Maybe that's a blessing," I said. "Good excuse to downsize. You could sell this place for at least a million dollars."

My mother shook her head with vehemence. "This house isn't for sale, David. Once I'm dead, you and the bank can do whatever you please, but I'm staying put till then."

"Ma, what sense does that make?"

"I like it here. What other sense is there?"

I shook my head, understanding her motives too well and yet baffled by the decision. My mother, the broke millionaire.

"I'll take care of it," I said. "This all the bank stuff?"

Mixed in with the envelopes was a pamphlet, on the cover a familiar white thunderbolt, and the words THE COMING STORM.

Woden's Bastards didn't appear by name on the literature, but the implication was there, the white faces on white paper. A simpler time. Waves of newcomers. Protection. Community. Remember feeling secure, and knowing your neighbour's names?

"You saved this?" I asked.

My mother shrugged. "They seemed like nice boys. And it is getting rougher out there."

"Skinheads, Ma."

"One had very nice hair."

I crumpled the pamphlet, thought better, then pocketed it. That too was my inheritance.

THIRTY-ONE

LEVERAGED

There was a second-floor bar in the Hilton, across from the Central Library. I returned *Richard II* and holed up in the bar. Couches and happy hour and a good selection of beer. I had a pint of Dark Matter and worked through my mother's legal correspondence.

The twenty-one thousand dollars was only the first problem. With that paid, plus whatever penalties they'd doubtless tack on, she'd be able to reapply for a mortgage. Which she'd no longer qualify for, not on her pension.

I'd never seen someone with a million-dollar asset whose finances were so thoroughly fucked. She'd deferred property taxes, and had only made the interest payments on her mortgage. Plus there had been other debts, some going back to my father's funeral. I'd need to find thirty grand immediately—even more difficult, I'd have to convince her to sell.

Or take over the mortgage myself.

An amusing thought. So amusing I needed another beer to celebrate how amusing it was. The only real chance for me to own a house in Vancouver, and it was the one house I wouldn't live in for anything. I'd rather see my mother sell it and take the money, live a worry-free life in a condo. Or she could renovate and rent part of it out. Would she be content with that, though? Inhabiting a part of the space she used to inhabit completely? I couldn't answer that.

I was meeting Naima Halliday for dinner at six. It was almost five by the time I got back to the office. Kay and Blatchford had left for their night shift. Jeff had given in to his wife's protestations and gone home to nurse his cold. Ryan and I were the only ones left.

"When's Nikki coming to pick you up?" I asked him.

"Quarter after. She's got to go home and get the van first."

"How'd it go today?"

Ryan scowled. "Jeff's a pain in the balls. But I guess he knows what he's doing."

"I won't tell him you said that." I took out my key ring and worked off the keys for the office. "You mind locking up tonight?"

It wasn't gratitude that I saw on his face. Something darker, an acknowledgement of the weight of the request, and some amount of apprehension. Unless I was mistaken. Ryan nodded and took the keys.

I met Naima at Le Crocodile, a French restaurant near St. Paul's Hospital frequented by doctors and judges. We were underdressed but it was early. Over salade niçoise and steak tartare, I asked how her day had gone and tried to suppress the thousand other questions.

Naima liked the hospital, got along with most of the nurses. The hours could be exhausting, and her feet had grown bunions from padding the hallway for hours on end. The patients were a mixed bag.

"Most of them are scared," she said. "They hide it different ways. Some of them become nicer. Too nice, too polite. Like they're ashamed of needing help. Sometimes it's easier when they get angry."

"Anger is easier?"

She smiled, forking a morsel of beef and letting it dissolve on her tongue.

"Not always," she said. "They scream, they yell."

"Throw things?"

"Sometimes. But then…" The fork made circles as she pursued the right word. "They feel bad. Ashamed. They apologize. And then I get to help them."

I wondered how many people Naima had ministered to in their final days. Not the worst end-of-life scenario.

"Was Kyle a person who got angry easily?"

I'd asked without considering the line I was toeing. Talking about one's ex was acceptable on a date. At least the last time I checked. No harm done. That the ex was deceased was no fault of mine, and it was only coincidence that I was investigating the death. Nothing unacceptable about that.

"Sometimes, yes," Naima said. "He could be proud. If he made a mistake, it was hard for him to say that."

"That's a big difference between us," I said. "I don't make any mistakes."

Laughter. The feeling of having swung a car out of the oncoming lane. But in the moment of relief, I felt myself jamming the wheel to the left again, knowing I was doing so, unable to prevent it.

"What kind of mistakes did Kyle make?" I asked.

The question hovered silently as our entrées arrived and the waiter cut the spine out of the Dover sole. You take a special person to a fine restaurant, to explore what the two of you could mean to each other. The ghost of her husband looms over the proceedings, his destroyed face and unknown motives clouding things. And you're the one who summoned him.

"Sorry I asked," I said.

"It's all right. It's fine." Naima speared a piece of the sole, severing it in two with a clack of the knife. "He lost money sometimes. He got into arguments. Kyle wanted…"

The fish wavered in mid-air as she thought through how to express the nature of her late husband's errors.

"Kyle wanted to be the one who fixes things."

"I can relate to that."

She chewed, nodded. "But we can't fix everything. He yelled at people over minor problems. Always an argument, someone who was wrong. You know those metal pieces on the front of cars?"

"Hood ornaments."

"Kyle broke those off for fun. I asked him, what does that accomplish? He hated rich people."

I remembered his collection, stuffed down behind his bed. But I refrained from mentioning it.

When the meal was over, we walked to her hotel. Foot traffic on Burrard was brisk despite the snow. A shirtless man squatted outside the theatre, asking for change. We stepped carefully through the crowds.

"What are you thinking?" I asked.

"I'm sick of winter."

"Anything else?"

She took my arm. "I want you to come up."

"Convince me."

We kissed under the awning of a jeweller, tasting of pine and olive oil, lemon. Her tongue pressed into my canine.

"No more about Kyle tonight, please…"

I kept my word through midnight, a long shower, then bed, and a shorter stint under the hot water to get clean again. When wet, Naima's hair clung to her brow, dangling over her eyes. She kept them shut, smiling as I sat her on the edge of the sink and dried her face.

"Did Kyle ever go for counselling?" I asked.

She pulled away. "I thought—"

"I know, I'm sorry—"

"You're not sorry," Naima said.

She left the washroom to hunt down her garments. Her bra had ended up behind the bed. As she bent, cinching her towel, I moved behind her, tried to help. She didn't want that. Naked, I sat against the headboard, my skin drying in the room.

"No, I'm not sorry," I said. "But I didn't and wouldn't sleep with you for information. And I can't stop looking for answers because we did."

Silence. She freed the bra with a snap of elastic.

"I'm not like other people, Naima. Work and home aren't distinct. My job is always the private life of somebody, and my home is usually where I find answers."

She inched down the towel, exposing her back to me, hooking on the undergarment. "I barely know you."

"You know everything there is."

"A mistake."

"Not for me," I said. "Among my many faults and quirks of personality is a stubborn need to know. It's why I'm single, why I still live in a city that doesn't want me. It's why I kill friendships and houseplants with reckless abandon. I'm just that person. The one who's not leaving without the answer."

"And what if there is no answer?" Naima said. "You think finding who hurt him will make me grateful to you? Care more?"

"No. Maybe when I was younger I cared about that damsel shit, but my work has never been about gratitude, or even justice. The looking is what matters. What I hold to. I won't for a minute pretend that it's noble, or even comprehensible to a healthy-minded person. But I can't apologize for it, either."

"All right," she said. "I should sleep."

It was a dismissal, but not a final one. A request for time to consider.

I walked down to Hastings in the direction of the office. You either say nothing, say it wrong or, worst of all, say it perfectly for deaf ears. Naima seemed to understand me, though. I hoped I hadn't damaged the possibilities for us.

At the office I made sure Ryan Martz had locked up properly. Everything seemed correct. The pinhole camera regarded me from above the desk as I reset the alarm and once again locked the door.

I was in the carport, keying open the Cadillac, thinking about repairing relationships and how to come up with thirty grand. I heard weeping and turned. Saw a flash of blond hair. A gloved hand pitched something toward my face.

THIRTY-TWO

KILL THE LIGHTS

Instinct brought my elbow up, turned my face away. I swung my forearm into the trajectory of the woman's arm. The reward was a screaming scalding pain through the fabric of my jacket. The cup clattered, the woman backpedalled out of reach.

Behind her, two men stood over a third. They wore dark blue hoodies, surgical masks. One was recognizably stocky and held a length of pipe in his hand. He was rhythmically striking the man on the ground, meeting no resistance, like knocking a tent peg into sand.

The other man was Dagan Moody's height and breadth, wore the same heavy boots. He soccer-kicked the prone man, who I recognized through the blood as Tim Blatchford. Tim sputtered and the stocky one clubbed him into silence.

Beyond them, the ramp gate was open. I could see snow falling, foot impressions leading down.

The elevator door had closed. The staircase vestibule lay to my right.

Understand there is no logic to a fight for your life. No perfectly choreographed sequence that prevents damage. The darkest thing you learn in boxing is that punches thrown take something out of you, too. That the breakdown of the human machine is inevitable, even in victory.

The woman pressed forward, the others rallying to her. Her blond wig was askew, blue close-set eyes below it. An aquiline nose above the mask.

I moved toward the staircase, then when it was clear I wouldn't reach it, I feinted the other way. Skirting Blatchford, trying for the elevator. Fighting panic.

The stocky man made a predatory dart toward me, my adrenaline feeding his. Expensive sneakers and black jeans, dark attentive eyes. He rushed, swinging the pipe overhead, counting on me to cringe in place.

I held ground until he'd committed to the arc of the swing, pivoted and olé'd him face first into the wall. Rabbit punching the back of his head as he went down.

My back was to Moody, and he struck me on the shoulder blade. I flicked out at his face with an open hand and he leaped nimbly out of range, agile for his size.

"Sorry for this, mate, but you wanted it," he said. His voice sounded sincere.

He stalked to my left, between me and the elevator. The stocky man hoisted himself upright, retrieving the pipe.

I barrelled into the woman, who seized my burnt left elbow in a respectable armbar. Helicoptering around, jabbing at her eyes, waiting for her hand to break off to defend, I turned my hip and flung her to the ground.

Up the ramp to safety, dizzy from the exertion. Guilt at leaving Tim behind, but too outmatched to do anything but die next to him.

At the top of the ramp stood another figure dressed in similar hoodie and mask. A woman going by shape. She held a pipe. Moody and the stocky one converged behind me. Hopeless. I lunged back into fists and hands, grabbed fabric, swung at a cloth-covered face. Impossible to tell how effective. The person I hit didn't fall.

A sick clang of metal off bone. My arm went instantly numb. My right hand flailed. Struck on the neck, ribs, thighs. Undisciplined, wild strikes. I was booted into the stocky man, saw a light brown fist swing at my shoulder. The collar of my shirt tore.

On the ground, barraged by fists, ill-aimed pipe blows. I was going to die here, in the concrete and snow.

Jail-yard instinct: take out the largest and hope the others run. I shouldered into Moody's legs with what I had left. The tall man reared back and I clung to his midsection, making my weight his responsibility to hold. He buckled and we fell over, through the others, my body landing atop him on the sloping ground. A pipe struck next to us.

My left arm was dead. Moody's hands were clutching at me, padded and with strength I couldn't match. I thumbed his face, felt him release me. Other punches rained on my back, a feeble attempt to pull me off him. Kicks, some hitting Moody instead.

As expendable as I am, I thought.

Moody wrenched my good arm back and away, roaring in pain and frustration. A white-hot *snap* as the pipe struck my ear. I landed beside him, my forehead on the pavement.

"That's enough," a muffled female voice said.

"You shut the eff up," the other woman said.

Processing what had happened took precious seconds. New damage. The roar of blood in ears, brain. I felt a boot on the shoulder, Moody's glove grasping my throat.

It was a galaxy of pains. Nothing I could do to stop them. My shoulder tore. Broken or dislocated I couldn't tell. Vision went murky. A hard shot to the stomach, one to the crotch. Blood filling my mouth. Choking.

Beyond thought. Beyond even desperation. My broken fingers felt someone's hair. A neck, a face. I brought mine closer. Sank my teeth into soft jelly. Heard a scream and held on, gagging at the wash of fluid, the ropy fiber of an eyelash.

That was it for me.

THIRTY-THREE
NOTHING

THIRTY-FOUR
AND THEN

Well hello there, love.

THIRTY-FIVE

CALLED OUT OF DARKNESS

There are lost hours before the hospital.

The video from the traffic camera on the corner of Hastings shows me crawl along the ramp, bloody-mouthed, bloody-everythinged. I crawl toward the street, legs pushing myself along, collapsing at the curb.

A nutritional counsellor nearly drove over me. I was babbling but conscious, and she called for an ambulance. Sensing I was concussed, she asked me basic questions. My name, what happened. I sputtered nonsense and gibberish until the ambulance arrived.

None of which I remember.

I awoke in increments. Pain, then the unsatisfying wash of anesthetic. Eyes open on the dull swirl of beiges and eggshells, before putting it together that I was in a hospital bed.

One eye was blurry. One arm refused to move. I could feel bandages on my face, looked and saw my right index finger bound in a metal splint. A catheter snaked out to a piss bag clipped to the rail.

Moments from the attack came back. My pulse raised. Soon I was out again.

It was hard to gauge the time of day from the grey February sky.

Someone was sitting in the chair next to my bed, a comforting blur on the side with the good eye. For a second, I thought it was Sonia.

Well hello there, love.

"Holy crap, you're awake." My sister's voice. Kay called, "His eye is open" to someone else. Commotion in the room, my little square of bedside becoming a high-traffic area. A white lab coat flitted into view.

"Not right," a doctorly voice said. "His temperature…"

I was back in the water next to Jeremy Fell, the cold sweeping over me, a delicious feeling of ebbing out, laying down a burden I didn't realize I'd been caring.

No tunnel of light. No choir to greet me. Only the tide, the water, the cold. Never dropping and never surfacing.

Eons passed. The water began to boil, volcanic fissures opening below, vents of scalding steam. Roiling in turbulent ever-crashing waves, incinerating, dissolving.

And then the cold again.

At the very end there was a voice, and it sounded very much like George Jones. A voice calling over the waves, through the darkness. Not moving toward me, nor I to it, but the distance between us closing.

A coincidence, maybe. The very first song I ever heard was "White Lightning," followed by "Who Shot Sam." Records playing while adults sorted out what to do with the kid. That unmistakable voice with its fantastic range from whine to growl, the kind of voice you never forget, like Nina Simone's or Nusrat Fateh Ali Khan's.

Opposite my hospital bed was another where a man who looked about ninety lay, eyes closed, hair like cotton candy over a checkerboard forehead. On his nightstand was a small boom box, and from it, George and Tammy Wynette sang about wings or winds of something.

The man in the bed may have been deceased. He may never have existed in the first place. Next time I opened my eyes, the curtains were drawn around my bed.

"You're back among us," the doctor said. Later on I'd learn her name. Dr. Ahluwalia had two children and positively hated country music. "Do you feel ready to listen to a few things?"

I wasn't sure how to respond. My mouth was dry as a Dutch joke-book, and my arms felt dumped in cement. I managed to raise my head off the pillow, the major accomplishment of my adult life.

"You were admitted with an assortment of horrendous traumas," Dr. Ahluwalia said. "To make things even more fun, you caught an infection during your third surgery. Now that's subsided and you seem out of the woods, we can focus on getting you better. With me on this?"

I approximated a nod.

"That word *better* is important, Mr. Wakeland. You will get *better*. You are not going to get *well*. Certainly not well enough you can absorb more punishment than this. If you were an athlete, I'd be telling you now is the time to open that car dealership. Hang up the jersey while you have one good kidney and your brain isn't gruel."

Dr. Ahluwalia sank down in the chair so we were eye to eye. She smoothed a few grey hairs off her temple.

"Apologies for being blunt. We're over capacity and understaffed, and this round of flu has been hellacious. Your charts lead me to believe you may have a few unreported concussions. What this means is, no more alleys. You're a housecat now."

I made an effort to point with my right hand, very generally, in the direction of the boom box.

"Beastly music," Dr. Ahluwalia said. "We make exceptions for the dying. I guess you've been close enough to count."

THIRTY-SIX

MY GOOD EYE

A day later I got a look at myself. A nurse brought a portable mirror. What I saw was sinister. A skull partially shaved, train-tracked with stitches. The skin a range of Easter colours from eggplant to buttercup to rose.

A partial bridge missing. Cheek swollen so the eye was half hidden. Beard growth, darker and lighter than before.

My first words with this face were, "They really knocked the shit out of me."

Kay was at my bedside the next morning, eating a muffin from the cafeteria. She'd set up the few get-well cards on the table near the water jug.

"We couldn't visit for days on account of the infection. You feel better?"

"Feel like stepped on dogshit," I said.

She brushed muffin crumbs off her shirt. "Yeah, you still don't look that good. I mean, you totally look better. I dunno, sorry."

"Tim?" I managed.

"That's right, you don't know." She put the skirt of paper in the trash. "He's alive. There's some head trauma, and the doctors still aren't sure how bad." Kay paused and held back a sob. "When you see him now he just stares at you. I'm so sorry, Dave."

"Not your fault."

"It is. Tim said he'd do my time sheet for me and I could go home and I was so tired, but I should have been with him, I should have—"

"Nothing you could do," I said. "Naima?"

"Who?"

In halting, see-spot-run sentences I asked if Naima Halliday knew what had happened and if she had visited me.

"I haven't seen anyone else here. Jeff said he'll come soon. I'll ask about her, though. Can I bring you anything? They're sticklers about food and stuff. Had to sneak my muffin in."

I nodded at the boom box, now to my right.

"Oh, sure, I'll grab some CDs from the Salvation Army or whatever. Cool."

Fatigue was setting in. It took effort to say "Gill" and to clarify, "Police."

"Yeah, they were in. Ray Dudgeon left a card. I'm sure they'll be back to talk to you. 'Specially now."

It took my sister a moment to realize she'd lost me. Her eyes opened wider, the tease of a smile accompanying it.

"Forgot to tell you. They caught the guys, Dave. About a day after they attacked you. It's over. Pretty great, huh?"

THIRTY-SEVEN

AN EXERCISE IN TERROR

There was a row of small houses on Nanaimo Street, earmarked for land assembly. Developers were waiting for the neighbourhood's last original Italian immigrants to either die or downsize. In the meantime, the houses already purchased were rented to people like Robert Whittal.

Whittal's house was a dilapidated Vancouver Special, the yard contained by a breezeblock fence. The grey stones crumbled as the breeching party forced the gate open and approached the front door, ready to execute the search warrant.

Whittal didn't answer the door, which was unhinged by two officers with a ram. The interior of the house was a mess, the ground floor and upstairs empty. The sound of the door giving way had given the occupants in the backyard garage time to prepare. Once the doors were barricaded and the windows blocked, they slipped on gas masks and Kevlar vests.

The first shots came through the wall of the garage. The breech team withdrew to the front lawn.

Proper warnings were uttered. *Lay down your weapons, face down on the floor. Hands on your heads and ankles crossed.* No response from the garage.

The door was rammed open and two cylinders of cs gas lobbed through the opening.

What followed would take months to reconstruct from the testimony of survivors and the officers involved. Six persons were holed up in the garage, including Robert Whittal and his brother James, Whittal's girlfriend, Mandy Carstairs, and a neighbour named Josephine Burns. Also present were Dylan Keeping and Magnus LeDuc, the two street-corner defenders I'd fought with days before.

As the breech team entered, Carstairs tried to run, was tackled by one of the officers. His armored body shielded her from the home-made incendiary device which went off a second later.

LeDuc and James Whittal immediately went up in flames. Robert Whittal's lawyer would claim this was the result of police action, while the prosecutor would claim this was part of an exercise in domestic terror. The review board would find the bomb went off accidentally, LeDuc having tripped it as he struggled to secure his mask.

Between the cloud of CS gas, the flames and the downed officer, confusion held sway. Officers would claim they were shot at, while Whittal would counter that he'd effectively surrendered by this point. He and Burns were in fact face down and weaponless, inching away from the conflagration.

Keeping was shot thirteen times.

In the aftermath police would remove from the property the following:

- six Chinese SKS rifles
- ten thousand rounds of 7.62 ammunition
- four thousand rounds of 9mm Parabellum
- one box of 10-gauge shotgun shells
- a Ruger Super Redhawk .480 revolver
- twelve cans of camping fuel
- a crate of empty organic cane sugar cola bottles
- six assembled Molotov cocktails
- two replica SS stormtrooper helmets
- a hand-painted Nazi flag
- a box of *How Safe is Your Neighbourhood?* pamphlets

On Whittal's computer were found chat logs with various sub-urban members of Woden's Bastards, along with bomb recipes, names and contacts for W.B. higher-ups in Oslo and Calgary, two drafts of a manifesto on how Jeremy Fell's death was only the start of the "Insurrekkktion to KKKome," and sixty-odd gigabytes of inter-racial porn.

THIRTY-EIGHT
JOHN ONE AND JANE TWO

My sister's care package from the VGH Thrift Store included four CDs from the SOUNDTRACKS–E spindle, *Eyes Wide Shut*, *Eddie and the Cruisers II: Eddie Lives!*, *Exit Wounds* and *We All Love Ennio Morricone*. They joined George and Tammy in the rotation. Kay also included a couple of Longarm paperbacks, and a Mack Bolan, The Executioner with a missing front cover.

I mended gradually. When Dr. Ahluwalia came to check on my progress, she'd often praise how one injury was knitting together, while mentioning another I hadn't realized I'd suffered. A dislocated shoulder. A second-degree burn on the wrist.

The doctor's warnings hovered over the bed long after she left. I'd been injured before, a few times seriously. The body had set to its repairs with gusto, and, perversely, I'd enjoyed the process. Getting stronger every day. Luxuriating in having survived.

But this time I'd grazed a bit closer to what a friend had once called The Great Disconnect. What I remembered most vividly from the encounter wasn't anything to do with me. Rather, the monotonous, workmanlike strikes to Tim Blatchford. No malice behind the swings of the pipe. No exhilaration. This was drudgery.

There are people who brutalize others for a living, who treat their occupation as a shelf stocker does, clocking in and out. Who feel as little for their victims as a mother jointing roast chicken for her kids. I'd met a few enforcers, both the good ones and the ones who thought they were better than they actually were. Most enjoyed the work on some level, but they might have swung as dispassionately as Blatchford's attackers.

But their swings would have been accurate.

You do anything enough times and you get good at it. I knew in a fight to avoid punching surfaces harder than my fist, to find weak spots, to be efficient with violence. An enforcer would have the same precision. Our attackers didn't.

The unadorned fact was, if they'd known what they were doing, or been more enthusiastic about doing it, both Tim Blatchford and I would be dead.

After a week, when I could shuffle around the room, I made the effort to visit Tim. He was on the floor below mine, in a glass-walled observation room. Eyes open, staring past the spray of chrysanthemums Paul had brought, at the sun breaking through the morning fog.

It was spring.

Since puberty my penmanship has been borderline unreadable. Writing with one finger in a splint didn't make it any more legible. On the blank back page of one of the Longarms, I numbered one to five and wrote down what I remembered of each assailant.

1. Dagan Moody
- 6'4" +/−, white, brown/brown
- leather jacket/gloves/boots
- eye trauma
- "mate"

2. Jane Doe One
- 5'9" +/−, white, blue(?)/short brown
- blond wig, mittens
- leader (?) "You shut the eff up," gave orders
- self-defence training (armbar)
- jailhouse napalm

3. John Doe One
- broad shouldered, stocky, 5'7"
- dark-skinned (?)
- nose and face bruised (wall)
- inexpert combatant

Moody's appearance was clear to me, while I'd recognized Jane and John One from the SkyTrain footage. I concentrated on the other woman, who'd been up the ramp, waiting.

4. Jane Doe Two
- impression of average height, white
- squeamish ("That's enough," hesitated to strike)

I'd only seen a flash of skin as John Doe One had punched me. I spent a silly four hours trying to account for the shade. Somewhere between olive and light brown, John One could have been Portuguese, Corsican, Nepalese, anything really. Under cage lighting in a parking garage, in the midst of a struggle for my life, I couldn't trust anything except the initial surprise, the shade registering as different from the others.

There were skinhead gangs who'd make an exception for a dark-skinned member or do business with international syndicates. It's a complex world. But Moody and company seemed inspired by something other than hate, something simple and powerful, which I could only guess at.

So guess, Wakeland. You're in here for the foreseeable future, and you've already read the dirty bits out of the novels.

I thought about what Naima Halliday had said about Kyle's motivations: "To make things better. He hated the rich." That impulse folded back upon itself. Get a gun. Kidnap a politician's brother. The others doing away with Kyle when he wavered from the plan. Eliminate the threat posed by my investigation. They wouldn't stop here.

Did all of them share the same motives? Did it matter so long as Jane Doe One did? The others followed her lead, even Moody. Why did Jane One go back to the beach where Jeremy Fell was killed? Why take a photo of him, if that's what she was doing?

Kyle Halliday's funeral had happened while I was in surgery. Naima had checked out of the Four Seasons the same day. She'd taken a leave from work. Family issues, a nursing friend who took pity on me said.

I hoped she was safe.

THIRTY-NINE

AN AUDIENCE

Days slid by like rush-hour traffic in a merge lane.

I was alternately exhausted, productive, bored, impatient, anxious, numb, thrashing in pain, and doped to the gills. My bandages itched. The ceiling offered no entertainment. Pissing while catheterized felt mildly embarrassing, and as I was weaned off anesthetic, began to feel like the Massey Tunnel had been piped through the spout of my dick.

On the first day I could walk a lap of the hallway without leaning on anything, I had a visit from Sergeant Ray Dudgeon. He showed me yearbook photos of the skinheads from the raid and asked if I recognized anyone.

"It wasn't Woden's Bastards," I said.

"Sure of that?"

I laid out what I knew of the quartet, explaining how Moody and Jane Doe One had been threaded through both murders from the start.

"Those cases are closed," Dudgeon said. "Didn't you hear the mayor, Dave? This year Vancouver is taking a stand against racism."

If the sergeant had qualms about the investigation, he wasn't volunteering specifics.

"The tall one," I said, pointing to the photo, remembering the thin neck and prominent Adam's apple.

"Magnus LeDuc."

"Was there any damage to his eye? A bandage? Because I remember in the fight—"

"LeDuc was burnt Cajun-style," Dudgeon said. "Extra crispy."

"I bit Moody's eye," I said, remembering enough of the taste that I was thankful not to recall the rest.

"We got the four of them on camera going down the ramp of your building," Dudgeon said. "Using what looks like a code grabber to open the gate. Our half-dozen skinheads also had one. Numbers match up, and mode of entry, and we found pamphlets there in Kyle Halliday's room."

"And what about Moody?" I asked. "You ever talk to him?"

"No, he's still worth a conversation, but Woden's Bastards fit our evidence. Gill is happy it's over, Dave. He's supported by MacLeish, and MacLeish has the mayor's approval on this. Legislative and judicial and whatever the third one is, all three branches of government agree we got our guys."

"I don't," I said.

"Your disagreement plus five dollars might still get you a Starbucks."

"Moody attacked me. I damaged his eye."

"You say so."

"John Doe had darker skin."

"And you recalled this pigmentation, what, a week after being concussed, while under all kinds of neat hospital drugs, plus fighting off the flu."

"I don't have a perfect memory," I said. "But certain details I'm sure of."

"Dave, I'm not saying you're a liar. Just pointing out that the evidence we got and the balance of probabilities don't line up with you. And no one is upset to see this shit over and done."

"I need to find Moody," I said.

"We'll find him, and if he's got an eye like a pirate, we'll follow up," Dudgeon promised. "Till then, focus on looking pretty for the mayor." And seeing my confusion, he smiled and added, "Your part-ner set up a little bedside photoshoot with you and Valerie Fell."

Jeff had bought a new outfit for the occasion: a grey pinstripe with sharp lapels. He and Valerie Fell and Evelyn Rhee walked into my room grinning like models in a resort commercial. I was conscious of my robe and piss bag, of my face resembling a ham steak that had been unevenly seared.

"We're committed to punishing those who attacked you and who killed Jeremy for the crime of being related to a proudly progressive mayor." Valerie Fell spoke to me but for the benefit of Natalie Holin-shed, the journalist representing whatever media conglomerate cur-rently owned the *Sun*. Rhee took photos.

Valerie Fell smiled down at me as if our last discussion hadn't taken place. That was the tack Rhee seemed to take as well. Polite strangers, now that our association was over.

"This business is at an end thanks to Wakeland & Chen, and the especially fine work of police officers like Sergeant Dudgeon. Hate has no place here in Vancouver. White supremacy can find no foot-hold under my administration. Our team is dedicated to reclaiming the city from hate, to unifying rather than dividing and to continuing the search—the *quest*—for justice."

She patted my head like a well-meaning aunt, but thankfully restrained herself from tousling my hair.

"The people who killed your brother are still at large," I said.

There was no need to look at Jeff to know his reaction. Evelyn Rhee stared at the floor. The mayor smiled even brighter.

"Well, in time we'll get them all," she said, adding a folksy twang to her exit line. "You heal up now."

"What exactly did you mean?" the journalist asked once the may-or's team had gone.

"My partner means we'd still like to know which member attacked Jeremy Fell." Jeff's voice was smooth, amused at having to clear things up. "Dave is still a little out of it, but he's what you'd call a dot-the-*i*'s kind of detective."

Natalie Holinshed got the story she'd been sent for, and she probably had a thousand other journalistic tasks demanding her attention. She'd only swing if I put the bat in her hand, trusted her with the full story.

"Is that what you meant?" she asked me.

No doubt Moody would count me out after the beating. If I talked to Holinshed, I'd be trading away the advantage of surprise for a story that might never be written.

Instead I grinned and nodded, trying to look weak and delirious. It wasn't a stretch.

FORTY

THE ARTIST AND THE STUDENT

After two weeks of convalescing, I pressed Dr. Ahluwalia for a release date. "Three more days, if there aren't complications. Checkups every week after that. And you'll have to go easy. *Very* easy, David."

Three days would be March 9. It hadn't snowed since the alter- cation in the parking lot. Instead it rained, and on warm mornings a fog cradled the hospital, encircling my view. I walked and stretched, listened to music, plundered the lending library for a Katherine Dunn book on boxing and a couple of Sue Graftons I hadn't read.

I flipped through newspapers. I healed. And I waited.

Last weekend's *Sun* carried the story of an accident involving an artist I'd met once, Alex Knowlson. He'd been commissioned by the Colville Development Group to craft a mural for the exterior of a West End high-rise. The project was notorious in Vancouver: long- term tenants had been evicted in order to renovate, adding floors and turning the existing apartments into four-hundred-square-foot micro suites. In court, Colville claimed that the renos had effectively made the building a new structure and any tenant agreements were void. Alex Knowlson's artwork had started going up among protests.

I'd only met Knowlson once and instantly disliked him. An art- ist who claimed to draw inspiration from the downtrodden, but who treated addicts and sex workers as raw material for his ego. His new direction was large-scale postmodern colour blocks. I didn't get it. I wasn't brokenhearted he was dead.

But my curiosity was piqued by the way he'd died. The mural had been constructed in his Granville Island workshop, then trucked to the building, the large canvas squares raised and pasted to the edifice. Knowlson had fallen out a seven-storey window, presumably while supervising the work.

Two things struck me. First, the poetic nature of dying at the foot of your own monument. Something about the accident's composition reminded me of Kyle Halliday, slumped beneath the *Gate to the Northwest Passage*.

Second were the questions. Why was Knowlson up there, unharnessed and alone, leaning out a window? Why was he there at all, when he had labourers and fine-art apprentices to oversee the assembly?

It would have been an odd death, but no more than that, if not for the student who'd died three days later.

"Student" was a self-description given by Kevin Novak, the son of an industrialist who'd gifted Kevin the penthouse suite of a Gastown apartment building. Kevin Novak was under house arrest, facing extradition for laundering fentanyl money into Lower Mainland real estate. For a twenty-two-year-old enrolled at a community college, his holdings were in the eight digits.

Novak had failed to show for an appointment with counsel. A day later, a realtor had found him in the foyer of an empty townhouse, one of several Novak had purchased to allegedly launder his money. His wallet was missing and the window of his Porsche broken, so it was likely a robbery turned violent. Cause of death was blunt trauma to the head. Similar to Jeremy Fell.

I didn't recognize Novak's name, but his lifestyle was familiar. The latest in a line of princelings who'd used Lower Mainland real estate as a means of legitimizing their wealth, usually adding to it in the bargain. Real estate prices rocketed as a result. A family looking for a two bedroom near a school now had to compete against investment concerns and crooks with unlimited funds. No one would weep over Novak, either.

The Death of Kings hadn't claimed responsibility for the artist or the student. Maybe their MO had evolved, the graffiti no longer necessary. Or maybe the deaths were what they seemed at face value—one an accident, the other a crime of opportunity.

It was only a hunch that connected the two. Maybe Moody and Jane Doe One were executing a list of deserving targets, their attacks growing more brazen, more confident. A war on the rich. "Death of Kings" was becoming an apt moniker.

How could I stop such a thing? I wondered.

And did I want to?

Jeff wasn't going to apologize for working the photo op, but dropped by to say it hadn't exactly gone as planned. "Bright side, Dave, we're getting movement on these invoices. Solis paid up through April. Nobody wants to get on the bad side of the mayor's new friends."

"If that's what it takes to earn a living," I said.

"Money is money."

"Speaking of."

I couldn't remember the exact sums my mother owed, but told Jeff it was in the ballpark of thirty grand. Did I have enough equity to swing that?

"As a gift, not even close. But as a loan, yeah, you could borrow that much." Jeff paused. "Has she visited you, your mom I mean?"

"She doesn't care for hospitals," I said.

"Parents. What can you do?"

Pay them, I thought.

He left me the final report he'd compiled on Jeremy Fell. What the mayor had asked us for. There was little inside that would surprise her—affairs and stints in rehab, car crashes and failed schemes and business ventures. Jeff had interviewed a night-club owner and former boyfriend and a private pilot who'd been photographed with Jeremy on the beaches of Maui. Neither had a bad word to say about the dead man.

I'd be leaving the hospital with one arm in a sling, with a chunk of my left kidney removed and with a face resembling the scraps from a butcher's floor. My energy waned at random intervals, and there were pains in my hip and spine which Dr. Ahluwalia had all but guaranteed were permanent keepsakes. I was becoming my own memento mori.

I had my final battery of tests and X-rays, lying at the centre of a cathedral of beige machines and harsh lights. When it was over a nurse helped me dress.

Back in my room, I found Ryan Martz waiting for me.

"You look like month-old roadkill," he said.

"But I'm ravishing inside."

Ryan looked uncomfortable being in the hospital. The picture of health otherwise. He was letting his hair grow in.

"Your sister's worried about you," he said. "Told me to talk some sense."

"Like asking Napoleon how to be happy with what you have."

"Kay's worried, Dave. She thinks you'll go limping after the guys who did this."

I nodded. Ryan watched me struggle with my new shoes, black New Balances with Velcro straps. Everything chosen now for ease of motion, to be done one-handed.

"You're going to get killed," Ryan said. "It'll happen again, another beating, only worse, and there'll be less you can do about it."

"I've got a pretty good plan," I said.

"Not even listening, are you?"

He pushed his chair forward, blocking me from the coat rack, driving me back to the visitor chair. I sat, indulging him, letting out a wheeze of pain as my stitched-up side compressed.

"You can barely take a seat, Wakeland. You're fucking up the people who care about you. And don't think the irony escapes me, my being the one to say this to you."

I let myself rest a moment, acknowledging the truth of what Ryan

Martz was saying, and also the effort it took him to say it. He was intervening to help me in a way I hadn't done for him.

"You're correct," I said. "I realize I can't go at these people head on."

"Avoid them entirely, is what you need to realize."

"There's a way to divide them," I said. "A group like that, anyone who knows their plans is a danger to all of them. That's why they killed Kyle Halliday. Nobody leaves."

"So what's your plan?" Ryan asked, showing reluctant interest.

"Make someone leave," I said.

FORTY-ONE

DRAW

Kay was picking me up at ten. The night before, she'd dropped off the clothes I'd asked for. Drawstring pants, black Velcro shoes and a billowy grey raincoat I could drape over my shoulder sling. A Soundgarden T-shirt, just so I'd recognize myself. A black knit watch cap completed the outfit.

The image in the mirror was insubstantial. A wraith.

"Smile, you fucker," I told the reflection. It took effort.

I'd packed up my books and CDs for donation, gave a last look at the cards on the bed stand. Jeff and Marie had left one, along with drugstore magnolias from the office staff. Some religious well-wisher had dropped off another. My mother a third, explaining that she didn't much care for hospitals, but would see me when I was out.

The fourth card was unsigned, the cover embossed with a bouquet of wisteria and baby's breath. "Thinking of you," written inside.

My paranoid side wondered if my attackers had left it. The nurses hadn't seen who dropped it off.

Sonia, maybe.

Couldn't be.

But I'd thought, upon waking up, I'd heard her voice—

Well hello there, love.

I kept the card, tossed the others.

Kay was on time, and picked me up out front. I'd told her what else to bring. It was on the passenger seat of the black Wakeland &

Chen work van, still in its lockbox. The .357 Smith & Wesson Magnum I'd bought and never fired.

"You sure you need this?" my sister asked. "You never carry a gun. You always say guns get you into more trouble than out of."

"They usually do. But I'm already in trouble."

Kay tapped the steering wheel. "If it makes you feel safer while you're at home resting up. That *is* the plan, right?"

The shoulder holster could fit under the jacket, next to the sling. I practised clearing the revolver, the gun heavy, my hand awkward and strength faltering. The splint had come off, and I could barely curl my finger through the trigger guard. I wasn't going to win any quickdraw contests. Hopefully it wouldn't come to that.

Instead of home, I asked my sister to swing by the apartment on Oak Street. I rang Naima Halliday's buzzer, thinking I could try her landlord next. But Naima herself answered, surprising me.

I waved for my sister to wait in the van. I'd be brief.

Jeff had installed a reinforced steel door with a triple lock and alarm. Naima unlatched it and let me in. She was wearing a robe and socks, her hair up. She looked exquisite. When she saw my face, her breath held for an instant and she reflexively clutched the throat of her robe tighter.

"They hurt you," she said.

"I worried about you. Couldn't get in touch."

"The funeral was a lot of stress," she said. "And I was angry at you. Your questions. And I didn't want your money."

"Good, because I don't have much."

"I mean the money you sent."

Seeing I was puzzled, she opened her purse and removed a manila envelope. "I never asked you for this," she said. "I don't need it. It's an insult."

She pressed the envelope into my hand, the flap open, inside a thick stack of twenty-dollar bills. Maybe five thousand dollars.

"Why would I send you money?" I asked.

"You didn't?"

There was a machine-ordered precision to the stack of bills, like they'd been spewed out of an ATM. Nothing else in the envelope. No marks on it.

"I think Kyle's killers sent this."

She flung the bills on the counter as if they'd suddenly grown fangs. Hands on her hips, agitated. I embraced her, letting her lean on my injured arm despite the discomfort. She smelled of tea and Ivory soap. When she kissed me, her mouth tasted of the cheap mint of gum. It was a good kiss, the kind I never thought I'd have again.

"Can you think of anyone who knew Kyle, a friend, someone who stopped seeing him? Maybe someone uncomfortable with the direction he was going. Who cut him out of their life?"

Naima pulled away from me.

"It's like it never happened," she said.

"What do you mean?"

"Before you were hurt, you asked me questions like that. You won't stop."

"No," I said. "Like I told you before, I'm not the stopping type."

There was grief in the way she nodded, an acceptance that we'd never regain that intimacy, and maybe it had only been proximity and need.

"Kyle had a study friend," she said. "A woman who helped him with economics. After he left college, they were still friends. And then something happened. I asked him why she never visited anymore. Kyle didn't want to say."

Naima gave me the woman's name. Christine Goss had graduated and was now a sessional at UBC.

"After this is over," I began to say.

But it was a thought too disingenuous to complete. I left, allowed Kay to drive me home, told her I'd be taking it easy for the next little while.

Kay had tidied the apartment for me, even made the bed. I sat down on it and told my sister I didn't need anything else. I'd be taking a nap soon. Thanks for everything, sis. Go home to my mother's place and I'll see you soon.

Once she left, I got back to work.

FORTY-TWO

THE HIDDEN MEANING OF ALL THINGS

When you're ugly, your coffee is always to go.

An hour later I sat in the end booth at Elysian on West Broadway, a few blocks away from the hospital. A London fog in a paper cup in front of me. My jacket rested on the bench beside me, the revolver concealed beneath it. Brandi Carlile on the café's sound system, "You and Me on the Rock."

There's a look certain young academics have, pretty, pale, slender and harried. The look of someone competent for the job they have, born into that world, always knowing it was theirs and that they belonged. A muddled blessing, maybe. Christine Goss epitomized that look. She dropped a Lacoste bag on the chair opposite me and joined the order line. She came back with an almond pastry and kept her eyes on the drink window, or on her food, rarely on my face. I didn't blame her.

"Would it be indelicate to ask what happened?"

"I was attacked," I said.

"Sorry to hear that."

Goss took small, agile bites, demolishing the pastry. Sustenance achieved.

"Why did you stop hanging out with Kyle Halliday?" I asked.

"He stopped hanging with me."

She leapt up and snagged her latte. Goss had compact, delicate features, animated by a roving, nervous energy. Kyle Halliday and I warranted a portion of her attention, at least for now.

"Since Kyle died I've been thinking about just when he got weird. After he met Naima, around when he dropped out, there was a palpable shift. I used to tutor Kyle in econ, and within a couple weeks he didn't want to engage."

Goss took a long foamy sip and continued.

"A better way to say it might be: Kyle didn't want to engage with the course material. Second year is about how different economies knit together, how macro and micro interdigitate. If you have ironclad ideas about how the world works, or the right and wrong of wealth creation, it's difficult material to absorb."

"And Kyle hated the rich."

"To be sure. Once I couldn't tutor Kyle, once he knew what he wanted to know, we'd still go for beers now and then. I'd invite him to lectures at the Marxist club. But he wasn't interested. In his mind, anyone not in outright rebellion was a hypocrite. Understanding the system held no value to him. Yet his ideas of rebellion were childish. Heavy on talk of violence and overthrow, but accomplishing zilch."

"Naima said he'd rip hood ornaments off sports cars," I said.

"That was Kyle. No shortage of fancy rides in the school parking lot."

"Did he ever use the phrase 'Death of Kings'?"

Goss made an amused noise, a not-quite-laugh. "His Shakespeare phase. He'd scrawl stuff like that in the margins of his notebooks. Little slogans. 'Distribution should undo excess' or whatever."

"Who shared his views?"

Christine Goss didn't have an answer. As she thought about it, I watched a pair of tall and thickset construction workers bang open the door of the café, voices loud, pawing the display case. Maybe nine feet from our table, with a right turn around the counter to negotiate. Say five seconds to reach us. I felt tension settle in my shoulders. The handle of the revolver was easy to grip. Toss the coat, raise the barrel clear of the table. Take the time to aim centre mass. If they tried something, I'd be ready.

But the men ordered coffee and muffins and jaw-jacked at the order line. Harmless. The scenario gripped me long after they left, the feeling of a threat galloping towards me.

I hadn't always thought like this.

"Kyle didn't have 'views,' per se," Goss said after some contemplation. "He was parroting things that made him feel special. Cherry-picking quotes, as if the quote was the entire meaning of the text. Have you ever seen that sci-fi film where putting on glasses allows you to see the hidden messages in the world?"

"*They Live.*"

"Right. Kyle got off on the superiority of being that person. What pundits don't grasp about conspiracy is how good it makes one feel. It raises you above people, especially people who might look down on you. Feeding that feeling becomes all important. Addictive."

"So who else felt that way?"

Goss chuckled, as if I'd asked a particularly obvious question. "I mean, it's college, so everyone, to an extent. But true believers, real true believers like Kyle became?" She remembered something. "There was a man who used to give presentations on wellness, and maybe not *him,* but the people *around* him."

"Dr. Mattias Van Veen," I said. "The Jericho Centre."

She snapped her fingers in affirmation. "That's him. He'd sit in our little auditorium, cross-legged, and invite people onstage. Naima must have told you about that."

"Why?" I asked. "Why would she?"

I knew what Goss would say. Apprehension stabbed through the painkillers and unanswered questions. Cold tea and milk sloshed my hand. I'd lost hold of my cup.

"Van Veen is how they met," Goss said. "Kyle and Naima. Onstage during one of his sessions."

FORTY-THREE
WORK EXPERIENCE

I cabbed home, no longer able to ignore the cries of exhaustion coming from my limbs. Confusion had triggered a cacophonous headache. Naima wasn't answering her phone.

She'd lied to me, leaving Van Veen out of her introduction to Kyle. Downplaying her knowledge of his friends. I needed to know why. But not as much as I needed sleep.

After doing a quick check of the apartment, and purging the fridge and mailbox, I stripped and showered and fell into bed.

This was sleep. What I'd had at the hospital was the off-brand, diet variety. I'd forgotten the real thing.

In the morning, I had black tea and dry cereal and vowed that next time I was critically injured I'd throw out my milk ahead of time. The apartment was quiet. The mail that had been delivered while I was in the hospital was disappointing, heavy on bills and NOW SHOWING UNITS FROM $999,000 brochures.

I took the SkyTrain to work, reaching the office around eleven. Ryan Martz greeted me with a nod from behind the reception desk.

Watching me free my sling from my coat, he said, "Guess you won't be jerking off for a while."

"Sacrifices of an honest, hard-working detective. They never end. Any messages?"

"Some clients heard rumours about you, called to ask what happened. I told them you'd been thrown out of a Christian burlesque show for getting handsy."

"There's probably humour in there somewhere," I said. "Ibuprofen?"

He tossed me the bottle from the desk's top drawer.

In my private office, I stared out the window at traffic as I tried Naima from the landline.

"It's me," I said when she picked up.

"David." Her voice neutral and resigned.

"Did you and Kyle meet at a Jericho Cure info session?"

"David, I can't—yes, but—"

"Why tell me you met in the school cafeteria? Why lie?"

"I did not lie. We saw each other there first, yes. The doctor asked for volunteers and we both went onstage. But we didn't talk. It was an exercise, a meditation."

"Did you know Van Veen?"

"I went to his talks."

"See Dagan Moody there?"

"No. I don't remember."

"Anyone you recognize? Any names you can recall?"

"Why are you upset at me?"

"It's a convenient thing not to mention," I said. "It connects Moody to your husband. And you."

"I didn't know it was important."

"Everything is important, Naima."

"Except my feelings. What I want."

She hung up.

I took a few minutes to calm myself and nurse my headache. Began to make tea. Fumbled the mug, and watched helplessly as it smashed on the floor.

Ryan pushed away from the desk, looked in my direction. "Something up?"

"A little help," I said.

He cocked his head, exaggerating. "Sorry?"

"I could use a little help, please."

He filled the kettle from the water cooler, then strung a bag around the handle of a new mug. "Was that so hard to ask for?"

"Yes, it was."

"'Magine how I feel."

With my cup of tea, I checked in on Jeff. He was going through Kay and Blatchford's hour sheets from the convention security job.

"Funny," he said, "how a gay ex-wrestler has the same handwriting as a college kid from Alberta."

"Kay might have filled out a form or two for him," I said.

"Or seven." Jeff straightened the pile. "From now on, everyone fills out their own. How am I supposed to know if Kay was covering for him?"

"You could ask her," I said.

Sighing, Jeff swept the papers into a drawer. "I just don't want any problems with billing. If Tim sues, I want to be clear what work he did and didn't do."

"You really think he'd take us to court for unsafe work environment?"

"You scoff," Jeff said. "But if there's damage that keeps him from working, he could decide it's our fault."

"It is," I said. "Pay him whatever he needs."

"I'll remember you said that." Jeff handed me an unsealed bank envelope. "Thirty thousand dollars. Borrowed against the business. Your mother know what a gem she has for a son?"

I didn't have a rejoinder for that. Or a straight answer.

I spent an hour scanning job sites, looking for a resumé from someone who'd worked at the Jericho Centre. Squinting, typing with half my usual two-fingered efficiency, it took ages and yielded zero results. No one seemed eager to advertise their time working for a disgraced guru.

But I'm crafty. Going back to Van Veen's corporate charters, I looked for names. Parminder Bhat was listed as chief financial officer for MVVBC, Inc. The job title could mean anything. Searching, I found

Bhat's CV: a receptionist by trade, with a curious two-year gap in her employment record.

I called and didn't get through, then pecked out an email asking if we could talk. I was debating whether to show up at her home or call it a day, leaning heavily toward the second, a cold beer and a bowl of dandan noodles from Peaceful Restaurant, maybe the Szechuan green beans, when Jeff opened the office door, cradling his phone.

"Evelyn Rhee," he said. "Dave can hear you, Evelyn."

"No one else?"

Jeff closed my door, ignoring Ryan's questioning glance. "Just us," he said. "Go ahead and tell him."

Rhee's voice, jagged with tension, filled the office. "There's been another kidnapping. How fast can the two of you get to the British Properties?"

FORTY-FOUR
EXCESS AND EQUITY

What do you expect for your money?

It's the question that faces everyone in the Lower Mainland. As real estate slides further from the grasp of the average person, the wealthy have to make tough decisions. Do you want a one-bedroom condo, downtown, with a view of the water? Or a sprawling house tucked away in the suburbs, with a three-hour commute? The housing crisis killed the notion that a person could have it all. Even the reasonably well-heeled.

For the unreasonably well-heeled, you could have the British Properties, a private community of estates and mansions, where the cheap homes held eight-digit values. Originally purchased by a group of wealthy Brits and Europeans, including the Guinness brewing family, and boasting a no-Blacks-no-Asians paragraph in its charter, the Properties now welcomed millionaires from around the globe. A collection of kingdoms pretending to be a neighbourhood and doing a decent enough job of it.

"If we had the money, this is where Marie and I would move," Jeff said.

Jeff's Prelude wasn't the most comfortable car, and the sling made buckling the seatbelt difficult. I shifted in the seat. "Yeah?"

"The schools are good. We like the area."

There was nothing not to like. West Vancouver had been built up to service the Properties and was a now a pricey but pleasant neigh-bourhood in its own right.

"You like the price tag?"

"It would be a hell of a mortgage," Jeff admitted. "But Marie and I both work. We'd manage."

"That's a lot of debt to take on," I said.

"But look at what you get."

The boulevards were wide and lined with willows and European birch, people smiling, walking their dogs. Scrolled iron gates with bronze javelins rose up. Manor houses, turreted castles, colonial palaces. I wound down the window, admitting the scent of cut grass and cherry. I'd lost the weeks spent in the hospital bed. My mind was still running on winter time.

"What about you?" Jeff asked.

Shrugging wasn't possible, given the sling, but I made an attempt at it. "I'll never leave East Van."

"You're just gonna rent forever?"

"My landlord's an all right guy."

"He's still a landlord, Dave. And it's still not your own place."

"How," I asked, "is going eight million in debt 'your own place?'"

"Build equity. Make the house you live in an asset."

I shook my head. "That *Richest Man in Babylon* shit doesn't fly when every home's a million dollars."

"A million isn't that much anymore," Jeff said.

The address Evelyn Rhee had provided was walled off from the lane by white brick, topped with pineapple and Cupid finials. The guard at the gate cleared us and we rolled up a hillside of gardens, pergolas, water features, a kissing bridge. Jeff parked next to a Hyundai with a government tag that probably belonged to Evelyn Rhee, at the end of a fleet of Italian machinery.

A short jog from the canopied turnaround was a modest little shack rising four teal-coloured storeys, a wraparound balcony on each, stretching out in two great wings along the crest of a hill. A modern plantation with the perimeter security of the exercise yard at Folsom. Not impressive at all. The helicopter parked on the lawn probably couldn't hold more than a dozen.

"You know French aristocrats used to dress up like shepherds?" I said. "One of their favourite pastimes, getting their picture taken in rags, holding a crook. The simple life."

"Probably stopped doing that once they could buy Ferraris," Jeff said.

My partner shot his cuffs and retied his tie. He looked me over, deciding there wasn't much room for improvement. He folded the empty arm of my jacket around the sling.

"You look like a Civil War general," he said. "Ulysses what's-his-name."

The front doors opened on a magnificent circular parlour, opulently decorated and vaulting to the second floor. A man no younger than eighty, wearing a white polo tee and grey slacks, sat on a quilted divan. The man was crying.

Evelyn Rhee sat on a rattan two-seater facing a sober-faced middle-aged woman, who eyed me and Jeff with both suspicion and relief. The woman was dressed in a silk blouse and skirt, business attire, but barefooted. A dozen silver bracelets shimmered on her wrist as she raised a cigarette to her mouth, the ash falling onto the polished maple floor.

"Mona, these are the men I was talking about," Rhee said. "Jefferson Chen, David Wakeland. This is Mona Tsai and her father, Edward."

Handshakes didn't seem desirable, so we nodded respectfully. Mona Tsai stared at us and smoked. She might have been fifty, was certainly beautiful, seemed sullen and insolent but leaning into these to partially mask her worry.

Eventually she said, "We were told no police. Of any kind."

"They're not the police, Mona," Rhee said. "They're private consultants. Val's office hired them to help with Jer."

"Guess that didn't work out too well for Jeremy, did it?"

It's understood that families under stress will sometimes take it out on those around them. You learned to judge genuine antipathy from the put-on anger of people who feel impotent, who use rage to take their mind off hurt. When that person was a client—or worse, a potential client—you had to strike the right note of polite deference, while showing enough backbone to suggest you were competent and could get the job done. It required a master.

Enter Jeff Chen.

"Ms. Tsai," he said, placing his hands on his knees, "I can't pretend to know what you're going through. My partner and I specialize in one thing only: getting the best possible result. Advocating for our clients is all we're interested in."

I noticed Jeff's accent downshift, his language grow formal while adding a pause here and there. Making himself familiar.

Mona Tsai pointed at me. "Who advocated for his face?"

"My parents did that, ma'am," I said. "Must've held a grudge."

"Dave was attacked by the same people who kidnapped Jeremy Fell," Jeff said.

Mona shuddered. Her face froze in a scowl, tamping down the emotions beneath it. The ash on the tip of the cigarette grew and curled downward.

"I thought they got those people," Mona said. "It was on the news."

"I hold a dissenting opinion about who was responsible," I said.

She shook her head, noticed the ash and flicked it. A spark died on the floor. "Maybe I should call the chief. To hell with what the letter says."

"Letter?"

Rhee passed us a slip of paper, on which was typed:

WE HAVE YOUR HUSBAND

PAYMENT IS DUE

PENANCE IS DUE

DISTRIBUTION SHALL UNDO EXCESS

NO POLICE

WAIT TO HEAR FROM US

FORTY-FIVE

CITY OF THE DEAD

The note appeared typewritten, but the letters hadn't been keyed into the page. Rather it was a 'vintage typewriter' font from a word processor, reproducing the splotches and fades of an old Remington or Underwood. The paper had been folded in half.

"Who's been abducted and when?" I asked.

Mona Tsai spoke as if resenting the time it took to mouth the words. "My husband didn't come home from the gym last night. I thought he might have gone back to the office, but then the note arrived this morning."

"Delivered how?"

"Dropped through the mail slot in the gate. I didn't see by whom."

"Your security system might have caught it," Jeff said. "Mind if I look?"

Evelyn Rhee stood. "I'll show him the footage, Mona."

"Do what you want."

When she and Jeff had left the room, Mona Tsai lit two cigarettes and placed one in her father's hand. The old man didn't move it to his mouth. The knuckles of his hands bulged from what seemed like a combination of arthritis and years of hard labour.

I balanced my notebook on my knee and gripped my pen. "What does your husband do for work, Ms. Tsai?" I asked.

"He's Adam Colville."

As if that explained it. And it did.

Colville built and Colville owned. His development company had ridden a twenty-year real-estate escalator, hauling in hundreds of millions, determining what the city would look like for decades to come. The building Alex Knowlson had tumbled out of was one of Colville's. So were dozens of others, luxury complexes with stratospheric prices and low square footage. The Vancouver skyline belonged to Adam Colville, had been constructed according to his specifications.

Colville's name reframed our conversation. It made me reappraise the woman lounging indolently across from me. She knew that, could sense the tempest of anger and disgust and respect the name summoned. It made her smile.

I focused on the details of the disappearance. "Did your husband usually go to the gym at night?"

"Always, even on holidays. Adam is driven like that. He gets his best ideas during workouts. We were putting a rock-climbing wall in our new home."

"Your husband doesn't live here?"

"This is my place," Mona said. "My father started Gold Mountain Food and Drug, and I've been chair for the last ten years. Seventeen locations and three signature stores."

Pride, along with an invitation to criticize or envy. I recognized the name, a grocery chain specializing in organic produce and Asian flavours. Good bakery, not enough checkouts.

"So with the proverbial gun to the head, pardon the expression, between you and your dad, you could put together a ransom pretty easily."

"Any amount," Mona said. "I love Adam. Maybe you don't believe me."

"Not important if I do, Ms. Tsai."

"It is if you want to work for me."

"Okay," I said. "I believe you love him. I believe you're Pyramus and Thisbe."

"Don't you dare mock me."

We needed a second to take each other's measure, drop the roles of princess-bitch and mouthy servant. Mona Tsai was distraught, dismissive, but deserving of professional respect, whatever my feelings about her husband. Whether I could muster that respect was another matter.

"Apologies," I said. "This is only my second day out of the hospital."

She pointed her cigarette in the direction of my face. "You'd maybe get beat up less if you watched your tongue."

Jeff and Evelyn Rhee rejoined us, Jeff shaking his head.

"Nothing on the street view except a stocky man in shades and a hoodie," he said. "Knows not to look up at the camera. Dropped the note through the gate and ran."

"No vehicle?"

"Not that we could see."

"Did you know Jeremy Fell?" I asked Mona in a conciliatory, down-to-business tone. "Or Kyle Halliday?"

"Halliday, no. We met Val's brother at a few parties, grand openings and such. We weren't friends."

"Does 'Death of Kings' hold any significance?"

She shook her head, then spoke to her father, translating the phrase, I assumed. Edward Tsai answered in a quavering voice, asking something. Her reply was curt.

"It means nothing to us," Mona said to me, in a tone that meant the discussion was over.

"Ms. Tsai, is there anyone you can think of who might be involved?" Jeff asked.

"Of course not."

"No enemies?"

"None." She allowed herself a long drag on her cigarette and a slow, thoughtful exhale. "Against Adam's company, you mean?"

"Against whomever."

"Of course there are a few disgruntled employees or activist types. Jealous shitheads, mostly, or people who want housing to magically appear for them, free of cost. But neither Adam or I have enemies."

I doubted anyone whose influence reached as far as Colville's had an accurate accounting of others' disposition toward them. If asked before this meeting, was I an enemy of Colville Development, what it stood for, what *he* stood for, I wouldn't have hesitated. Yes, absolutely, of course.

"How do you want us to proceed with this?" Jeff said.

"Find my fucking husband. That would be nice." Mona lit herself another cigarette. Her father's had snuffed out between his fingers.

I looked to Jeff, who looked to Evelyn Rhee.

"The note said not to contact the police," Rhee said.

"The note always says that." I scanned the windows, thinking how hard it would be to defend a place this size, an echo chamber with branching hallways and twinned staircases. Pacino at the end of *Scarface*, with tonier decor.

"Mona feels bringing them in at this time wouldn't be wise," Rhee said.

"If that's your preference," I said. "That case, we wait here till they contact you."

She looked to the millionaire for confirmation. Instead of a reply, Mona Tsai stormed out of the room, snatching a bottle from the well-appointed sideboard on her way. Her cigarette she left burning on the table. A door slammed somewhere upstairs, the noise like artillery above us.

The back patio of the Tsai home stretched out to an infinity pool in a plinth of heated tile. The deck's roof retracted. Next to the pool were a couple of cheap plastic deck chairs. Jeff and I parked ourselves there.

"You feeling okay?" my partner asked me.

"Stitches ache. Otherwise, I'm fine."

I'd pilfered one of Mona Tsai's cigarettes, tapped it on the arm of the chair. If I knocked it out of shape I'd be less tempted to smoke it.

"What are we doing here?" I asked.

"Like you told her. We're waiting for further contact."

"I mean morally. What can we do for an Adam Colville that the police can't? If the system doesn't work for the Colvilles of the world, what's the point of the system?"

"Maybe you came back to work too quick," Jeff said.

"Maybe."

"You forget this *is* the job."

"And you never feel you're maybe on the wrong side?"

Jeff didn't answer. The sun was going down below the gently sloping lawn, which ran miles in the direction of English Bay. A darkening expanse of green and grey.

"All that land," I said.

"It's a really great spread, isn't it?"

Somehow the cigarette still looked very smokable. I kept tapping.

"What did the father say about 'Death of Kings'?" I asked.

"Cantonese is like my third language, Dave."

"But you caught some of it."

"Sure. Some talk about emperors, hell. Stuff like that. Nothing that helps us."

"You never know," I said.

Jeff sighed. "Youdu is the Dark City. It's underground, totally dark all the time. That's where King Yan rules over the dead, passing judgment on them. Death of Kings, Ruler of Death—maybe it was a translation thing. Or maybe Youdu was on the old man's mind." He shifted his weight, causing the slats of the chair to exclaim. "You really care about old myths and shit, I'll buy you a book."

"I make no apologies for having a curious bent."

"The whole city's supposed to be lit by candles."

On the other side of the silver-red water was the black mass of Stanley Park. Vancouver beyond it, lit up but not by candles.

We waited. We didn't have to wait long.

FORTY-SIX

A REASONABLE RANSOM

I woke up to Jeff prodding my arm, harder than necessary. "Mona just got a text from them," he said.

Getting out of the lounge chair one-handed was awkward. In my pocket was a vial of T-3s. I'd dry-swallowed one instead of lighting the cigarette. The result had been a numb and patchy sleep.

We assembled in the living room, all but Mr. Tsai who I gathered was still sleeping. Mona sat splay-legged on the carpet, her phone in front of her on the glass coffee table.

The single text instructed her to install a peer-to-peer conversation app called KLOAKr, which instantly erased messages and call logs. Seconds ticked by as it downloaded. The four us stared, waiting, feeling nervous and ineffectual.

Evelyn Rhee took her own phone out. "Babysitter check-in," she explained.

Mona's screen woke up, a screech from an incoming call. The caller ID read [BLOCKED].

Jeff nodded, ready, and Mona tapped the ACCEPT button. "Yes, I'm here." Her voice was soft, threads of tension through the last syllable.

"You're very fortunate, Mona Tsai."

The voice was electronically detuned, metallicized, but clear and husky. Female, I'd wager.

"Is my husband all right?"

"He's alive, yes. You're fortunate because you have the chance to keep him that way, by keeping others that way."

"I haven't involved the police," Mona said. "I'm willing to pay whatever to get Adam back safe."

"And you will pay, but not to us. Take this down."

Mona mimed writing. I passed her my notebook and pen. She tore a page out, wrote directly on the table, the pen rasping the glass through the sheet.

"Two million dollars," the voice said, "goes to the Surrey Gurdwara Food Bank. Two to the Gospel Mission on Hastings. Two to the Society for Sex Worker Safety. Two to the Committee for Tenants' Rights. Two to Safe Supply Vancouver. These donations need to be made publicly and made within twenty-four hours. I'll repeat the names."

Mona underlined each as it was spoken a second time. Charities and organizations that fed, housed and advocated for the city's most vulnerable. A ten-million-dollar infusion would help countless people. That must have been what the voice meant by keeping Colville alive by doing the same for others.

Jeff was watching the screen. I looked at Evelyn Rhee, whose eyes met mine and turned quickly away. An instant, no longer, yet I'd caught something in her look. I tried to figure out what it was.

"I'll send the money as soon as I can," Mona said. "My husband. When will he be released? How do I know you haven't hurt him already?"

There was silence on the connection.

"I need some sort of proof," she added.

No answer. I thought the connection had gone out, then a distorted yelp could be heard. A man's voice, in pain.

Jeff winced, and Mona sobbed in recognition. "Please, you don't have to hurt him."

"He's going to be fine," the voice said. "Once the money has been sent and all five charities have publicly acknowledged the donations, he'll be dropped off unharmed."

"All right, I believe and trust you," Mona said.

"We haven't asked for an unreasonable amount. Not considering your combined holdings. Any tricks, any delays, any *anything*, Mona Tsai, and your husband will drown in his own blood. He'll be buried under his treasure. You'll never see him again. That's it."

The line cut out, and we watched the app scrub the record of the call.

"There might be a way to recover that," Jeff said.

Mona wasn't listening. She was already calling up her bank account.

"Can you move that much, in that amount of time, without a personal appearance?" I asked.

"I'm looking up the manager's name. Maybe Adam has his home number in the office upstairs."

I stopped myself from remarking on that. A different world for the wealthy and the connected. A fortune she could move in a second, that she could easily live without, and could have donated at any time. No hesitation in doing so now, though. Maybe that was a sign of true love. For richer or for slightly less rich.

I left her to the money and Jeff to work with the app and followed Rhee down the hall. Photos of Adam Colville and Mona Tsai, photos of a much younger version of the old man under the awning of his first market. Valerie Fell handing Colville some sort of civic award.

I caught up to her in the kitchen, which could have accommodated comfortable stations and *mises en place* for an entire culinary school. Rhee removed a Perrier from one of the refrigerators.

"Water?" she asked.

"No thank you."

"Mona's a friend," she said, accounting for her familiarity with the kitchen. "Adam, too, though he's closer to Val."

I nodded.

"Mona phoned us the second she got the note. Why are you looking at me like that?"

She had paused mid-twist, the bottle cap still between finger and thumb. I leaned my good hand on the cutting board island. It might have been larger than my kitchenette. Or it might not. I didn't have a tape measure handy.

"You already knew," I said.

"Sorry?"

"You've heard all that before," I said. "The voice, the spiel, was familiar to you."

"Bullshit, Wakeland."

"Dollars to doughnuts, if I looked on your phone, I'd find that same app. Wouldn't I?"

Her hand went to her pocket reflexively, a gesture I caught, and she saw I'd caught it.

"Are you working with them?" I asked.

"Fuck you for asking that. Of course not."

That left only one other explanation. "You never told the police, did you? When Jeremy was kidnapped, they contacted you in the same way. And you never told Gill. Did you?"

"No," Rhee said. "That's why I wanted to hire you. Why I recommended you to Mona."

"You could go to jail for withholding evidence."

"I suppose I could," she said, too distraught to pull off the matter-of-fact tone. "And you could lose your business."

"What does—"

"You signed an NDA," she said. "You work for Val. You breathe a word to anyone without her say-so, you'll be sued and then blacklisted by every business in the city. Your job, your life savings, your reputation. You'll end up doing security at a mall. Your partner's kids will be able to visit him at the food court on his break. Understand?"

"I've never understood anything less," I said. "Didn't you want Jeremy back?"

"Of course."

"Then—"

"Come outside," Rhee said. "I'll try to explain."

What could I do but follow.

FORTY-SEVEN

SPARE ME

Rhee dialed up the gas on the patio's fireplace. We shifted the deck chairs closer. The pool, lit by pink and yellow underwater lights, burbled as the filtration system kicked in.

I lit the mangled cigarette. If ever there was a time.

"Maybe I should have told you the truth sooner," she said. "No one can understand the pressure on Val. First female mayor of one of the biggest and most diverse cities in North America. Bisexual, but downplaying our relationship to keep Sonny out of the spotlight. She walks the finest of fine lines. A fucking filament."

"Can't be easy," I said. The smoke was harsh. I regretted and welcomed it.

"On the flip side you have Jeremy, who stomps through life doing whatever he feels like. A good person deep down, but you summed him up correctly with what you wrote that first day."

Another lifetime ago. I tried to recall.

"A flake," Rhee said. "Val was constantly coming to his rescue. Paying Van Veen when Jeremy walked out of his clinic, covering bad debts, loans and lines of credit. I'm not saying all this to make it sound like Jeremy deserved what happened. I want you to appreciate the lengths Valerie had already gone to for him, what it had cost her. She'd do anything in her power."

"Except pay his ransom," I said. "That's what we're talking about, right? The kidnappers offered you the same deal and you turned them down."

"It wasn't the same deal," Evelyn said. "They contacted me, yes. But do you know what they wanted Val to arrange?"

"Dinner at the Keg with Ryan Reynolds?"

"To empty the prisons and legalize drugs. That's what they asked for. *And* ten million dollars. Think of her options, Wakeland. Even if Val could borrow that much, she can't remake the laws at whim. And say she could, say magically Val could give these people everything they wanted. Then what? No guarantee she gets Jeremy back. Her career, her ambitions, all destroyed."

"So she chose not to try."

"Idiot, no."

Rhee kicked her chair back as she stood, pacing in front of the fireplace. I smoked and tried to put myself in her position, thinking what I would do. Tell the police, even though that meant putting Jeremy in the hands of political adversaries. Pay. Don't pay. Make it public. Each had tremendous downsides. An impossible position to be in—if you knew you were in it.

"You never told her," I said.

"No, I didn't." Evelyn rubbed warmth into her shoulders. "These people knew enough to call me. I never responded, never told Val. You're the first person I've told."

"And because of that—"

"Yes. Jeremy's dead. Kyle Halliday, too. And what happened to you and your associate."

"My friend," I said, thinking of Tim Blatchford's empty gaze from a cold hospital room.

I finished the smoke and considered tossing the butt in the pool, watching ash cloud the just-filtered water. The pointless revenge of the not-wealthy, like Kyle ripping hood ornaments. Futile. I crushed the filter with my shoe and tossed it in the fire instead.

Gill's task force, and the entire police operation, had been hamstrung from the start, told only that Jeremy was missing. No wonder they'd come to the wrong conclusion. Not a single person would mourn the skinheads, but if Adam Colville wasn't returned in reasonable health, the fault would lie with the woman pacing in front of me.

"Did you tell Her Worship that you spared her from making this decision?" I asked.

"She knows without me saying it," Rhee said.

"It's a neat snip of the Gordian knot. If she pays, she's the Mayor Who Kowtows to Terrorists. If she refuses, she's the Heartless Bitch Who Let Her Brother Die. Must've confused the Death of Kings when you simply didn't answer."

"Have you ever been in love?" Rhee said. "Really, truly loved a person?"

"I like to think so, yes."

"Were you a hundred percent honest with them?"

"In everything that mattered."

She gave an amused shake of the head. "No, you weren't. No one is. Love isn't honesty, it's loyalty. Doing what the other person needs. Taking on what they can't bring themselves to do."

"Funny," I said, "that's how *Richard II* ends. The King hints he wants Richard dead. Someone in his court jumps at the chance. Thy will be done and all that."

Rhee frowned, then nodded, seeing the connection. "Love," she reiterated.

"Maybe one type."

My thoughts ran to Sonia and her move to Montreal. Was that a test I'd failed? Or her way of trying to break the circuit I was trapped in, a circuit that had led me eventually to the beating? Either way, I reckoned, if I'd been in Montreal instead of here, I'd have fewer stitches and a prettier face. Not to mention I'd be with her.

"Anything more you can tell me about these people?" I asked.

"Just that they had my cell number. They knew that to get Val's attention, they'd go through me."

"Which didn't work out so well for anyone."

"I did it for her, to spare her," Rhee said, sorrowful but meaning her words. "Maybe some day you'll do an awful thing for someone you love. Or they'll do an awful thing for you. Judge me then."

FORTY-EIGHT

VOW OF POVERTY

I needed to get out—out of the British Properties, out of this ultra-lavish and empty home that piled luxury upon luxury, drowning in expensive things. Most of all I wanted out of the predicament I'd found myself in.

Working when things didn't make logical sense was one thing. I was used to pushing forward without a map. But this didn't make *emotional* sense. I couldn't square my conscience, found myself sympathizing with the people who'd beaten me to within an inch of my life, despising the people I worked for and represented.

Leaving Jeff to help with the ransom, I took his car home, stopping at a Gold Mountain Food and Drug to buy a pack of cigarettes. Call it trickle-up economics. In deference to Jeff, I smoked with all the windows down.

Bedevilled on both sides. Was terrorizing the rich a crime any worse than the way they held money and political power above human life? How did I end up carrying water for people whose greed and negligence were choking the life out of the city?

But kidnapping and the violence that followed was sick, wrong, and excusing it was a slippery slope. The Death of Kings had elected themselves to speak for the city's downtrodden. Yet Dagan Moody collected rent from Van Veen's property, and Kyle Halliday had left a middle-class marriage to go slumming in an SRO. They were proletarian poseurs, whatever their aspirations.

What plagued me more than anything was the gun next to me on the passenger seat. What it said about these people, and about me. Before this was over, I'd have to kill someone. I'd accepted that possibility by not running away. But it nagged at me, how easily I'd accommodated to the idea.

Since when did we decide collectively that human life meant so little? Death is inevitable, omnipresent. We are brief.

I tossed the half-smoked cigarette. Then the pack. They whipped by the window of the Prelude, inhaled by the night.

I was in this to the end. I'd try to prevent anyone else from dying. Myself included. Mercy was a principle I could hold to in the darkness. The only principle that made sense.

At home, there was barely time to remove my shirt before my phone rang. A number I didn't recognize, from the city's 778 area code.

"Wakeland," I said.

"Still want to talk?"

The voice was unfamiliar. Young, female, barely above a whisper.

"If you have something to say."

"Roof of the Sinclair Centre in twenty minutes. Empty pockets. No phone."

"How do I get to the roof of a closed shopping complex at night?" I asked.

"I'll leave a door open for you. But I'm not waiting around. Twenty minutes."

It took me five to shrug my clothes on, another six to wheel the Prelude downtown. Driving pell-mell, hoping to get lucky with the lights.

The Sinclair Centre was a mall built by connecting the city's former post office, customs house and two other concrete buildings from the 1930s. I parked near the familiar clock tower on the Hastings side, across the street from the Wakeland & Chen office. Had the caller chosen the meeting spot because of that?

Before I left the car, I texted Jeff my whereabouts, and practised drawing the gun. My guess, the caller was Parminder Bhat, Mattias Van Veen's former receptionist and CFO. She had reason enough to avoid being seen speaking with me. Of course she could be working with the others. Setting me up for them.

True to her word, the door leading to the fire escape was wedged open.

Nowhere but up.

FORTY-NINE

A CONFESSION

Shoulder first through the staircase door. I was huffing a little, my good hand gripping the handle of the .357. On the exposed roof, a wind whipped down the corridor created by the surrounding office towers, sharp as a freshly stropped razor.

A figure sat hunched behind the peaked skylight, eating from a bag of Doritos. Between her feet, a bottle of root beer. The hood of her North Face jacket was up, tendrils of black hair lifted by the wind. Parminder Bhat was twenty, if that.

"Cripes, is that a gun?" She tensed, hand thrust in the bag.

"You told me not to bring a phone."

"I didn't think you'd come strapped, mate."

Parminder Bhat had the post–high school amusement at the world and the language employed to describe it, though her smirk was subdued by experience. Older than her years in some way. I watched her tilt the bag and gulp down the last mouthful of crumbs.

"Late dinner," she said. "Wow, mate, who gave you that face?'

"The subtractions were done by four people in hoodies, one of whom is named Dagan Moody."

"Sky," she said, recognizing the name. "The Doc gave all of us nicknames. Mine was Jazz. Jasmine, first, but he changed it when I told him I didn't envision myself as a Disney princess. Or a bag of rice." She crumpled and pocketed the bag. "Sometimes part of me still misses that asshole."

I turned my back to the wind so I was standing next to her, like two people at a bus stop. "You must have been young when you started there."

"I was skipped two grades, so I was seventeen when I enrolled at Langara. Met the Doc the same year, so, yeah. Time flies when you're having fun."

"You can help me," I said. "I don't understand how this New Age self-help group, or whatever it was, spun off into whatever it's become."

"Tell me about it," Parminder said. "When I saw the footage of Boss burning that transit cop, I wanted to tell someone. But I don't even know her real name, just that she was with the Doc."

"With him how?"

"He fucked her, but he fucked a lot of us. Boss was more like the Doc's understudy, his number two. Boss and Sky were special to him. They called the shots when he wasn't there."

"This must be rough," I said, "but please take me through what you can."

Parminder nodded. Maybe she'd been waiting to tell someone.

The Jericho Centre rented out college auditoriums, community centres, and church basements, giving free info sessions, which were glorified meditation exercises with a sales pitch at the end. Van Veen used the sessions as a means to recruit clients for the clinic, but also seeking out volunteers. Young students, attractive, idealistic, looking for guidance and reassurance. The Doc worked pimp-like on them, nurturing their self-esteem, making them dependent, crossing boundaries, worming their confidences out of them. They adored him, and they adored what they became under his guidance.

Dagan "Sky" Moody and "Boss" lived in Van Veen's home, the elder siblings of their alternative family. Most of the members worked jobs or studied, spending their spare time at the house, in the orbit of their guru.

The volunteers ate well. They drank nice wine. They meditated and studied together. Van Veen cultivated habits of respectability and good hygiene. You needed to move through society to impress it, to eventually conquer it.

And conquest was what his teachings led to. Becoming rich, famous, successful, unlocking your potential, driving out doubts and hesitations. Becoming powerful. Desirable. Whole.

Their new names were a part of this. You never called a volunteer anything other than the name Van Veen bestowed. Parminder had confessed to the Doc that her secret desire was to run her own business, have a work force under her. As a precocious student whose truck-driver father talked her into community college to save money, she'd felt misunderstood, caught in a stasis of ambition and doubt.

"College is a respectable path for Parminder to take," Van Veen had cooed. "So let her take it, mate. And when you're at Jericho, you're Jazz, and Jazz is on track to run this business. Maybe take it over if she chooses."

Parminder couldn't believe it. "He was giving it to me to run. I could have shit I was so happy."

Van Veen convinced her that as she trained with him, volunteered as his receptionist and serviced him sexually between workshops, she was inching closer to her dream of being a captain of industry. Adding her to the articles of incorporation as chief financial officer was proof this was her way to the fortune she wanted and deserved. How many late teens were officers of a corporation raking in millions every year? This was success, wasn't it?

And then, within two weeks, Van Veen had disappeared, the door to the clinic was locked and the funds the Doc had promised had dried up. Confusion reigned. Sky and Boss were the most defeated by this. Without Jericho, who were they?

She'd learned later, as the story broke, that Van Veen had fled to Malaysia. A patient, the daughter of a yoga-wear designer, had suffered a complication while getting an abortion. The family had found out that the Doc was the father. While it was kept quiet to avoid scandal, Van Veen lost his licence and his upper-class clientele. The clinic was shuttered. All of it over.

"That's when I tried killing myself," Parminder said, uncapping the root beer. "I wasn't the only one. We lived for this guy. If the Doc had stuck it out, we'd have defended him all the way. But he ran, and it became clear he was just a guy who'd scammed some easy blowjobs and cash. He didn't give a flying fuck about us."

Parminder tried to go back to school, but the environment made her remember the info sessions, the clinic. She'd taken a reception job, supporting herself while she worked things out.

"He got deep into my head, mate. Way deep. If you were around him long enough, you'd start to speak like him, use the same mannerisms. Our families didn't know what volunteers really did, and if they objected to all the time we spent, we just cut them out. I still can't face my dad."

A person that young shouldn't have been so knowingly cavalier about self harm and abuse. Parminder Bhat had been victimized by Mattias Van Veen, misled, disempowered. I was glad she was now beyond his grasp.

"How did the Death of Kings form out of the clinic?" I asked.

"Sky came to visit me in the hospital after I cut. There's this nice little duck pond behind the recovery centre, and we walked around it, fed the birds and talked. I was so tranked up it was like being underwater. And then he told me the Doc was back, and it was like breaking the surface."

Even the memory caused a flinch. She bit her lip, looked down into the soda bottle.

"He was back, yeah, thirty pounds lighter, addicted to heroin. Being spoon fed and shot up by Boss and Sky at his compound in the hills. The power was off, Sky told me. They were starting something new, he and Boss, and I was welcome to be a part."

She laughed, a caustic, defensive sound.

"Part of me really wanted to go. Isn't that messed up? I almost did. Guess I knew it was bullshit. Even Sky stopping by, it was more of a recruitment drive than checking on a friend."

"When was this?"

"Six months, maybe a little less."

"You look like you're pulling through," I said.

"Oh, yeah, I'm really thriving."

I'd need an entirely new vocabulary to find words to console someone who'd gone through what she had. The best I could do was finish my interrogation and leave her be.

"Did you know Kyle Halliday?" I asked.

"He was getting into it near the end. He and a few others from the college. Didn't know them very well."

I went through my description of John Doe One.

"Sounds like Driver," Parminder said. "I'm pretty sure he's the one in the video with Boss attacking that Transit cop. He used to drive the Doc around, pick things up for him. He wanted to be a professional driver, stuntman or something. It's weird, but I feel like I'm betraying him, telling you his dreams and shit."

"Do you know his real name?"

Parminder shook her head. "I only know Sky's because he had to sign in at the recovery centre when he visited me. The people he and Boss recruited are probably like me. Smart, mixed up, no confidence. Sky and Boss are probably even using the Doc's same pitch. Join us, make something of yourself, leave your mark on the world."

It sounded like something Kyle Halliday would go for. I recited the description of Jane Doe Two. "Know her?"

"Could be Rio. She started around the same time as Kyle. The same age as him, or a little older."

"Did you know Kyle's wife, Naima?" I asked. A troubling possibility, one I wished I could shake.

"No, I didn't spend much time with the new folks. It sounds messed to say, but I felt I was better than them."

I tried to think back to the garage, the woman in the hoodie. Her hesitation to join the fray. I knew Naima Halliday's face, her body, but covered up and seen in the middle of a fight, by someone already injured and panicking—I couldn't be sure. I didn't want to be sure.

"The Death of Kings seem to be targeting rich people," I said.

"Funny, huh? The same type of clients the Doc loved to work with. Only time you'd see him suck up."

"Any idea where they'd hide out?"

"Nope," Parminder said. "And I don't want to know. I am so fucking done with them."

"I can imagine."

"No," she said, "you really can't."

I told her I'd transfer some money to her, suggested she leave town for a few weeks. Maybe check out Montreal. She didn't argue or agree. Maybe what she needed more than anything right now was to decide things on her own.

"Do me a solid and wait here a few minutes, mate," Parminder said. "I don't want us to leave at the same time."

I nodded, and as she headed to the door, asked, "How did you end up with the keys to this place?"

"Driver used to work here," she said. "Bike courier for one of the offices. I took the keys when he quit. He said he wouldn't come back here even if he was dead, so I figure it's pretty safe."

A smile formed, or something near to one. Parminder Bhat made her exit. I waited ten minutes, thinking of how a person could go on from something like that. I wished her safe travels and a long life, one hopefully devoid of creatures like Mattias Van Veen.

FIFTY

SEASON OF HOPE

Sinclair Centre boasted roughly sixty offices, which meant sixty potential employers for a broad-shouldered bike courier. That didn't account for turnover. I started at nine sharp with Ahmad Investments and hoped to hit Ziegler and Ziegler Florists by the end of the business day.

I was on hold with Coach House Cleaning, and had just filled the kettle for the second time, when Ryan Martz shouted at me from reception. "The first one is up."

I read over his shoulder that Surrey Gurdwara, a feed-the-poor initiative run by Lower Mainland Sikhs, had received "a generous donation" from Mona Tsai and Adam Colville.

The press release trotted out all the hits—*the start of a partnership, an investment in our most precious resource, recognition of the tremendous work they do.* Two million would fund meals in hard-to-reach northern communities, help people displaced by climate disasters and cushion city folks who had fallen on hard times.

I was desensitized to the praise, aware that proportionally, what Tsai had given would be around five hundred dollars for me. But I couldn't deny that this was meaningful.

"Two mil pays for a lot of samosas," Ryan said.

Within the hour, similar messages had been released by the Society for Sex Worker Safety and the Gospel Mission, praising the generosity of the couple from the British Properties. A rival developer claimed she'd match the funds. "What can *you* give?" was the trending phrase of the day.

Kay showed up early, and I filled her in on my search for a stocky bike messenger nicknamed Driver. She couldn't hide her disappointment in me, her fear in where this might lead.

"I know you're probably real pissed about what happened," my sister said. "It totally sucks, but you're making it way worse. You need sleep and soup and all that." She sniffed. "And a shower. Your shirt's a bit stank."

"She's right, Pig Pen," Ryan called.

I didn't protest. The joint pain hadn't subsided and my temperature had gone up in the night. The hours spent on a rooftop talking with Parminder Bhat hadn't helped.

Before I left, I gave Kay the task of finding Driver's real name and address. She nodded, sitting down at my desk with the list and sliding the phone closer. "I'll totally wake you if I find anything, I swear."

I left, doubting my sister would wake me for anything less than the boiling of the seas. For my part, I meant to keep my promise and go home. Honestly I did.

By noon, the press would be calling this the Season of Hope, articles written in praise and condemnation of the millionaires' largesse. Weren't people being helped? Shouldn't we have taxed them in the first place?

But by then I was speeding off to meet Jeff at a warehouse on Kingsway. The kidnappers had texted Mona Tsai an address.

FIFTY-ONE

A DIVIDE

Across from Science World, on Main and Terminal, was a row of empty wood-framed buildings that looked out of place amid the new and improved Vancouver. Quaint peach and lavender paint jobs had been scraped away by rain and years. One still bore a sign for the carpet shop that had once occupied it. Next to Warehouse Row was a grey cube of modular housing boasting bright murals by Lawrence Paul Yuxweluptun.

Jeff had taken a screenshot of the text before it disappeared. A coordinate for the warehouses. Nothing else.

We set up in the surveillance van in the McDonald's parking lot, Mona and I sitting on milk crates in the back, Jeff outside, walking the perimeter of the warehouses. No sign of Adam Colville or his kidnappers.

Alone with a multimillionaire, both of us exhausted, neither with much to say to the other. Mona wore a black leotard with a drawstring sweater, fresh makeup. She'd brought a plastic cannister of slime-green juice to sip from.

The van's tinted side panel provided a good view of the warehouses. Through the back door I could see a pair of apartment towers connected by a cross bridge, a crystalline *H* overlooking False Creek.

I pointed at the towers. "That one of your husband's?"

Mona looked away from the warehouse, briefly, and nodded.

"You know what was there before?"

"No idea." Not looking forward to an answer.

"I can't remember, either," I said. "Isn't that odd. My whole life I've lived here and I barely recognize anything."

"And that's Adam's fault, right?"

"Him and those like him."

"Meaning me."

I didn't deny it.

"I'm fifth-generation Vancouver," Mona said. "You know the shit my father went through? How many people like you told us we don't belong?" Picking up steam, she added, "You know why you hate buildings like that? Because they're full of rich Asians."

"And rich Americans. Rich Saudis."

"But they're not who white folks think is ruining the city, are they?"

"No," I said.

"Stealing the country from you. As if you didn't steal it from the Indigenous people."

"Your white husband doesn't give a shit who lives there, because his home is a gated castle. Soon to have a rock-climbing wall."

"You don't know him," Mona said.

"I know the net effect of his existence," I said. "He's made this city harder to live in for most people. Which is no mean feat. He'll probably be celebrated for it."

The slap came from the sling side. I could only watch Mona's palm as it connected. I've been struck harder, with far better reason. But she put enough emphasis behind the slap to sting.

Mona fumed and clasped her juice bottle in both hands, anger washing out slowly.

"I apologize," she said. "I just thought Adam would be here, that this would be over. Why isn't it? We gave them what they wanted."

I had no answer.

After another hour Jeff began prying the boards off the warehouse windows and looking inside. No trace of Adam Colville.

There were several likely possibilities why the Death of Kings hadn't showed. They'd never meant to bring Colville here. They'd meant to, but didn't, or couldn't. Or else they wanted Mona's attention focused here.

From the standpoint of cold logic, killing Colville made a certain sense. He could likely tell the authorities something useful about his kidnappers. Allowing him to go would put them further at risk. And considering everything they'd already done, abduction to homicide was only a slight escalation.

But no sign of the man, living or dead—what sense did that make?

I watched concern and doubt gnaw at Mona. She veered from barking commands to sullen fidgeting, to demanding results, to asking questions outside our expertise. I couldn't deny she loved Colville, and watching the rich woman rip herself to shreds provided no satisfaction.

"I think we should take you home," Jeff said. "Do you have anyone who could stay with you? Any family?"

"Just Bàba, and I look after him. Adam has a niece, but Susan goes to school in Spain."

"One of us will stay with you."

He looked at me, hoping I'd volunteer. Jeff probably hadn't seen much of his family over the last couple of days.

But I shook my head. "I'll spell you tonight."

His expression over Mona's shoulder told me I'd better.

FIFTY-TWO

TEAM PLAYER

En route to my flat, I remembered the cheque and hung a right to Laurel Street. My mother was on her porch clipping coupons. She had time to absorb her son's new appearance as I negotiated the lawn and stairs.

"You look like pure hell," she said.

I grunted in response and balanced on the rail, keeping watch on the street. I had the envelope in my good hand but didn't float it across the porch to her. But I let her see it.

"You didn't visit, Ma."

"I know. I'm just not a hospital person."

"Hospitals and funerals," I said, remembering her words. "So if I died, I shouldn't expect you at the wake?"

"Well, you'd be dead," my mother said after a moment. "You wouldn't be expecting much of anything."

I could only shake my head at that. She turned to a Safeway flyer while I tracked a delivery truck rumbling down between the parked cars. I waited for a clear view of the driver, a bored-looking woman with earbuds in. Not Dagan Moody.

"I guess I don't expect much of anything from you," I said.

"What do you want from me, David? I did the best I could."

"Did you?"

My mother dropped the Easter insert. Chocolate eggs, chicken drumettes a dollar off. She crossed her arms.

"Your generation makes everything so complicated. It's exhausting, David. Instead of a good job and saving to buy a house of your own, you're out at all hours, getting into scraps like a damn high-school kid. You manage to find yourself a nice girl, and maybe she's not what I expected, but you don't make her feel special, so now she lives in a different city. And you ask why I don't want to see you in the hospital."

"You don't approve of the way I live," I said.

"There's no living in it, son."

I watched cars pass, a man push a stroller up the block. *Ma, the things you value aren't easy to come by anymore, and to be honest, I like what I have, what I do. I'll take stitches over a cubicle any day. Even the broken heart, it's mine. I earned it.*

Telling her as much would be like kicking sand into the tide. Generational argument is so much emptiness. I gave her the envelope.

"This should get you square with the bank," I said. "You'll probably have to sell the house and downsize. Kay could help you with that."

My mother wasn't looking at me, though she clutched the envelope. It wasn't pride, or not *only* pride. Taking money earned from my business meant accepting the business, if not approving of it.

"That's another thing," she said as I took the stairs down. "You let your sister go."

"Kay's her own woman." I unlocked the van door and slid onto the seat.

"Lord knows why, but she looks up to you." My mother stood, her voice rising. "You want to end up like your father, that's your choice, and nothing I can do about that. But she's just a kid, she has her whole life ahead. She shouldn't make the same mistakes."

Love you, too.

Ryan Martz was locking up when I returned to the office. "Kay took an evening shift," he said. "Left you a message. We struck out on your list."

"We?"

"Slow day, so I took half the names. Maybe this Driver worked nearby, or for an outfit that folded in the last year."

"Could be," I said. "You have time for a drink?"

"Got time to watch you take one."

There was a bottle of Buffalo Trace on the top shelf of my office closet. I poured a dram and diluted it with water from the cooler. The whiskey ran over broken teeth and a stitched gumline like brushfire. I coughed.

"Right when I have these people figured," I said. "They get what they want, arrange a dropoff, and then no-show. To what end?"

"You're asking your humble secretary?"

"Don't start with that."

"All right," Ryan said. "You want to know why you can't figure these guys out?"

"Enlighten me, please."

"You don't understand groups, Wakeland. You've never functioned in one, not successfully. Being part of something bigger than yourself, that baffles the shit out of you. Scares you."

I finished my drink, wishing I'd left the bottle within reach. "There's a business to run," I said. "With my name on it, case you forgot."

"Jeff runs it. He built you a little playpen to splash around in, make you feel part of the team. At heart, scrape away everything else, you're a loner. And that's why these people have your number."

My response was knee-jerk and feeble. "This from a guy who treats people like shit, pushes his friends away."

"I got things to work on, too," Ryan admitted. "But I spent twelve years as a cop. And I'm happily married, despite going through shit you couldn't fucking imagine. I know how to play my part, Dave."

"So what am I missing?" I said.

"A guy like you goes full steam after something till he gets it. That's not how a group works. A group's got competing interests, political shit, compromises, favours. A group needs to learn how to be itself."

"So how does that apply to the Death of Kings?"

"Don't assume there's one motive," Ryan said. "Or that all of them want the same thing. There's probably someone in there regretting what they've done."

"Like Kyle."

"And there's probably at least one who thinks they aren't going far enough."

A dark thought. "So Colville's kidnapper could be different from whoever was supposed to release him," I said.

"Sure, or could be the same person with that much more experience under their belt."

I thought about this as he finished locking up. Together we left. On the curb, as Nikki pulled up, I remembered about Kay's message.

"Naima Halliday called for you," Ryan said. "Kay got excited, thinking you might try to sample the lady's broth house rather than chase after another beating."

"Broth house?" I asked.

Ryan held his middle and index fingers as a V and flicked his tongue out in simulated cunnilingus. Then waved goodbye before greeting his wife.

As they drove off, I thought of what to do next. I considered calling Naima, but decided the time wasn't right. I wanted to apologize, to make things okay between us, to sweep her into bed for a week. But there was no way to separate desire for her from my need to see this through. I couldn't untangle that in the time before I relieved Jeff at Mona Tsai's home.

Sinclair Centre was next door, so I headed there instead. I showed Driver's photo to security guards, store owners, the janitorial staff. No bells. No exclamations. Not only do I know the son of a gun, I have his address committed to memory, along with his birthday, social insurance number and his list of top ten Canucks, not counting goalies or Mark Messier. Would you need anything else, sir? Next week's lotto number, or the secret to living a righteous life without feeling you've missed out?

On the drive to the British Properties, I turned over what Ryan had said. What was the Death of Kings becoming? Crimes from graffiti to assault, all the way to murder. Some professionally planned, others haphazard and spur of the moment. Facing down the four of them, I'd seen no coordination. At least one of them hadn't wanted to attack at all. And what of the money left for Naima? Penance or pay-off?

Assuming the one called Boss was still in charge, how had she gone from Van Veen's assistant to taking vengeance against the rich? And were the others only on board to a lesser degree?

And supposing Kyle had been the moderate, compassionate one, and he was now dead, what were the others capable of next?

Approaching the turnoff that led up to Mona Tsai's gate, I saw a van make a left, heading the opposite way. It took the turn a few miles per hour faster than would make me comfortable if I'd been at the wheel. It didn't jounce down the slope or careen over the centre or leave a Goodyear peel behind. Just an insistent, slightly reckless speed. Enough to summon my attention.

I debated following the Jeep. And then I saw what looked like mist, cloaking the hillside around the home. Smoke.

FIFTY-THREE

A CASTLE BURNING

Green Cherokee, or possibly a Wrangler. Recent but not too recent, say within the last ten years. First three letters of the licence plate B-K-O.

Busy steering with my good arm, I couldn't jot down the make of the Jeep or the snippet of license plate. I recited the information to myself as I slowed to the gate, saw it hanging three quarters open. The van nudged through into mist. Plumes the colour of gypsum trailed off the house. No flames I could see. *Green Cherokee or Wrangler. Probably from the last ten years. Licence starting B-K-O.*

Treads pitted the lawn. A dark swipe along the side of a white Porsche. I halted the van on the turnaround, where a rattled-looking couple watched the creep of fumes. The woman was on her phone, hopefully to Emergency. Barefoot, backing up as the wind shifted. The man looked young, agonizing between Doing Something and not knowing what to do.

"Mona inside?" I asked.

"I don't know, the dude just said to get out to the lawn."

"Jeff Chen? Late thirties, overdressed, decent pinstripe suit?"

The man nodded.

"He's still inside?"

"Think so."

The double doors were gauzy with smoke. I jogged around the side, thinking Jeff would only have sent out the others if he had things under control. Or thought he had.

Green Cherokee or Wrangler, last ten years.

I opened the back door, called out for Jeff. Heard footsteps upstairs, a thud of body weight at least one floor up. The smell of burning insulation. *Licence plate starting B-K-O.*

Up the stairs slowly. *B as in Bob. B as in Barbara Mandrell.* Calling out on the landing. No answer. *K as in my sister Kay, K as in Kenny Rogers, with or without The First Edition.* A headache from the fumes. *What stood for O? Nothing stands for O.*

Up to the third floor. There'd be a point I would have to turn back. Client or no client. Jeff or no Jeff.

The heat was above, and I was climbing into it. I would have turned back but I heard voices, Jeff saying "That's enough, help me with him."

I remembered the old man.

Jeff approached the stairs carrying Edward Tsai like a bride, Mona holding his air tank and something else under her arm. The three of them coughing. I took one of Edward Tsai's legs and some of his bird-like weight.

"I hoped that beating might've knocked some sense into you," Jeff said.

"No chance."

What we lacked in coordination we made up for in speed. Above us the house snarled and grunted.

"Anyone else in here?" I asked.

"Nobody," Mona said. Under her arm was a valise of some sort. It seemed heavy.

Through the kitchen and out the back, into fresh, cold air that tasted like a teen's first beer. We put the old man in a chaise longue and dragged him off the poolside, into the safety of the grass. Smoke and particulate unspooled into the night.

Evelyn Rhee had left her Perrier bottle on the fireplace. We rinsed out our mouths with the remains. The fire department soon arrived and ran hose around the side of the property. The eastern wing of the house would survive, albeit with some grievous ventilation on the fourth floor.

As the paramedics inspected the Tsais, I led Jeff across to one of the flower beds.

"You see who did this?" I asked.

"No, we were talking and heard the explosion." He spat into a patch of crocuses. "It wasn't loud, just *whoosh* and the place went up."

A zigzagging staircase connected the back patio to the decks of the upper floors. Someone who knew the house could get up to the top floor that way. There were probably enough pictures of the house online that *anyone* could learn its layout.

"We should've been ready for something else," Jeff said. "My fault. Careless."

"There's enough blame to go around."

Mona and her father were whispering, the old man stroking her hand. Consoling her. Mona's eyes shone as she watched her home go up. The valise rested at her feet.

"What's in the bag?" I asked.

"Jewellery and papers. I told Mona to leave them, but she wouldn't."

"Just when I was feeling sorry for her."

"Don't bring it up," Jeff said, spitting something grey-green onto the lawn. He wiped his mouth, coughed. "We got the old guy out safe, that's the important thing."

"Actually," I said, "the important thing is a Jeep. Cherokee or Wrangler, I'm not sure of the model. You like Kenny Rogers and Barbara Mandrell?"

FIFTY-FOUR
START LOW

"A hospital isn't the ideal setting for us to have this conversation," Inspector Gill said. "If I had my druthers, we'd be downtown. But I don't. So what's this about a Jeep?"

The inspector had commandeered an empty examination room at the clinic in West Van. Jeff and the Tsais were in nearby rooms. I sat on the paper-covered exam table, legs swinging, leaning back against a poster urging drug users to carry naloxone and space out their doses. START LOW AND GO SLOW! was the slogan. The room beat a VPD holding cell.

Gill was no dope, but he was a politician who sometimes did policework. His career depended on anticipating the results desired by his superiors, and being able to supply them.

"We should have been alerted to Mr. Colville's kidnapping immediately," Gill said. "If I find out you and your partner convinced Ms. Tsai not to, I'll hold you responsible for whatever happens to him."

"You'll hold us responsible anyway," I said.

"Finding Mr. Colville and ensuring his safe return is all I care about."

"Don't let me stop you."

"You won't." Gill uttered his threats in a softer voice than his questions. "Your partner didn't see who started this fire?"

"That's what he said."

"Curious that he was there at close to midnight. With the majority of the household staff away."

"Waiting for instruction from the kidnappers," I said. "Don't waste time on whether my partner knows his job, because no one knows better."

Gill looked over the room. Posters of healthy and blackened lungs, photos showing a woman's methamphetamine journey.

"You're wearing a gun these days," he said.

I'd gotten used to its weight, the feel of the holster against the sling.

"It's registered in my own name, don't worry."

"You're aware how dangerous these people are, Mr. Wakeland. Your face is living proof of that. Go home, or better yet, leave the city. There is nothing you can do for Mr. Colville. Except stay out of our way."

"The Death of Kings is going to kill him regardless of what any of us do," I said. "When they're done extorting and terrorizing Colville's family, they'll knock him over the head like they did to Jeremy Fell. Or worse."

"And how exactly do you know that?" Gill asked.

"It's right there in their name."

FIFTY-FIVE
THE FIX

I'd given Gill the partial plate number, the decade and the general make and model. That might be enough to go on—if he held my eyewitness account as reliable. Could the Jeep have been a GMC? The colour black rather than green? Could that *B* in fact have been an *8*? Gill's people would be nice and thorough. Adam Colville didn't have time for thorough.

Marie had picked Jeff up from the clinic. I imagined a long convalescence in his future. As I drove the van over the Lions Gate Bridge, I thought about my next move. What I needed to know, and how to find it.

Evidence: Parking ticket for Naima Halliday. Incurred by her husband, Kyle Halliday, at Sunset Beach in Stanley Park.

(*so she claimed, but push that thought aside*)

Evidence: Jeremy Fell's body found in the waters off Sunset Beach, by Vancouver's most brilliant, under-appreciated and bow-leggedly hung private investigator.

Evidence: Kyle Halliday's body found in Vanier Park.

Supposition: Kyle (or whoever) had done reconnaissance of Sunset Beach prior to killing Fell.

Hypothesis: Someone—Boss, Driver, Dagan Moody or Jane Doe Two, had done a similar reconnoiter of Vanier Park.

Possible Proof: A parking ticket for a green late-model Jeep.

If Ryan Martz still worked for the department, I would have asked him to find out. Instead I plugged Evelyn Rhee's number into my phone. It was five in the morning and she answered without a trace of sleep in her voice.

"Any word on Adam?"

"There was a fire at Mona's place," I said. "Everybody's fine. You know someone who can fix parking tickets, right? Could look up when they were issued and to who?"

I explained what I was thinking. It took Rhee an hour to get hold of her contact, and then get back to me. I could tell by the triumphant note in her voice she had something.

"A week before Kyle's ticket," she said, "a green Wrangler 4xe was ticketed near Vanier Park."

The Jeep was registered to Peng Liu, who lived in a house on Victoria Drive. An eight-minute walk from my apartment. The rush of guessing correctly dissipated, leaving confusion and a sense of danger.

Peng Liu was twenty-seven, stocky and moon-faced, balding and with broad shoulders exaggerated by his forward-leaning posture. Photos of cars, stills from car movies, clips from racing video games smothered his social media. No posts more recent than a year ago, but a backlog of tweets about hating his job, wanting a Mitsubishi Lancer.

Peng was Driver. Now what to do with that information?

I looked around my apartment. The blanket Kay had used was folded neatly on the arm of the couch. The same stack of Criterion films, the same bookmark faithfully holding place in the same chapter of *The Nashville Sound*. Like I hadn't lived here for months, and in a sense I hadn't.

"Will you phone Gill and give him the address?" I asked Rhee. "He'll take this more seriously coming from the mayor's camp."

"Mona said no police."

"That was before her house was set on fire. She might feel differently now."

"But these people still have Adam," Rhee said. "If the police show up, they'll kill him."

If they hadn't already, I thought. "I'm in no shape to storm a house."

"We'll just drive by the place. If we see something, we'll phone Inspector Gill. If there's a chance to get Adam back safely, alive, we have to take it."

Rhee was downplaying the danger, making it sound reasonable and necessary. Maybe guilt over Jeremy was motivating her. Guilt and rage. I wondered if this was how I sounded to Jeff.

One step more and then another. All the way to hell.

FIFTY-SIX

STOPPING POWER

During rush hour, Victoria Drive was busier than the neighbourhood had been built for. The roads were jammed with cars trying to circumvent the traffic on Hastings or First. Flocks of school children turned every intersection into a four-way stop. By ten, though, it resumed being a placid residential street, though one you still couldn't afford to live in.

Peng Liu's house was indistinguishable from its neighbours, save for a tangle of Christmas lights hanging down over the porch like the forelock of a Golden Age superhero. No yard, just a brief stretch of gravel which led to the staircase. Curtains drawn upstairs and down.

Rhee had a box of protein bars in her Saab, along with a cold cup of rooibos tea. Cars and cyclists came and went. No Jeep. No Peng.

"You think he's inside?" Rhee asked.

"No idea."

"So we just wait?"

"Pretty much the definition of a stakeout."

She checked her phone, fidgeted with her keys, plucked a grey hair, shuffled the contents of her glovebox.

Ten became ten-thirty. At 10:31 she sighed and threw open the door.

"Back in a jiff," Rhee said.

"Don't," I called over the chime of the door. She'd left the keys in.

She darted across the road, up the steps of Peng's house. She pressed the buzzer and knocked. In her dress slacks and blouse, Evelyn Rhee could have been a teacher from the school down the block, a parent, a census taker.

A minute passed. I watched her inspect the mailbox, crane her neck to peer through the bay window.

Peng wasn't home. Good to have that established. *Now come back to the car. We'll call Gill, tell him the address in case he doesn't have it already.*

But instead of a retreat, Rhee left the porch and crossed the gravel to the side of the house. She reached over the gate, on tiptoe, and unlatched it. Her phone was in her other hand, whether for talking or taking photos I couldn't tell. She moved out of my line of sight. The gate closed behind her.

10:32 on the Saab's dashboard clock. 10:33. A grey squirrel flitted over to the gravel and paused to examine some possible treasure.

The curtain in the upstairs window swayed. Nothing suspicious about it. Nothing that couldn't be caused by an open window, a drafty attic, a ceiling fan left on. A small movement. Meaningless.

10:36. I texted Peng's address to Jeff, just like I'd done before my rooftop meet. I made a meaningless check of the cylinders of the revolver. Six metal-jacketed rounds of .38 Special ammunition, 130-grain weight, propelled at eight hundred feet per second. Less stopping power than a Magnum cartridge, but I might be able to hit something I aimed at.

At 10:38 I left the Saab, looked both ways and crossed. I followed the route Rhee had taken, omitting the porch. The squirrel watched me approach, and when I cleared that invisible safety line, she lit out for the nearest maple. I didn't blame her.

The house had been extended all the way to the alley, over what had once been a sizeable backyard. This left a long-shadowed gulley along the side. Each crush of stones echoed.

I drew the gun. Called Rhee's name. No answer.

The path spit me out close to the back fence where the house ended in a white scaffold of stairs and landings. Three separate suites, one per floor. Peng's address didn't have an apartment number. Was he the building's owner?

The door to the top-floor suite was open. I took the steps as softly as I could, feeling the wood squeal as I went. As soon as I passed the landing for the middle suite, the middle door opened. Evelyn Rhee. A gun to her head. Peng Liu's forearm locked around her throat.

"Inside, dude," Peng said.

FIFTY-SEVEN

TRAPPED

I've had guns pointed at me, and I've pointed them at others. It's not something I take casually. When you've seen what a gunshot can do, or felt it, you tend to approach firearms with a healthy respect, if not apprehension.

Peng was different. He gripped the small pistol too tightly, his knuckle too far inside the trigger guard. He crackled with nervous energy. And yet the impression I got was of someone holding a video game controller, at heart unconcerned with the consequences of what his toy could do.

Peng tapped me on the shoulder in an after-you gesture. A gunman in drawstring pants, a Forza tee and round-the-house slippers.

"Shut the damn door, man."

I did and he sighed, more worried about being seen than of our resisting.

He led us through a foyer, past the kitchen, to the living room. Rhee was taller than Peng, and as he moved, her stance widened, stooping so as not to choke. His forearm bore a tattoo, the word "Fearless" in gangster cursive. The letters thrummed against his hostage's throat.

He shoved Rhee onto the sofa, made me stand in the centre of the living room. Family photos on the wall, Peng with a middle-aged couple, his parents probably. Brown leather furniture, big-screen entertainment centre, chess and Go boards on the coffee table. Comfortable and middle class in every respect.

"Both hands up," he said.

I gestured at my sling. "Kind of hard to do that."

"I think I've got to search you."

Peng didn't know what he was doing. It was a movie pat-down, divorced from the actual goal. He'd never seen an ankle holster or a knife sheathed close to the spine. He slapped my ankles and paid far too much attention to the cast and sling, as if I might have built a crossbow into it.

"You were Kyle's friend," I said. "Kyle Halliday?"

Peng finished his search, studied my face, then patted down my trapezoids. The gun pointed away from me at times. With two hands, I might have grabbed for it. As it was, I'd have to talk my way out.

"Kyle was a good dude," Peng said. "That whole thing was rough."

"Why'd it have to go that way?"

"That's the thing, mate—it *didn't* have to. Kyle kept changing his mind, wanting it both ways, wanting not to hurt anyone. Finally Sky was like, 'Listen: you *can't* have it both ways. You want out? Fine. But you keep quiet.'"

"And he wouldn't keep quiet," I said.

"Dude *couldn't*. Little hints to his wife or whoever. He was proud of what we were doing. Tagging walls all the damn time, talking about change. But the second it got real, dude made like he wanted no part."

Peng, lulled by the rhythm of our conversation, kept talking.

"We agreed, all of us, that whoever pulls the trigger is only doing the will of the group. It's all of us together or nothing. No generals, only soldiers, each with a voice as loud as the rest."

"You should shut the eff up, Driver," a female voice called from another room.

"It's nothing you or Sky haven't said a billion times," Peng replied.

"Maybe, but don't you know who this is?"

"Course I do," Peng said, to me adding, "Boss thinks she's the only one who knows anything." Yelling to the other room, "Sky said not to hurt him."

"Did he say you should spill your effing guts?"

Peng sighed and sat down. The gun was pointed sideways across his thigh for the time being. Rhee watched it carefully.

"My goddamn parents' house," Peng mumbled.

Boss entered from the short stairway opposite the foyer. She stared at me, the first time I'd had a good look at her eyes. They carried the dead stare you saw on the face of child soldiers. Pitiless not from evil but from the forced simplification of things to a survival level.

With sunglasses and a wig, that expression had been hidden. Now she wore a tank top, no bra, her sternum tattooed with flames up her throat to her chin. The woman called Boss couldn't have been more than twenty-five. A generation younger than me, harder, a warrior mobilized against a looming threat.

"Are you expecting Moody and the others?" I asked.

"Soon enough."

"And is Colville still alive?"

"Maybe," she said. "It figures you're working for that pig."

"His wife, actually."

"We should do both of you now."

Rhee shivered. Boss didn't spare her a glance.

"That's not what Moody wants," I said.

"He doesn't run things," Boss said. "It's by group decision."

"How many in the group?"

"Enough."

"I just want to know what my chances are."

Boss sat down on the couch beside Peng, tucking her legs beneath herself in a lotus position. She fixed that cunning expression on me. Her eyes gave us slim odds.

FIFTY-EIGHT
RECRUITMENT

After minutes spent standing in the centre of the room, I eased myself onto the sofa next to Rhee. Our shoulders touched, and I could tell her pulse was racing. She kept her eyes downcast, letting her breath out in sips. She didn't want them to know how rattled she was—or how ready to act if they let their guard down.

Across from us, Peng adjusted the gun on his lap. Boss kept up her stare. I gathered we were waiting for Moody.

There are monsters in human form. And then there are confused, conflicted souls who do evil by accident, out of fear or passion. There are also the self-righteous, who see what they've done as justified. Peng and Boss seemed closest to this last category. Yet there was something else, something uncanny. It was almost as if they believed they hadn't done anything at all.

"What the eff are you staring at," Boss said.

"I was thinking I've never seen killers so at peace with what they've done."

"Seen a lot of killers, have you?"

"My share, yeah."

"Your share." She hunched forward, maintaining her lotus. "The others think you might come around."

"That's why you haven't shot me?" No answer. I wondered if I could sell an ideological transformation. "I'm always willing to listen, if you think I can understand."

Boss's expression marked her as impervious to being swayed—by reason, mercy or charm. The more I looked at her, though, the more I sensed that it was at least partly a put-on. That whatever she'd gone through had shaped but also damaged her, and the gunfighter stare was an attempt to conceal those wounds.

But I could've been wrong.

After a while she said, "I can't explain as well as Sky can. But you live here. You see how things are. How the poor get effed over by the super-rich."

"The kings," I said.

She gave a vigorous nod. "And some of us decided enough's enough. This isn't how it's 'sposed to be, is it?"

"No," I said.

"Real action is needed. Meaningful change. So we decided to start making change."

"What change does killing Jeremy Fell bring about?"

"His sister's the mayor. She's never given an ess about the poor. People are overdosing, freezing in the streets, and it doesn't affect her."

"So it's punishment," I said.

"You want to think that, go ahead."

"It's not about her," Peng said. "Or any of them. It's what they represent."

"The artist who fell to his death?" I asked. "The student with a crooked fortune?"

"There's a whole class of folks that think they're above us. Like nothing they do ever has, what's the word?"

"Consequences?"

"Results," Peng said. "Yeah. They need to know there's gonna be results."

I heard a door shut, farther in the house. Peng immediately brought the gun up and pointed it at me. Bootsteps through the halls. Rhee took a long breath. I tried to transmit patience to her.

"We're in here, Sky," Boss called.

Dagan Moody moved through the doorway, holding a bottle of water. Hair now peroxide blond, most of it hidden beneath a Blue Jays hat. Visored shades, a bandage beneath, covering his left eye. He saw me and grinned.

"Wakeland," he said. "You look rough, mate."

"Guess I've been better."

His smile was affable, mocking as if he knew something I didn't. He finished his water and tossed the bottle in the fireplace.

"I could use a hand moving our guest outside," Moody said to the others. "Is the van in the alley?"

"It's good to go," said Peng. "Only six-cylinder, but it can move okay."

"Take our guest, then. I'll stay and watch Wakeland and the other."

Moody perched on the arm of the sofa. It tipped slightly under his weight. Peng took the pistol with him, Boss following. Moody had no weapon in sight.

"I feel we know each other pretty well," he said. "You're maybe the most tenacious person I've met. Warnings and beatings and yet here you are. How's your arm?"

"It hurts."

"I've never been punched like that," Moody said. "Someone told me you used to box. You must've been pretty good. One against four, and you're still here."

"I'm not sure why."

His smile was capacious. "We feel you'll come around to our way of thinking. If we can't warn you off, you could be a tremendous asset."

I gestured at the eye. "You don't hold a grudge?"

His fingers touched the adhesive over the gauze. "Oh, I was furious, mate. But it seems like it'll heal."

"You had it looked at by a doctor?"

"By someone in the medical trade. But I have to admit, I kind of like it. It's a symbol of commitment. A small sacrifice for the Death of Kings."

An absurd tableau, sitting across from a genial one-eyed man, listening to him speak of beatings and murders with an absolute, fervent sincerity. Days after we'd torn into each other, Dagan Moody was pitching me like a bank teller recruiting for his branch softball team.

"I'm not expecting you to get it all at once," he said. "Just keep an open mind. And ask yourself if our goals are wrong, or do they just seem wrong because they target the ruling class?"

"Wasn't your buddy Van Veen part of that class?"

His expression turned maudlin, regretful, but only momentarily. "The Doc put us on the path but he lost his own way," Moody said. "He thought he could change the rich by appealing to their spiritual side. But they have none. The kings of this world don't care about anything except their own comfort and property. Every good impulse in the Western tradition is a movement away from a ruling elite. And yet we're still yoked with one—the Valerie Fells, the Adam Colvilles."

"And the Kyle Hallidays?" I asked.

Again, that brief nod to regret. "Kyle was one of us. It was his idea to effect change by using their own money to fund it. But Kyle lost faith in the project. Even that we probably could have forgiven."

The stairs clattered. Peng and Boss returned, both now wearing their hoodies, Boss's blond wig showing beneath hers. Between them they led a man in socks and underwear, a potato sack secured over his head with a cheap dog collar. This had to be Adam Colville. The millionaire's hands were bound behind his back. Boss prodded him forward with an antique over-and-under scattergun.

Evelyn Rhee gasped and moved to stand. I gripped her arm, keeping her beside me. Not yet.

"Dude is freaking heavy," Peng said.

Colville shuddered. His body was well-proportioned and defined, chest bruised and scratched. One white athletic sock was dotted with dried blood.

Moody stood up. "I'll carry out our guest."

As he stood, he noticed something out the window and made a harsh shushing sound. Through the jewel-shaped windows in the door, I saw a head of black hair. Heard the knock.

Peng put the barrel of the gun to my temple.

A hand tapped the window. Feet scraped on the porch. A voice called through the door, "Mr. Peng Liu? Are you home, sir?"

Peng's attention was on the entrance. I felt Rhee's weight shift away from me, moving to the balls of her feet.

The knocking grew louder.

Peng looked to the others, struggling with whether to answer. His mouth moved silently. As he started to speak, Rhee launched herself off the couch, swatting his arm, knocking the pistol to the floor. Yelling "Run" as she bolted toward the foyer.

She ran all out, counting on confusion to give her a head start. Not seeing Boss raise the barrel of the shotgun.

The room thundered and all sound seemed to rush to a rumbling crescendo before plunging into silence. I threw myself down. When I looked up, Evelyn Rhee was struggling on the ground by a cabinet of busted china and Hummels, a pulpy red abyss the size of an apple on the back of her blouse.

Boss swivelled her hips so the barrel lay between a cringing Colville and me. She nodded with satisfaction, like a cleaner sweeping an errant strand of cobweb.

"She worked for the mayor," Boss said.

FIFTY-NINE

HOSTAGE

In the aftermath, Moody stooped, retrieved the pistol and jammed it back into Peng's hand. Peng barely noticed, transfixed by the figure on the floor. Rhee's arms splashed in the glass and broken plaster.

"Keep Wakeland here," Moody said, prodding Colville hard enough to stagger him. Next to Moody, the millionaire looked small and vulnerable. "We'll meet you at the other place."

Peng nodded as they left through the back. I felt the gun tremble against the side of my face. Whoever had been on the porch had ceased knocking.

Evelyn Rhee coughed.

"She's still breathing," I said, more calmly than I felt. "We should help her before they come back."

"That crazy—she didn't have to—" Peng's gun wavered.

"The longer we stay here, the more likely we'll end up like her. That what you want?"

"I can't—I can't—"

"It's all gonna go to shit fast, Peng. Let's help her. Come on."

The rev of an engine carried from the back. Peng turned in its direction. The gun still looked at me. His shock, *our* shock, was a shared point I could build on.

"They're running out on you, Peng. Leaving you to pay for it all. And in your parents' house. You can't want more of that. Let's get her help while we can."

"They're not leaving me," he said. "We're together on this all the way."

"That's what they told you. The dirty secret of life, Peng? You're in this all on your own. All that 'each voice as loud as the rest' stuff is how they get you to go along. You make the grand sacrifice. They ride away to safety."

His eyes pearled with tears. The gun looked loose in his hand now, as if he'd forgotten it. One-handed, could I take it from him? And did I have a choice?

"You can save her," I said. "You joined them to make a difference, and here's a difference you can make. Life and death."

He seemed almost convinced. Or maybe I was just hopeful. But then we saw lights through the curtains, blue alternating red. Peng's demeanor changed. He clenched his fist around the gun and pulled away the curtain. Chargers and police vans blocked the street, one parked up on the curb directly in front of the house.

"Oh fuck," he said. "Fuck fuck fuck fuck *fuck.*"

"Take a breath," I said.

He did, the gun barrel rising and bobbing. He looked at the curtains again.

Rhee twitched. I told myself it was only pretend. An hour ago we were sharing stakeout detail, passing the dregs of a cup of tea between us. It's not her lying there. She's out front, probably, with Gill and the police. There's plenty of time.

Peng laughed. There was a manic edge to his laughter. With his gun hand he scraped tears off his cheeks.

"It's over," he said. "I'm gonna die."

"No one has to. We walk out. Give ourselves up. This all gets resolved without more blood."

"After what I've done?"

"What exactly did you do, Peng?"

"The dead people." He made a fatalistic shrug, the gun slicing diagonally through the air.

"We can still help this woman. That counts, Peng."

The tears returned. He sobbed out his words.

"We split up, two and two," he said. "Each does one. Boss and Sky took the mayor's brother. They said Kyle would suspect if it was them. Me and Rio met Kyle at the statue in the park."

"You shot him?"

"I couldn't," Peng said. "He was my friend. I got him to look at the water, and she…"

His voice trailed into a sob.

"You were coerced," I said. "Kyle was ratting you out. You had cause." I didn't believe a word of that. Kidnapping Jeremy Fell might have started as an abstraction, but murdering him was a calculated act. An assassination. Kyle's death had been a pragmatic choice, accomplished to protect the mission.

"He thought—" Peng blubbered, started again. "Kyle thought we were meeting to turn in Boss and Sky. The rest of us were all gonna stop this together. We should have."

"Mr. Peng?" the voice called out through the door. Inspector Gill's, I recognized.

Looking through the gap in the curtains I could see officers gathered behind the cars. I saw someone who looked like Jeff, dressed in Jeff's tan overcoat.

"Need you to step outside, please. This is Inspector Gurcharan Gill of the Vancouver Police. Talk to us, Mr. Peng."

"Fuck fuck fuck," Peng said. He looked between me and the injured woman on the floor. Rhee's chest rose, faltered, fell. Dying in front of us.

"Mr. Peng, if you don't talk to me, this won't end well. You don't want that and neither do we. How 'bout it?"

Peng stole a look through the curtain, then sidestepped away as if worried about sniper fire. I could see Gill standing on the porch in tactical gear and helmet.

"Do you want me to come in?" Gill asked.

"No."

"Am I right to think you got some hostages in there?"

Peng looked in my direction. "Sort of."

"I can take that as a yes? You have hostages?"

"Yes."

"All right. We heard what sounded like the discharge of a firearm in there. That's the situation, if I understand correctly. What will it take to resolve this?"

"Resolve?"

"To get these people out, Mr. Peng."

Confused, Peng looked around, finally in my direction.

"Don't look at me," I said.

SIXTY

TACTICS

For thirty minutes, all attention in the world was focused on the heart-beat of a single person. At times Peng's pulse seemed to wind down, like a toy in need of cranking. Then it would rocket up as if he were on an amphetamine jag. He cackled. He wept. He paced the living room, avoiding the window when he remembered to.

"Let's at least get things in motion," Gill said. "What is it you want out of this, Mr. Peng?"

He looked at me again. "I never done this. It's so fucked. I am fucked."

I was kneeling by Evelyn Rhee, holding my jacket to her chest. Asking your hostage to collaborate on your demands seemed only mildly absurd, given our predicament.

"First things first," I said. "He wants to know if you're gonna shoot anyone else."

"I don't want to."

"Tell him that."

Peng called, toward the door, "I'm not gonna hurt anyone."

"Tell him there's a woman here needs help. That way he'll know you're a man of your word, and not some kill-crazy nut."

"I'm not," Peng said.

"I know that. You need to show them. Let them bring her out, get her medical attention. You'll still have me."

"If they come through the door—"

232

"We can head to the kitchen," I said. "Let them stretcher her through the front door. No one else comes in."

"It's stupid. I'm gonna die. It's hopeless."

Gill was saying something calming. Peng walked a circuit to the foyer and back. He transferred the gun to his left hand and flexed his fingers, shook out his wrist. Nearing exhaustion, I thought. It was a big club.

In the back of my mind was my revolver, sitting on the landing outside the back door. If I were to get there. If I were fast enough. Was that what Rhee had been running for?

"All right," Peng called to Gill. "Nobody come in but paramedics. Everyone else back up to the street. 'Cluding you."

"You and I need to keep in contact, Mr. Peng. You have a phone there? I'll slip my card beneath the door."

We heard the porch creak. A white rectangle fell through the mail slot.

"Now back," Peng said.

He crouched and worked a fingernail under the card to pry it off the floor. He fished out his phone, attempted to dial one-handed, then motioned me forward.

"You dial. Speaker phone."

I did as he asked. Gill picked up immediately. We watched his shadow recede from the door.

Peng gestured me toward the kitchen. His gun in my ribs. We heard the front door open, the murmurs of paramedics making judgments on treatment. They lifted Evelyn Rhee, and we heard the stretcher roll across the parquet floor, catching on the lip of the front door.

"That was the right move," I said. "You're doing good."

"I don't know what the fuck I'm doing." Peng leaned close to the phone. "Okay, you got her?"

"We do," Gill said. "Good man, Mr. Peng."

"All a sudden everyone thinks I'm great."

"Now how do we get you and Mr. Wakeland out of there?"

"I don't got a fucking clue," Peng said.

He sat on the stove, kicking the oven door. I'd have to pass him, turn the corner, to get to the revolver. I looked at the nearest window and wondered if it opened, and how easily, or if the sill had been painted over.

"How you feeling, Mr. Peng?" Gill asked.

"Got a headache. Tired."

"You have water there? I can send some up."

"Probably poison it. Knockout drops or something."

He hopped off the stove, looked out the window. Listening for a second.

"I'm going to die," he said. "I just know it."

"We can walk right out that front door," I said.

He was shaking his head again. Tears flowing. "My parents are in Singapore till June, but if they come back to this. I don't want my mom to think I'm—"

He broke off in sobs. Peng Liu looked even younger than his twenty-seven years.

"I'm never gonna see them again," he said, snot waterfalling off his lips. "My mom."

"No reason you can't," I said.

"All I wanted was to drive cars."

Peng held the gun toward the ceiling. Then tilted it so the barrel rested against his head. His eyes closed.

Maybe I could make the stairs before he could shoot me. If he planned to. Some essential part of him was broken, and he deserved no sympathy. But he'd let Rhee go, and that meant something. Maybe it meant I was sick as them, thinking Peng Liu could be walked back from self-slaughter.

"I need a favour," I told him. "If I don't make it out, pass a message to Sonia Drego in Montreal."

Peng snuffled and blinked. The gun retreated a half inch from his ear.

"I want you to tell her," I started, and went blank. Anything raw and honest and lovely would be obscene coming from someone else. Especially since I hadn't made time to tell her myself.

I found my own eyes watering up.

"Just say that she was—is—better than I deserved. And that I'd've found the courage to go to her sooner or later. She'll probably roll her eyes at that. She used to call me a Jerk in Progress, which about sums it up."

I looked at the floor, thinking what a sight the two of us must make. "Can you remember that?" I asked.

Peng sniffed. "Would you tell my mom something if it's me?"

"Go ahead."

"That I'm so sorry, and I miss her, and I fucked up so bad, and I'm just, I dunno, real sorry."

"I can tell her that, sure. Might mean more coming from you."

Peng wiped his eyes, grabbing a roll of paper towels off the counter. He turned to see a helmeted woman in tactical gear step out of the foyer, a semiautomatic rifle pointed at him.

"Drop the gun," she ordered.

Peng's hand fluttered and she fired twice, into his chest, and he dropped both pistol and the roll of paper towels. He leaned back on the counter and she shot him again, this time aiming higher. She swept in through a gunpowder cloud to watch Peng fall drunkenly, face first on the tile. One of the bullets had left a gory bloom on his cheek.

The officer said something like "All clear." I felt her gloved hand come down on my shoulder, pushing me against the wall. I stared down at Peng. That heartbeat, which had held the universe captive, gurgled and then stopped.

When I blinked there were two more officers in the room. Then I was downstairs, being walked across the gravel toward where Jeff stood, grinning at me with a relief I should have been able to feel.

"Fuckface, you made it," my partner said.

I couldn't complete the walk. Instead I sank down on the curb, head on my knees, and bawled my eyes out.

SIXTY-ONE

IN THE AFTERMATH, MICE

Interviews.

Endless, one after another. Some with people I knew, like Gill and Sergeant Dudgeon. Others focused on the police shooting, or the culpability of Evelyn Rhee. I gave descriptions, statements. I accounted for myself.

Dagan Moody and the woman called Boss were still at large. Their descriptions were public. The identikit sketches looked enough like them, though the pick-and-mix features couldn't capture their expressions. Moody, the True Believer; Boss, the Holy Executioner.

Gill's first impulse was to get me to admit it had been my recklessness, my need to stay involved, that had put Evelyn Rhee in the line of fire. There was enough truth to that to make me ashamed. I could see his tactics, and couldn't defend myself. I stopped talking, asked for my lawyer to be present.

Ray Dudgeon's efforts were more personable and informal. When I stopped by the station to pick up my revolver, he asked if he could buy me a cup of coffee.

"Long as it's fresh and not from a vending machine."

He took me to a break room, where half a pot of inert blackness sat on a burner. He tossed it, began the process of brewing a fresh pot.

"You didn't pull the trigger on Evelyn," he said.

"Nice of you to admit."

"All joking and bullshit aside. I mean it. You shouldn't've been there, but it wasn't your fault what happened."

The machine hissed and Dudgeon fetched two mugs.

"None of us saw those kids for what they are. You take moo?"

"No thanks. What are they?"

Dudgeon watched the piss-trickle of coffee begin to fill the glass carafe.

"Wolves," he said.

I thought he exaggerated. Cops often do, though they never admit it. Good guy/bad guy is a clear-cut definition, and the Death of Kings were bad. They were evil.

Dudgeon wasn't entirely off the mark with that. Peng Liu had lured his friend Kyle Halliday out to Vanier Park, telling him he was right, Boss and Sky were way too extreme. They took this from a fun little exercise in civic resistance to something dark and whirling out of control. Together the others would turn in Boss and Sky and tell the police everything.

And when Kyle showed up they made him look out at the water and shot him from behind. Staged the body beneath the *Gate to the Northwest Passage*. Peng and the woman called Rio left their friend's corpse in the snow, and went on as if nothing happened.

Yes, that was evil. And they felt justified in doing it, which was hypocrisy on top of cold-blooded murder.

So sure, they were wolves, and they'd murdered four people and left a trail of injuries and scars. Their culling was necessary. And Peng's tear-stained face staring into the barrel of the rifle was something I'd carry with me.

I'd once watched a poisoned mouse in an alley, watched it run in mad circles with no heed for direction or safety. Just running, till it ran out.

Make that five people. In the long-term parking lot at the airport, a few days after the ordeal with Peng, police found an abandoned panel van. The stall had been paid up for a week, on Adam Colville's credit card.

Colville was in the trunk. He'd suffered a heart failure at some point in his captivity. His body and the car's interior had been doused with bleach.

Wolves.

My left arm came out of its sling, knitting nicely according to Dr. Ahluwalia. My face improved. I felt better.

A shotgun is the most dangerous of small arms when the distance and load and mechanism are all correct. In that regard, Evelyn Rhee had been lucky. A cluster of bird shot, propelled by decades-old powder, had punched back-to-front through her abdomen, missing her spine but costing her several yards of small intestine. When I visited her, I brought presents, tokens of my own recovery. She smiled at the boom box and the crappy CDs, nodded approval at the dog-eared copy of *One Ring Circus*.

"I'm sorry," Rhee said. "You told me not to go."

I squeezed her hand. "If I was healthy, I'd have done the same thing, only faster."

"Nice of you to say." She adjusted the bed to sit up. Took some water. "What are you going to do now?" Rhee asked.

"Get drunk, play records. In the immediate future, at least. Beyond that I don't know."

"But what about them?"

I knew who she meant. Images of Peng flickered on the screen of my mental projection room. Jeremy Fell in the water. Evelyn Rhee lying in glass.

I could only shrug.

"'Flutter' is an interesting word, Mr. Wakeland."

Detective Lee Fontaine was a soft-spoken woman from Skwx̱wú7mesh Úxwumixw, the Squamish Nation. She was heading the investigation into the use of force that led to Peng's shooting. To her credit, she didn't treat it as open and shut.

"It's the only word that fits," I said. "His hand fluttered."

"Peng could've been raising his gun?"

"Sure."

"Drawing on Officer Devereaux."

"It's possible."

"And yet you say *'flutter.'*"

Fontaine nodded and tapped a mechanical pencil against her desk. We were in her office in Delta, walls decorated with commendations and Coast Salish art. A lacrosse trophy gathering dust next to a printer.

"In your opinion," Fontaine said, "did Officer Devereaux fire recklessly?"

"I don't know."

"Was there another option?"

"Couldn't say."

"Off the record. Your reading of the situation."

I closed my eyes, reliving the moment, something I was trying to limit myself to doing only thirty times a day. It called to mind a whole gallery of images I'd rather forget.

"I wish I could tell you something else," I said. "That's how I saw it. Ambiguities and all. Sorry."

"Quite all right, Mr. Wakeland." Fontaine smiled and showed me out. "We all have to live with doubt. That or lie to ourselves."

Adam Colville's funeral was held in a picture-book chapel in West Van, on a day with clear skies and a warm spring breeze.

It was a smaller affair than I'd anticipated. The benches in the non-denominational chapel were only half filled. I learned later that there'd been a public remembrance at Colville Development HQ.

Mona Tsai nodded absently at my condolences. Grief had struck her as a general listlessness, aided by some sort of sedative. Her designer mourning wear looked uncomfortable, and she uncinched her belt before sitting down. Her father smiled as if the ceremony wasn't real. An usher led him to the front pew.

Valerie Fell was one of the speakers. She paid tribute to Colville's sense of civic responsibility, the practical jokes he'd loved to play on his friends. Her security detail roamed the aisles. A child I took to be Evelyn Rhee's son sat with the mayor's retinue, including a blond man who spent the service on his phone.

After the playing of Colville's favourite Aerosmith song and a hymn by the choir he'd sponsored, Jeff and Kay and I filed out. In the parking lot, the blond man stopped us. He introduced himself as the mayor's PR person.

"Val would like a brief word, if you two don't mind."

The mayor waited in the chapel's vestibule along with the child. Behind them stood the mayor's body man, a hulking Malaysian with a crewcut. We submitted to a pat-down. Kay took Sonny aside, showing him a video game on her phone, while Jeff and I followed Valerie Fell into the storage room.

"I'm holding you responsible for this," she said to me. "For what happened to Evelyn, too."

"Dave couldn't have anticipated—" Jeff began.

"She insisted on hiring you, the Great Fucking Detective, went out of her way to get you. And for what?"

If we weren't on sacred ground, she might have spat. The mayor contented herself with staring daggers at me. I'd seen daggers before.

"So what are you going to do about this now?" she said.

"Get drunk, play records."

"You think this is funny? I just buried one of my closest friends. My brother before that. I want these people found."

"I couldn't give a shit what you want, Your Worship."

Jeff all but shoved me toward the door. "Dave is still shook up from all this, ma'am," he said. "He doesn't mean anything."

"Like hell I don't. Gill has been on the wrong track from the start, and you were happy enough to go along if it meant wrapping things up with no fuss. If you'd listened to us at all—"

"And maybe if you'd said yes to Ev way back when, she wouldn't be injured, and Jeremy and Adam would still be alive." Valerie Fell picked a silver hair off her jacket. "You can continue to play pass the buck, or you could try doing what you're paid for and find these people. Your choice."

We collected Kay and headed to Jeff's car. Real smart. I'd only attended because of a nagging thought that maybe someone unusual might show up. Someone connected with the Death of Kings. But no one had.

As we drove back to the city, Jeff said, "Take as much time off as you need. And then add two weeks. You need it."

"What about what the mayor said?"

"To be honest, Dave, I don't think you're an asset to her right now."

Kay was in the passenger seat. She turned around to face me and smiled. "I'm going to see Tim tonight. He's getting better all the time."

"That's good," I said.

"You want to maybe come with me? I'm sure he'd like to see you."

"I will, but later. A couple days."

"Dave?" my sister said. "You seem kinda distant."

I'm distant, I thought. I wondered if I'd ever come all the way back.

SIXTY-TWO

THE POLITICAL

True to my word, I uncorked a bottle of Buffalo Trace, had a drink and played records. Mad Season, Rosanne Cash, an R.L. Burnside live recording, an album of French love songs by Jill Barber. Somewhere on the B side of *Carry Me Home* by Mavis Staples and Levon Helm, I started writing to Peng Liu's mother, fulfilling the promise I'd made him. Or trying to.

> *Your son told me he was sorry. He expressed his love for you, and some measure of contrition for his crimes. He craved your forgiveness. While he was holding a pistol on me at the time, that fact does not lead me to doubt his sincerity. You see, Mrs. Liu, I shared certain traits with your son. Emotional cowardice and a consuming regret.*

Nothing I put down would console Peng's mother. I left the letter unfinished, like everything else about this. Violence upon violence, radiating out. Like a tide, like an infection.

Rhonda Bryce attacked for her gun. Jeremy Fell kidnapped and murdered. Kyle Halliday killed by his friends for voicing dissent. Tim Blatchford and Evelyn Rhee critically wounded for getting in the way. Mona Tsai's house set on fire. More deaths. Alex Knowlson, Kevin Novak, Adam Colville.

I'd left myself out. No other case had exacted such a toll. Physically diminished, psychologically run ragged. And still trying to catch up.

Over ten years now in the PI business, and what had I learned? That my body was more fragile, my existence more precarious than I'd previously believed. And my noble motivations only served to justify whatever I chose to pursue. Whether or not it was healthy. Whether or not it mattered.

Dagan Moody had sought to reason with me, possibly recruit me. As if I was no different from them. He'd showed up at Naima's apartment, I'd thought to threaten her into silence. While I was in the hospital, she'd been given five thousand dollars. Had Moody gone back to pay her? Had that been his intent all along?

A change of clothes, a swill of Listerine. I cabbed to VGH. Naima Halliday was on the Palliative floor but had a break coming up.

I waited outside. Rain crackled off the awning. Two ER nurses smoked and talked about the shift they'd just had. A steak knife through his cheek. Walked in with the darn thing sticking out. Sixteen years old. Just glad Robertson wasn't on call, you know he's botched the last two? Marriage trouble.

Naima nodded at the others as she came out, her leather jacket over her shoulders like the first time I'd seen her. The nurses watched her join me, no doubt filing our meeting away for when the Robertson gossip ran dry. Her greeting to me was the same nod, pleasant but formal. Naima stood at the edge of the overhang, risking rain rather than move closer to me.

I had more questions than ever, but couldn't put a voice to any of them. Seeing her, all I wanted was to apologize and try to wind things back to where they'd been before I'd chosen her husband's killers over her.

Before I could ask anything, though, Naima said, "You're working for the police."

"For the mayor," I said.

"That's different?"

"Her brother is dead. A friend of hers, too. She wants to find the people responsible."

"One of them was killed by the police," Naima said. "A young man."

"Peng Liu. Did you know him?"

"No," she said. "Maybe I saw him once. I don't know."

"You don't want them found, do you?"

"I don't want them killed."

"They killed your husband," I said. "Kyle was going to turn his associates in. You called him naïve, but I think Kyle was the only one who knew where this was heading. Only Kyle tried to put on the brakes. And for his troubles he got a hole where his face used to be."

"I know what happened to his face," Naima said. "I see worse every day. You think I don't know what they did?"

Naima pulled the lapels of her jacket together. Her shoulder was picking up droplets of runoff. The faux leather glittered under the fluorescents.

"Everything is complicated," she said. "It's political."

"A bullet to the face is pretty damn non-partisan."

"Personal and political, they overlap, they're the same. You can't understand, David. Living here, you don't know like I do. The government and the police, what it feels like when they kill your friends. When you have no power."

"Kyle is dead and your sympathy is with his killers," I said.

"That's not true." Naima stepped into the rain. "I have to go. I don't think I want to see you anymore."

"If you know where they are."

"I don't," she said.

"And even if you did, right?"

Her expression was sorrowful verging on a smile. It slashed right through me.

"I would never tell the police, if I knew," she said. "But I would have told you."

SIXTY-THREE
BEGINNING AGAIN

The personal and political. Naima's words were a metronome, their pulse running through my head as I returned home and poured another drink. I needed an idea, something to break the tempo.

Kay and I had made plans for a Kurosawa marathon, but between her shifts and her visits with Tim, she hadn't been by. I watched *High and Low* and half of *The Bad Sleep Well*, feeling run down rather than tired. The metronome kept going, a steady hundred and twenty beats per minute.

To drown it out I stuck my head beyond the edge of the balcony and let rainwater run down my neck. The shock of cold—I thought I'd caught a glimpse of the idea I needed, a tease—

Nothing. A wet head and no clue as to how to proceed.

I towelled off and lifted the lid on the Rega. The second Johnny Cash *American* recording, with his cover of "Rusty Cage." No song had been with me longer. The lyrics were fantastically miserable, a barrage of Pacific Northwest ugliness that the singer vowed to break through. I wish him luck, swapping out the platter for *The Magnolia Electric Co.* From bleak to apocalyptic.

The personal. The political. What did that even mean? That our everyday actions had consequences. That we willfully blinded ourselves to these. Too comfortable. Too distracted.

When you're desperate for a breakthrough, you can almost imagine one coming. What it might look or sound like. But every glimpse only sent me back through the things I already knew.

The letter to Peng's mother still lay on the coffee table. A few empty words in a rain-soaked Moleskine. No wonder I couldn't finish writing it. I'd survived, and still hadn't made my own apology.

Almost three now. It would be six in Montreal. Too early to phone Sonia. But I phoned anyway, dousing my apprehensions with another pull of bourbon.

Sonia Drego's voice, low and sleep-addled. A voice I'd fallen in love with as much as its owner. It yawned out my name. "Well hello there."

"Just wondered if you were up," I said.

"I am now, you prick."

I laughed. "Missed you too. How is it?"

"How's Montreal? It's Montreal. Amazing food, shitty weather. You can get by without a ton of French. The cafés do this drink called an *allongé*, it's the best goddamn coffee I've ever tasted."

"And the job?"

No hesitation. "I fucking love it, Dave."

"I'm glad for you."

"I actually believe you are," Sonia said. "And how are you?"

"Same old same old," I said. "Seeing anyone?"

"I have, yes. Not seriously, but I'm not keeping chaste waiting for you to come out. What about you?"

"Gave it a try," I said. "Work got in the way."

"Should be the Wakeland family motto," Sonia said. "Miss me?"

"Of course."

I remembered in the hospital thinking I'd heard Sonia's voice. Hoping it was her. Now I knew I'd been hallucinating, and the realization hurt. I felt the distance between us, every kilometre.

"Did you ever catch a case with a political bent?" I asked.

"You mean like terrorism?"

"I guess I do, yeah."

"Not overtly," Sonia said. "But politics are behind everything, aren't they?"

"The personal and the political overlap. Someone told me that today."

"It's sure as shit true in Quebec," Sonia said. "If it's not the French and English, it's Catholics and Muslims, women and men, the police and everyone else. Government officials aren't held in high regard."

"Maybe I'll visit," I said. "When I'm all done with this."

"Which'll be never. Let's not kid each other."

"But if it was," I said, "maybe I can crash on your couch?"

A long pause on her end.

"I don't have a couch for you, Dave. But I—hold on."

An electronic squeak, then a minute and a half of waiting. When Sonia came back on the line, she said, "I've been called in. Which is fine. Four hours of sleep is all I wanted anyway. We'll talk soon. Take care of yourself."

"What were you going to say?" I asked an empty line.

I took a long drink. Not only had I said nothing of what I'd meant to, the possibility of reuniting with her in Montreal seemed dead. My last chance at escape had been bricked over. Here I was.

There it was.

A jumble at first, more raw excitement than refined idea. But I mulled over it as I showered and dressed.

The personal was or wasn't the political. But the political was personal, always, in the end.

The violence had started with the Jericho Centre and a fraud named Mattias Van Veen. He'd used and manipulated a handful of college kids, who went on to do the same to others. Selling them the idea they were destined for greatness and glory. When that was ripped away by Van Veen's fall from grace, the group curdled. They took aim at the class they'd been promised entry to. The people who'd torn down the clinic would be torn down in turn.

Rather than admit their own complicity in the game, the role their own unmitigated thirst for power had played, they'd spun righteous, gone fanatic and turned to murder. The Death of Kings would do a great service, make *them* great, by cleansing the city of the privileged and guilty. Maybe Moody and Boss knew that at heart this was the personal, dressed up as political terror. Maybe those two were the ones most in need of the delusion.

It didn't matter. There'd be a grievance behind each of the attacks, a reason these people were chosen. Jeremy had walked out of the clinic once. Maybe that was why he'd been the first victim.

The metronome had stopped, replaced by a breathless silence. I knew what I had to do. Go back where it started. Find their reasons. And from there, find them.

SIXTY-FOUR

SPAIN

Rain slapped the Cadillac's hood and curtained the windshield. The downpour had reached ark-building proportions. Half of Broadway was flooded. The wheels tore through the pools, shooting sheets of water across the empty sidewalks.

Rhonda Bryce lived on St. George Street, close to Fraser. A wall of decrepit breezeblocks ran across the front of the property line, broken up by a cement staircase. One section of the wall now curved toward the street, defying gravity, its crumbling blocks permeated with weeds and tufts of grass. Holding on out of sheer stubbornness.

In contrast to the ruined wall, the blue house was in good repair. The flower beds were staked out with twine and white flags, anticipating a break in the weather. A hopeful gesture, I thought. A light was on inside.

I knocked on the door. It was answered promptly by a man of about sixty.

"Rhonda home?" I asked.

He nodded, then seemed to recognize me. "You're the fellow she hired, aren't you? Little early for a home visit."

"I like to get a jump on the day."

Mr. Bryce shook his head and admitted me. "Coffee's about ready. Ronnie will have her face done in a jiff."

I waited in the foyer, ducking below an electric ceiling candelabra. A rack near the door overflowed with boots, sandals and shoes. I was happy for any distinguishing feature, since they kept comparisons with Peng Liu's house out of mind.

Rhonda Bryce came down the stairs, wearing white slacks pulled up past her navel and an avocado-coloured pullover. Her eye was still milky, but looked better than it had. The skin around it was healing. At this rate we'd all be healthy for Easter.

Bryce's husband set out three coffee cups and an old-fashioned glass pitcher of milk. Bryce filled her cup to the brim with equal parts of both.

"The people who blinded you," I said. "I think they were working off a grudge. My guess is you'll know at least one of them."

"I went over all that, a million billion times. I don't have much in the way of war stories on the job. Never pulled my gun, with Transit or VPD."

"There's someone you pissed off, sometime."

"Sure of that, are you?" Bryce quaffed grey coffee and refilled her cup. "Gurcharan Gill tells me this is a political thing. 'Stead of white power, now they think it's whacked-out kids trying to make a statement. They picked my gun to do it. My bad luck is all."

"I don't doubt any of that," I said.

"So why're we talking this over at five-thirty in the morning?"

Bryce's husband took his coffee and leaned a hip against the kitchen stove. It was an expensive-looking machine, glass-topped, brushed stainless steel. It matched the fridge and the various small appliances on the counter. Stainless steel and butcher block, lace curtains and tile flooring. A beautiful kitchen in a beautiful home, owned by people who couldn't imagine how anyone could ever hate them.

"When you hired me," I said, "at first, I thought like the police do now. That this was a statement."

Bryce nodded, following me. Her husband split the remains in the coffee pot among us.

"What I think now is that the act itself was meant as a statement, as a trial run for more elaborate crimes and as a means of getting hold of your gun. But choosing you was personal. Specific."

"Why would you think that?" Bryce's husband asked.

"Because of how these people operate. Imagine you've dedicated years of your young life to a spiritual leader who promises wealth and power. And in a moment, that's all taken away. You're crushed—not only are you adrift karmically, but you don't even have the money for bus fare. The worst period of your life, and along comes some dipshit with a ticket book—no offense. And as you make plans to bring the city to its knees, and someone says we need a gun, whose face comes to mind?"

"A job like mine you see thousands of faces every day," Bryce said. "But I don't forget the real dangerous ones. And I didn't recognize the two who jumped me."

"Someone else, then. A ticketing that went poorly."

"Nobody likes getting them, kid."

A feeling crept over me like persevering in a fight, gaining that elusive second wind, only to expend it fruitlessly. A double exhaustion. Muhammad Ali had called that feeling "the closest thing to dying."

Mr. Bryce said, "Could this perhaps be a little thing?"

"What do you mean?" his wife asked.

"How many times at dinner have you started by saying, 'Ruben, you'll never guess how this uppity so-and-so or this drunken so-and-so reacted'?" To me he added, "What if this was someone who blew some little bitty thing Ronnie did way out of proportion? That's in the realm of possibility, isn't it?"

"Definitely in the realm," I said.

Mr. Bryce set his cup down, opened a closet in the adjoining dining room. At the bottom, sitting atop a deluxe-model vacuum, was a cardboard box. He lifted it out and set it on the table.

"This was stuff the hospital sent home with me," he said. "Of course it belongs to Ronnie's work, and we've been meaning to drop it off. Just haven't got around to it."

He handed his wife a small tablet in a heavy vinyl slipcase. "All her tickets are in the system, so maybe the son of a gun is in here."

"How long's this go back?" I asked.

"Year, at least. 'Course I've been off a while now." Bryce powered it up, began tapping through the tickets. "Yeah, I don't recognize any of these. Maybe this one. Guy shat himself on the platform. During rush hour, too. You don't forget that, try as I might."

I copied down the name and the man's particulars, not exactly thrilled to be chasing that lead. A fifty-three-year-old incontinent man wasn't the profile I was looking for.

Bryce flipped through, making an effort with each to recall their circumstances. I copied down another name, a woman with a French passport who refused to pay bus fare.

"I sought you country ees socialeest. Ees not? Zen fack yew." Bryce chuckled. She reached the end of the tickets and frisbeed the tablet back into the box. "Sorry, but no one else really stands out."

"May I?"

Bryce clicked her tongue but didn't stop me from retrieving the tablet and scanning through the tickets and dates.

I stopped on January 4. A 3:14 ticket for failure to produce valid fare, issued to Susan Colville. Adam Colville's niece.

"Remember this woman?" I asked.

Bryce squinted at the window, frowned. "Maybe. I think it was on the 99. She didn't want to show ID. Yeah, I remember. Tried to say she didn't have any, then when I said that meant we'd have to go to HQ to sort this out, she magically remembered she'd brought some in her purse. Funny how often that happens. Anyway, she ponied up her license. Sulked but didn't talk back or anything. Why, that significant?"

"I think so," I said. "According to Mona Tsai, Susan has been out of the country. Kind of hard to rack up tickets if you're not in town."

A quick search of Susan Colville found an active social media presence. A student at the University of Valencia, she posted pictures every week. Susan in Bilbao, in La Mancha next to a Don Quixote statue. On January 4, she'd posted from Madrid.

Bryce scrutinized the photos and shrugged. "Couldn't say to a certainty."

I could. In the pictures, Susan's fair skin was deeply tanned. Her smile was wide and carefree. Her eyes held none of the annihilating menace they'd held when she shot Evelyn Rhee. But the resemblance was unmistakable. Susan Colville was the woman called Boss.

SIXTY-FIVE

MONSTROUS INGRATITUDE

Racing down the Causeway, over the Lions Gate Bridge, I beat the rush hour traffic into West Van. There wasn't much rushing around the British Properties. I didn't see any other people until I reached the gates of Mona Tsai's home.

Jeff had posted a half dozen sentries around the property. One recognized me, but thinking this was a test, they insisted on phoning the house to ask if Ms. Tsai would see me. She would.

Tarps covered part of the roof. A scaffold clung to the side, rising from the top patio. I doubted the smell of smoke had even reached the other wing of the house. I knocked and let myself in.

Mona was sitting at the bench in the kitchen, a notepad in front of her. Her robe was loosely belted, one nipple exposed. I stared at the wood grain on the island until she noticed and adjusted.

"I keep making lists of what to do, and then not doing any of it," she said. "In the last week I must have made twenty or thirty lists."

"You're bereaved," I said. "Don't beat yourself up about it."

"The trunk of a car," Mona said. "I keep thinking about his last moments. Adam must have been so frightened."

There was no comforting reply to that.

The kitchen lights were off, but the curtains were drawn and Jeff's new perimeter lights flooded through the windows. A spotlight on the loneliest person in the world. I hadn't taken her love for Colville seriously, but Mona's grief was undeniable, filling the room like a haze. The enemy bleeds, too.

"Adam's niece wasn't at the funeral," I said.

"Susan said she couldn't get away. School stuff."

"But she phoned you?"

Mona gave a listless shrug. "Why?"

"I need to know exactly where Susan is."

"Spain. She's studying—"

"She was in town on January 4. She got a transit ticket."

"Identity theft," Mona said.

"I think she's been here for a while. Susan is one of the kidnappers." To head off any questions, I asked one of my own. "Do you have a number to contact her?"

"Just her email."

"But no way to talk in real time. Nothing to prove she's where she's supposed to be."

It was clear Mona didn't want to entertain the possibility. But something was nagging at her.

"Susan was going to send us a number for emergencies," she said. "I had to email her about Adam's funeral."

"She never gave you a number?"

"No. Adam would get an email from her every few weeks."

She picked her phone out of a ceramic bowl on the island, found the email and turned the screen to me.

The message from Susan Colville's school account read:

> Hey Uncle A and Auntie M,
> Did you get my Xmas presents? I had a friend who's a chef pick them out she says the pots are top of the line hope you like them. Sorry they were late I've been incredibly busy.
> Midterms are coming up. I'll be studying like crazy so if you don't hear from me that's why. The reading list is insane and so is the prof though he's nice.

Thinking of you, XOXOXOX
Suzie

Mona put the phone back in the bowl. "We were thinking of visiting her, Adam and I, before all this insanity. Do you really think Susan has been playing us?"

To answer, I showed her the footage of Susan in a hoodie, blinding Rhonda Bryce.

"Could be anyone," Mona said. "Her hair is dark and naturally curly."

"A wig," I said. "She attacked me, and shot Evelyn Rhee, and probably set fire to your house. It's Susan."

Mona let out a moan, and seemed to deflate. I wondered when she'd last slept or had a decent meal.

"She hated being called Suzie," Mona said. "That should've told me she was stringing us along. Telling Adam what he wanted to hear. Damn her."

Mona hadn't seen Susan Colville in two years. Susan's Christmas gifts arrived with no postage. Her emails avoided questions about visits or calls. Cheerful missives about studying hard, seeing the sights, and vague plans for visits that never materialized. She sounded happy, so what did it matter? They'd thought it was a sign of maturity.

"She's always been a little distant from me," Mona said. "I told myself that was normal for a girl who lost her parents at eighteen. Adam's brother Roger drove drunk, killed himself and his wife. Adam tried to look out for Susan. And for this. What kind of monster..."

I nodded, thinking of how difficult it had been between me and the people I called mother and father. At times in my teens, my mother had reminded me that raising her sister's boy wasn't her choice. I hadn't always been grateful or understanding, either. Nothing much had changed.

"Does Susan have friends she'd stay with?" I asked.

"I wouldn't know. It's clear I never even knew the girl."

"Did Adam keep anything of hers? Papers? Anything about his brother's family?"

"We can check," Mona said.

It was a monumental struggle to her feet. I followed her up to the second floor, where the whiff of the fire was more prevalent. A home office overlooked the front yard, two workstations with separate desks and printers. Mona shuffled to the filing cabinet, knelt and dug a large manila envelope out of a folder. In black marker and an even hand were the words *Roger Colville* and the date *2018*.

She cut her thumb on the metal fastener and sucked the wound. The envelope held stapled documents, a police report care of the Jamaican Embassy, a will and various legal correspondence.

"I'm going to smoke a cigarette," Mona said. "Would you care for one?"

"I can't think of anything I'd care for more," I said.

Sitting at her desk, we smoked half a pack of Kools. The room grew hazy. At the end of two hours, my throat felt furry, but I had a better understanding of how Susan Colville had become Boss.

Roger, her father, had worked for Adam as a vice president. As Vancouver real estate took off, and Adam's holdings grew, Roger's role had only expanded slightly. He'd drawn an eighty-thousand-dollar salary, nothing to sniff at, but fly shit compared to the eight-digit years Colville Development was having. A decade of uninterrupted prosperity.

Roger and his wife Myrna had been on vacation in Jamaica at a resort. The police report stated he'd lost control of the vehicle, pancaking into an oncoming semi rig. Roger was killed instantly, while Myrna died a day later. The coroner's report listed Roger's blood-alcohol level at .3.

Susan had been attending summer school to make up for a French class she'd flunked. Otherwise she might have been on vacation with her parents. A heavy burden for an already fragile teen. It would get heavier.

At the back of the file was a cover letter from a forensic accounting firm, chasing down $334,000 in "misallocated" funds from Colville Development. The accountants had pinpointed the dates and departments responsible and which projects had been leached. Did they have Mr. Colville's permission to proceed further and examine employee emails?

Evidently so. Sandwiched between Roger's will and a letter from his executor was a sheet of company letterhead, a note handwritten in shaky script.

> *Adam,*
>
> *We both know what was done and why. I won't apologize, and I don't expect forgiveness from you. I always made my own bed. Let's forget forgiveness.*
>
> *I hope you'll always look after your niece and not let our silly crap affect how you treat her. I'd like to believe you won't hold it against her future.*
>
> *Myrna is with me on this and insists I tell you it was her idea. I guess we all want things just out of our reach.*
>
> *Love you, kiddo. Believe it or not.*
>
> *Your brother,*
>
> *Rog*

Mona hadn't lit the last cigarette. It dangled from her lips, movie-cowboy style, awaiting a match.

"Adam never let me read that," she said. "He told me Roger took the money and probably drove into that truck on purpose. But nothing about the letter."

"Could Susan have seen this?" I asked.

"It's possible. She stayed here a few times, and used the office for homework."

"Did she have a trust fund? An allowance from Adam?"

"He took care of her school and sent her money when she needed it."

"Roger Colville didn't leave a house, a portfolio? Shares in the company?"

For a brief moment Mona looked like her old self, vexed that I'd mention anything remotely negative about her husband's family. But she couldn't sustain her ire and slumped down. I lit the cigarette for her.

"Even I thought it was a shitty move," she said. "But Adam was upset. And it was company money, not his. He had to."

"You're saying Colville sued his brother's estate?"

She nodded. "Susan got the rest, a hundred grand or so."

I pried open a window, letting in fresh air.

"Did she ever mention the Jericho Centre, or a doctor named Van Veen?"

"That quack," Mona said. "I have friends who went to him. I know Adam wanted Susan to see someone. It might have been him."

There was a sick irony: Colville sending his niece to the person who helped form her into his kidnapper. The things we do, not knowing they'll wreck us down the line.

"When you emailed Susan that her Uncle Adam was dead, did she phone you back?"

Mona tapped her ash into a Colville Development mug. "That's right. I wrote to her a few days ago, just saying it was urgent and for her to call. She did. From the university, I assumed, but I don't know that for sure."

I ran down the stairs to retrieve her phone. Mona unlocked it and pulled up the list of received calls. None with a Spanish country code.

"How did she sound?" I asked.

"Sad, surprised, but I couldn't say it was genuine. I was upset myself." Mona smoked for a moment. "She sounded older, too. At first I didn't recognize her voice."

"The fire," I asked, "was anything of Susan's or Roger's lost? Maybe taken?"

"Actually, yes. Adam was storing some things in the room where it started. There was a box labelled ROGER, but I never had reason to go in there."

"What happened to the box?"

"Damaged or destroyed, I assumed."

I looked through the rows of digits on her phone, most with 604 or 778 area codes. One number looked familiar. I had to check my own phone to make sure, but it was the number Kyle Halliday had given when he was looking for the gun. The Van Ness Hotel. Susan Colville was staying there, too.

SIXTY-SIX
LAST RUNG

Ryan Martz was the only one in the office. He nodded at me with more benevolence than I deserved.

"Jeff's at a breakfast meeting with the CFO of Solis Incorporated," he said. "Some new contract they're hashing out. Kay's with Blatchford and his boyfriend. No messages."

In my office I took the Maglite and a box of shells for the .357. I found a tactical vest in the closet, white Kevlar with thin plates. A floor model from a convention I attended years ago. I practised unholstering the gun across the padded chest. Exhale. Pull in one smooth motion. I wouldn't beat Doc Holliday at a quick-draw, but the movement was easy enough to remember.

Walking out, I passed Ryan, who said, "Hey, Joe."

"Huh?"

"The Hendrix song. What's with the gun in your hand, Dave?"

"I have a lead on one of the members. Adam Colville's niece Susan."

He reacted to this with surprise. "Damn. And let me guess, you're not calling the cops?"

"Thought about it," I said. "Last time they were involved, Susan shot Evelyn Rhee. The best chance I have to end this without more bloodshed is to surprise her."

"You're not gonna wait for Jeff to back you up?"

"If he was here, I'd ask him. Kay, too. But end of the day, Jeff's got a family and Kay's mine."

"All right." Ryan scribbled something on a notepad, stuck the sheet to the computer screen. "I'll lock up."

"I can't ask you to," I said.

"Not up for discussion. When it comes to taking doors, I got more experience than you."

Ryan picked up the phone receiver, held down one of the buttons that did who knows what. He said, in a bright, cheery receptionist voice, "You've reached the offices of Wakeland & Chen. We can't come to the phone right now, since our services are needed saving our idiot co-founder's hide. But please leave your name and number and we'll get back to you soon as we can."

That done, he pushed away from the desk, maneuvered around the reception island. "Now let's you and I pick up this niece."

I parked the work van in the alley behind the Van Ness. A couple of men were smoking crack in a nearby doorway. I set Ryan's chair on the ground and held the door. We'd stopped at his house to pick up his gun, a SIG not unlike Rhonda Bryce's, and a shoulder holster concealed beneath the ugliest vomit-beige warm-up jacket I'd seen.

"My undercover coat," he said.

"You never worked undercover."

"Never had the need till now."

"There's no elevator from the lobby," I said. "Just a rickety-ass set of stairs."

"Well, that is a clear violation of accessibility bylaws."

"Judging from the mould inside, I don't think the Van Ness gets a lot of inspections. You rather wait in the van?"

"Fuck no," Ryan said. "From here I can cover the front door and the fire escape."

"You'll get soaked."

"It's Vancouver, dipshit." Ryan zipped his jacket and wiped the droplets from his head. "Next time choose a skel who likes dry weather."

I took the stairs, the smell of rot no longer disguised by cleaners. I saw my reflection in the glass door at the top. Wild eyes and a desperate set to the jaw. *Use that*, I thought.

The same mummified clerk sat on her perch behind the grungy counter. The smell of burnt coffee in the air. She folded her hands on the desk.

"Susan Colville." My voice left no room to brook argument.

"I don't know that name, sir."

I showed her a photo of Susan in Spain. The clerk looked at my phone, looked at me. Nodded.

"What a pill that one is," she said. "I'll call up."

"Better in person. Less chance of violence. What number is she in?"

"Three-three-one. Gimme a sec." The clerk stood and picked a key ring the size of an ankle bracelet off a nail on the wall.

"You probably want to stay down here," I said.

But she didn't relinquish the keys. Following behind her with my adrenaline spiking and the weight of the vest against my heart was agony. The clerk took each step of the stairs in turn. I considered throwing her over my shoulder.

She paused on the second-floor landing to catch her breath and to let a wild-haired man pass us going down. He smelled like a bus terminal washroom. We reinitiated the climb. Another recuperative pause before we were ready to walk down the third-floor hallway.

At 331 the clerk stopped and knocked. The doors were slightly recessed, and I stood a foot to the right, out of view from the peephole.

"Message, ma'am," the clerk called out.

I heard rustling and soft footsteps. Then a pause and silence, as if the other party was gauging who waited outside their door. A snap from inside, panicked footsteps stamping across the room, a window latch being struggled with.

"The key," I said.

Once the clerk selected it, I snapped up the ring and threw the bolt, earning a sigh of disgust from her.

The door inched open. The chain had been slotted in. Through the crack I could see thin arms working at the windowsill.

"Five steps back," I told the clerk.

Given the decrepitude, I assumed the door would snap open with one emphatic size eleven. But then in a place like this, security was probably tested on the regular. It took three boots to snap the chain free.

Susan wasn't inside. The window opened out to a fire escape. Clothing, bandages, garbage and food had been scattered across every surface. Pamphlets on the bed, military manuals. The old coach gun was propped in a corner, the breach open on empty barrels.

I moved to the window, stuck my head out, heard the vibrations of wrought iron. Susan Colville was escaping down the sharp-angled stairs. Barefoot, in a ragged blue sweater. I pursued down the first flight, calling out to her, "Susan, it's over!"

We slashed by each other, Susan a staircase ahead. Recognition and hatred in her eyes.

She reached the drop-off point, the square-cut hole ten feet up from the alley. Moody had made a similar leap in the snow. Susan hesitated, stepping to the edge. I increased my pace. Reached the platform before she jumped. Grabbed for her, my hand grasping air.

She landed in a crouch with a grunt, took a few seconds scrambling to her feet. The alley was dirty broken brick, puddles seeping over the uneven surface. No sign of Ryan Martz.

Susan Colville limped a few feet, looked back at me. Like her, I hesitated. I had shoes on and knew how to fall, but there was also more of me to drop. I took hold of the grate with my good hand and swung down, holding on a second, then fell.

The drop sent a shockwave up to my teeth. But I landed on my feet and stayed on them. I was in time to see Susan Colville pass the two smokers and reach the end of the alley.

I drew the gun, trying to slow my breath.

She was limping but moving fast and darted around the corner before I could reach it.

There was a clatter of aluminum and pavement and human bodies. Rounding the corner, I saw the source of the noise.

Ryan Martz had tipped over in his chair. Purposefully—he'd lunged for Susan Colville's neck and had his arms snugly around it. Susan was struggling, kicking at Ryan. He cinched up, she howled, and her kicks turned to flutters, soon stopped altogether. Her eyes wheeled between us, frightened. And rightly so.

"Struggle some more, miss," Ryan said, "and see if I don't snap your fucking neck."

SIXTY-SEVEN

MARTYRDOM

"Maybe a round of introductions is in order," I said.

We'd had a bitch of a time moving her. I'd brought the van alongside the two grounded individuals, ignoring the looks from the neighbourhood folks. VPD sometimes placed undercover officers in wheelchairs, in an initiative to bust people who prey on disadvantaged citizens. Perhaps the downtown regulars thought we were cops.

Without relinquishing his hold on Susan's neck, Ryan had me toss the wheelchair into the back of the van. He relaxed the tension enough for Susan to sit up. With my assist, he moved them together so Susan was sitting on the middle seat of the van, with Ryan between her and the sliding door.

The van was used for surveillance. As far as I knew it had never been used as a mobile prison. I didn't have cuffs or zip ties, but made do with a microphone cable.

I drove us to the parking lot of a White Spot. Then I turned off the engine, got out and took a seat behind Susan and Ryan.

"You know who I am?" I asked Susan.

"Stupid trash who doesn't know eff-all."

"That's Dave, all right," Ryan said.

Gone was the menacing poise, the cold-blooded distance. Her hostility was bratty, a pouting teen's. Fear beneath it. Desperation, too.

"I want an attorney," she said.

"I want to look like Paul Newman in the seventies."

"I'll scream."

"Knock yourself out." I tapped shave-and-a-haircut on the tinted glass. "We soundproofed these vans pretty good."

"I'll tell people you tried to rape me."

Ryan flexed his bicep. "How about you stop threatening what you're gonna do, princess, and do as we fucking say?"

"Eff you, you dumb cripple."

"Susan," I said, "I know a lot about you."

"You don't know eff-all. You're so in the dark it's funny."

"I heard about your parents and I'm sorry."

Not a beat passed. "Entitled effing a-holes. My dad thought 'cause his brother was rich he could do whatever he wanted."

"You take after him," I said.

Her anger intensified, but there was nowhere for it to go. "That's not true."

"Then how do you explain the Death of Kings?"

"We're making them see how their actions hurt others. Have consequences for the masses."

"'Them' being the rich."

"Un-huh. And you can't stop us because we're a destiny. A movement. Even caught and executed, we'll be the start of something."

It sounded memorized, rote. I let her run on about the subjugation of the ordinary decent citizens for a while, until she coughed, in need of water. There was a jug in the van. I broke the seal and passed it to her.

"Don't just let her drink like that," Ryan said. "Withhold that shit until she talks."

"I'm never saying ess to you," Susan said between gulps.

I studied our position for a minute. The three of us were standing on a battlefield between the Death of Kings and the police. A clash was imminent. My hope was that even Susan could see that.

"I'm not going to argue ideology with you," I said. "Or try to convince you of the error of your ways. You have a choice. You're big on consequences, so I'll set them out for you. We can take you straight to the police—"

"Effing do it," she said. "Take me to jail."

"Sure," I said. "We could do that."

"So do it."

"With you out of the way, the others should be easy enough for the cops to find."

I paused to give her time to absorb that.

"No one's luck holds out forever," I said. "Knowing what you know about Dagan Moody, is he likely to surrender? Or more likely to blaze-of-glory things, end up like Peng?"

Susan didn't have a response. Ryan raised the jug to drink, and I watched her watch him.

"The alternative," I said.

"Eff you."

"Just have a listen, in the interest of fairness. Ryan and I are not the police. We picked you up without harming you."

"Though the day is still young," Ryan said.

"Susan, I watched Peng die. And think what you want of me, you know I didn't want that. And I don't want to see anyone else go that way. You. Your friends. Or me."

She nodded. She believed that.

"If there's even part of you that doesn't want to see your friends die in a hail of gunfire, please tell me where they are. We'll pick them up non-violently, I promise, and arrange the terms of their surrender."

"You bit his effing eye," she said.

"In self-defense. And he's still alive to gripe about it."

The three of us sat quietly, each with their thoughts. There weren't a lot of options left if she didn't go for our offer. Handing Susan Colville over to Inspector Gill would be far from ideal, but maybe he could leverage her to give up Moody. I doubted it, though.

Susan Colville held her hand out for the water. Chugged some and wiped her mouth. A fucking kid, I thought. Younger than Peng, and mired in more bullshit than any ten adults.

"She told me you didn't like violence," Susan said.

"Who? Rio?"

"And Sky said you might even help us."

"He was wrong," I said. "You're the one in a position to help him."

She nodded sarcastically as if I was conning her. "You won't ever come around because you're weak. Like everyone else. You see what's going on in this city and you do nothing."

"Tell us where he is, Susan."

"No effing way," she said. "I'm not like you. I won't sit by. Do what you want."

"To hell with this," Ryan said.

He clenched his fist around her elbow and wrenched back until she winced.

"We don't have time for you to dick us around," he said. "Tell us where your one-eyed buddy is. Now."

"Don't," I said, more a request than an order.

Susan spat on Ryan, who increased the torque. She thrashed in her seat until I forced Ryan's hands off her wrist.

"He'll kill you," she said. "Kill you both, you get in the way of our truth. You, your partner, even your sister if that's what it takes. Cut off my hand if you want to. Our work is too important. And I'm not saying ess anymore."

SIXTY-EIGHT

HAZARDS

There was no other play except to turn her over to the police. That move had advantages, number one being I'd have Susan Colville off my hands. If it felt like personal failure, or an abdication of responsibility, maybe that was inevitable. Positive, even. She and Moody had set in motion something neither of them could foresee. I anticipated its outcome would be bloody.

I called the task force number, asked for Gill. Was put on hold. After a few minutes the inspector came on, not thrilled to be talking to me.

"I have one of them," I said.

"You're being serious?" Gill went from skepticism to cheer in a beat. "That's terrific, Wakeland. Send us his particulars."

"Hers, and I mean I have her physically."

"I see. Well, as the rappers my son listens to would say, ain't that some shit. Where abouts are you?"

"The White Spot on Kingsway."

"You needed a Triple O burger before you brought her in?"

"Just a head's up we're on our way."

I drove toward the station. On Main Street, the shops were busy, people lining up for brunch or vegan cheese or graphic novels. Dogs tied up under awnings, couples with kids. The rain didn't dampen their mood. A lazy Sunday afternoon.

I made eye contact with Susan in the rearview. "The oppressed, teeming masses," I said.

"Don't talk to me."

"Most of them think your crimes were done by Woden's Bastards, a white supremacist group. What does that tell you?"

"I'm not racist," Susan said.

"Massively entitled, oblivious to the suffering of others. If that's not kissing cousins to white privilege."

"You're the one that's oblivious."

"What do you mean?"

Susan's smile was ominous and condescending, similar to Moody's, though his smile seemed more beatific, less vengeful. The two of them looked down on me. Maybe on the world.

I turned on Seventh, let a couple of cyclists cross the street to Jonathan Rogers Park. At the next intersection I checked my phone. A message from Mona that said *Urgent*.

When I phoned her, at first, she didn't pick up. An idea came to mind. Maybe Susan's aunt could get through to her, put a human face to the misery Susan was causing. Looking at those eyes, I very much doubted it, but it was worth trying before handing Susan over to Gill.

The station was close but I pulled over to dial again.

"What are you doing?" Ryan said.

"There's someone I'd like Ms. Colville to speak with."

"Who, Mona?" It's hard to jeer with your hands bound, but Susan pulled it off. "You think I'll effing talk to *her*?"

"We'll find out."

Mona picked up. Only it wasn't her voice I heard.

"Why the *hell* would you send them away, Dave?"

It was rare to hear full-on fury from Jeff Chen. Irritation and disapproval, sure, but hardly ever did my partner forsake his cool.

"What are you talking about?" I said.

"The shift rotation at the Tsai home. Six on, six off. You sent them home early."

"I haven't done shit with your scheduling," I said. "I've been busy, and anyway I was just at the house. The guards were there."

I waited for Jeff to tell me what I could already guess from his tone.

"No one's here now," he said. "Not the shift. Not Mona. And not her father, either."

"Christ." Not knowing what else to do, I set the hazards. The van's interior filled with the click of the lights.

"Just to be clear, you didn't send an email to the day shift?"

"Of course not. Why would I?"

"You log into your account in front of anyone recently?"

"No," I said, with more assurance that I felt. In bed with Naima in those first days of intimacy, I'd certainly checked my account. Shielding the screen would have been out of the spirit. I didn't have secrets worth keeping. So I'd thought.

"Moody has Mona and the old man," Jeff said. "The outgoing shift didn't see anything, and the cameras are off. I'm the only one here."

Behind me I heard Susan Colville begin to laugh.

SIXTY-NINE

LIFE IN CAPTIVITY

I turned off the hazard lights. Sat there with my hands on the wheel, ten and two, like a tentative student driver. Waiting for my mind to catch up to its circumstances.

Edward Tsai with his breathing apparatus, fragile in Jeff's arms. Mona sitting at the table, dwelling on her husband's last moments. *He must have been so frightened.* Mona now living that for herself.

This wasn't about ransom or demands. They'd be killed either way, for what they stood for. I despised what they stood for, but they were clients, and I was duty-bound to risk my life for theirs. Ryan's, and Jeff's, and Kay's, too. I'd work out the why, and the right or wrong of it, after.

To stop Dagan Moody, I'd likely have to kill him. That weighed on me, but I accepted the possibility. To find him, I'd have to get the information out of our prisoner.

Susan Colville looked gleeful. Her apprehension seemed to magnify that. No regard for human life beyond her own, and maybe Moody's.

Ryan leaned over the passenger seat. He could sense what I was debating.

"I can get it out of her," he said. "Go take a walk around the block."

"You can't do effing anything to me," Susan said.

Everything about her made the case for it. But I couldn't. Years ago, I'd wound up on the wrong side of a biker gang. I'd been held at gunpoint, taken up a mountain and forced to dig my own grave in the wilderness. The experience had made torture a reality to me, in a way it wasn't before. I wouldn't be a party to it. And I hadn't talked then, so its effectiveness wasn't guaranteed.

"Lady, take a good look around here." Ryan gestured at the ladder, the toolbox, the road cases of AV equipment. "There's bound to be something that'll make you chatty."

"I won't say ess, you gimp."

He shook his head. "Makes me sad that you're too much of a ree-fined lady to say 'shit,' but 'gimp' rolls off that fat little tongue so easy."

"Swearing is uncultivated," Susan said. "It shows you have no control over your emotional self."

"I got control over your finger getting snapped like a fucking chopstick."

"She's just repeating things her guru told her," I explained. "How did Van Veen end up dead, anyway?"

"He just died." Susan's face showed something close to melancholy. "He loved that property, so we put him there."

"Overdose, probably," I said. "He really hurt you, didn't he?"

"Doc set us free."

Could Moody have returned to the compound with his hostages? Unlikely, I thought, given the police had combed through it. He'd likely go some place new.

I started the ignition and swung the van around, back to the Van Ness. There had to be an answer somewhere in Susan's apartment.

Parking a block away, in case anyone in the neighbourhood had seen us load Susan into the van, I told Ryan I'd be quick. "Do what you have to to keep her here," I said. "But no torture. I won't condone that."

Ryan nodded. I pictured him waiting till I left and doing it anyway, sparing me from responsibility. Like the king at the end of *Richard II*. I made him promise not to.

As soon as the engine was off, Susan began to struggle. When she couldn't free her wrists, she banged her knees into the side panel, making as much noise as possible. I put a Neko Case album on the stereo, filling the space with Case and Mark Lanegan's vocals on "Curse of the I-5 Corridor."

"Alt-country," Ryan said, with a metalhead purist's disgust. "And he says no torture."

The clerk called "Sir?" as I passed her, but didn't follow me up the stairs. One excursion per day was enough for her. She'd closed Susan's door but hadn't locked it. The chain still lay on the floor.

Something in here would tell me where Moody and the hostages were. Parking ticket, restaurant bill, diagram of the safehouse. Instead I found mounds of sweat-salted clothes and the same embedded filth as Kyle's room. No Death of Kings graffiti in Susan's. No trophies. Susan didn't care about graffiti tags or names. There was only power— through persuasion, through force, through holding others hostage.

And now I held her. Unless I could find an address, though, she'd continue to hold the upper hand.

I didn't find an address. In a gym bag on the floor, I found medical supplies, gauze and Band-Aids and distilled water, a few pain pills. Susan's wig and hoodie were bunched in there, too. A small code-grabber, which looked like an old portable radio. An empty leather wallet, cut for European bills. A Cartier watch inscribed from Roger Colville to his wife on the occasion of their tenth anniversary. An envelope of family photos.

There wasn't time to examine any of it closely, but after combing through the rest of the room, uncovering bed bugs and mice, I was drawn back to the bag. Susan had kept the important things here, the incriminating things, the keepsakes she'd retrieved while setting the fire.

The Band-Aids had come in a tin. Shoved inside was a set of keys on a Hyundai fob, the hood ornament of a Lexus. At the bottom of the tin, folded at the edges so it would fit, was a Polaroid. I recognized the faces of Susan and her accomplices. I also recognized the kitchen where it had been taken. A nurse's shift schedule was visible in the background.

Sky and Boss, Driver and Rio. The Death of Kings in Naima Halliday's apartment. Kyle no doubt had taken the picture.

I leaned out the window, feeling vertiginous, my mouth dry. Deceived from the start. And culpable in my own deception. It explained why Jane Doe Two had hung back when the others had swarmed me. Why they hadn't simply killed me before now. I'd been no worse than a nuisance to them. Maybe even useful.

Rage. I'd never even known what it was before. Guilt, either. Now they avalanched over me, a landslide of fury and despair. If I'd had time to weep, if I'd had an enemy's throat to crush, if I could have blown up the world for an instant—

Then the avalanche was over, and I was left to pick my way through the rubble. Clear-eyed, with no doubt of what I had to do. The gun a comfort now.

I left the Van Ness. Walked back to the van, and turned the music off. I lifted out Ryan's chair.

"I need to talk with Susan alone," I said.

Never in the decades we'd known each other had Ryan Martz passed up an opportunity to jibe me. Seeing my expression, though, he nodded and vacated the van.

"I'll head back to the office and coordinate with Jeff," he said. "Don't do anything I wouldn't, Wakeland."

Soon Susan and I were alone, driving east on the highway, in the direction of the Second Narrows Bridge. In search of a quiet place to have a talk.

SEVENTY

SWIMMING LESSON

"Where the eff are we going?"

On the other side of Burrard Inlet, east of the market at Lonsdale Quay, is a marina operated by the Squamish Nation. Yachts on one end, a flotilla of houseboats next to them. And on the far side, a row of aluminum sheds for long-term moorage. Narrow plank walkways between them.

That's where I headed.

Rain fell on the windshield at a stately tempo. Graphite clouds hung low. Patches of blue to the west.

"Don't effing bother trying to scare me. I know all about you from Rio."

I was sure of that. My own carelessness had led me here. And Susan Colville would provide the way out. Voluntarily or otherwise.

Beneath the bridge, the green-grey water roiled. No ships smaller than the SeaBus, which rode the chop like a brick on a basketball. The marina parking lot was empty, no one sailing today.

Susan struggled and flexed. I climbed over the seat and put a hand on her wrist, pulling up like throwing a power switch. She jackknifed forward to ease the pressure, grunted and stopped fighting. I opened the door and helped her down.

My moves were deliberate. The lock on the aluminum gate leading down to the boats gave way to three sharp strikes from the butt of the revolver.

"What the hell," Susan said. "You're taking me on a boat?"

I started her forward, down the planks. Steered her left through a narrow alley between two of the sheds. Corrugated metal on either side of us. Ahead, the water.

"Hey. *Hey*. Don't. Effing don't, okay?"

The jetty rocked with our footfalls. I steadied myself by gripping the side of a shed. Susan could only stumble and try to ride each lift of the tide.

In the bad old days of Vancouver policing, when my father and his partner had wanted to intimidate someone, they'd take them to the docks. Petty thieves, dope dealers, members of the youth gangs that hung out in the parks. "Swimming lessons," they'd called it, laughing about it over drinks years later. Cops could do things like that.

"Effing don't," Susan said. "Please. A-hole."

I shoved her and she teetered to the end of the dock, heeling back, her sweater already wet with perspiration and rain.

"Only two ways to see land again," I said. "One of them involves swimming to Japan. If that doesn't appeal to you, Susan, the other is telling me where Moody is. Think it over. In you go."

I nudged her into the bay, waited as Susan bobbed to the surface, sputtering, legs cycling frantically. I pointed the gun at a spot just over her shoulder, took two-handed aim and fired. The report caused Susan to gulp saltwater and cough. She was sinking and treading and trying to breathe. The second shot was closer. The third closer still.

"Okay, okay, I'll fucking tell," Susan said between gulps of saltwater. "His home. They're in Uncle Adam's home."

"The one you set on fire?"

The shots had startled the gulls sheltering in the eaves of the sheds. For an instant the sky was alive with them. I took aim at a spot in front of Susan.

"Not that home," she said, blubbering. "His new one, the one that's being built. I'll take you."

I believed her. I holstered the gun and squatted at the edge, grabbing a cleat with one hand and reaching for her with the other. "Roll back so I can grab your leg."

Susan did. It was a stretch but I caught her ankle, dragged her close, hefted her onto the dock. She gasped on the wood for a while. I remembered the last body I'd pulled from the water, remembered Susan standing over Jeremy Fell on the breakwater.

"Why did you take a photo of Jeremy?" I asked.

"What?"

I repeated the question as I helped her up. Susan Colville was slight and looked even more so with her hair matted to her ears. Freezing in her waterlogged sweater. A frightened creature. I'd done that to her.

"I didn't take photos," Susan said. "Only Kyle ever took photos. I just needed the light on my phone to make sure he was dead."

"You weren't sure when you hit him?" I asked.

"Sky hit him." Susan closed her eyes. "When we saw him up on the rocks, we were worried you'd brought him back."

"No one could. That's the meaning of dead."

"I'm cold," Susan said.

It was a long road to killing someone. For most of us, anyway. As I herded my hostage back to the warmth of the van, I couldn't help but think that I'd just taken one step farther down it.

SEVENTY-ONE
DEPLOYMENT

Lashing Susan's wrists to the steering wheel took a second cable. I put the van in drive for her, counting on old-fashioned self-preservation to keep her from flipping us off the Second Narrows. The heat was all the way up. Sitting beside her, with the gun casually pointed at her hip, I called Inspector Gill.

"I've been on tenterhooks waiting for you to deliver my kidnappers," Gill said.

"Just one. Her name is Susan Colville."

Susan grimaced and she looked at me. I pointed at the windshield, *eyes on the road.*

"You're referring to Adam's niece?" I heard the chittering of Gill's computer. "She's out of the country."

"She's been posting old or doctored photos to make it look that way," I said. "In point of fact she's sitting right next to me. Say hello, Susan."

"Eff yourself," Susan said.

All the idle amusement had left Gill's voice. "If this is true, then it's crucial that you bring her to the station."

"I need her for a quick errand first," I said.

"You realize Mona Tsai and her father are missing? Possibly in jeopardy?"

"I believe that's a safe assumption."

"God*damn*it." Something clattered on Gill's end of the line. His voice had turned to rolling thunder. "Haven't you cocked things up enough, Wakeland? Do you have *any* idea what it's like watching you and the mayor and every other arrogant shithead act like the rules don't apply?"

From the bridge Susan took the Cassiar Connector onto First. She was biting her bottom lip, stifling a grin at the inspector's vexation.

"The answer to both questions is yes," I told Gill. "See you soon."

As I dialed Jeff, Susan said, "They don't even realize whose agenda they serve. Even you see that."

"Even me," I said.

"You were a cop. Your father, too. And the woman you were seeing."

It was still eerie to hear how much Susan Colville knew about me. How far behind I'd been each step of the way.

She was saying something else about the authorities and the rich. This woman whose inheritance had only been six digits, who'd decided a continental education was somehow not enough, explaining how law and order were tools of oppression, how the system brutalized people in order to protect itself. She wasn't entirely wrong.

"The law is a complex institution," I said. "I don't pretend to understand it. It's in need of change."

"The state is a tool of the rich."

"Sometimes. Other times it's a woman getting a face full of jailhouse napalm from a spoiled college kid who didn't like getting a ticket."

"That pig effing deserved it."

The van surged through traffic along the viaduct, dropping us onto Terminal Avenue. Warehouses gave way to waterfront apartment towers. Susan cut across Quebec to Second, Second soon becoming Sixth, becoming Fourth, in the logicless layout of False Creek.

"Doc was the first person who ever believed in me," Susan said. "I was so messed up about my parents. He showed me a way to live and treated me like an adult. Like I mattered. Sky was living in his car before the Doc gave him a home. We were effing lost. And then he was accused, this whole witch hunt against him."

Susan changed lanes without signalling, the speed creeping up to seventy. The wiper blades too slow to clear the glass.

"When Doc came back, he barely weighed a hundred pounds," she continued. "One day he just kept throwing up, couldn't stop. I was bringing him medicine and that pig pulled me off the bus, asked for my transfer. I didn't have a free hand to swipe my fare card, big effing deal. And then you know what she said? 'Have a better day, ma'am.'"

Her fingers pulled at the vinyl on the steering wheel.

"How horrible," I said. "Worst hard-luck story I ever heard. You poor thing."

"A-hole."

I got through to Jeff, told him where to meet me. Kay was en route to the office. I asked if Ryan Martz had returned.

"Ryan's here," Jeff said. "He told me what you're doing. I don't know what to say about that."

"Me neither," I said, thinking he ought to see what I had planned next. "Can Ryan get himself to Naima Halliday's place? Keep an eye on her door, and anyone who comes and goes?"

"I'll drop him there. Leaving now. Be careful, Dave."

Passing through Kitsilano, we neared Point Grey, where Van Veen had lived. Susan turned her head, recognizing something of her surroundings. Her expression didn't change. How many times had I looked at a space feeling hollow and angry about what had once been there? A city of lost memories and ghosts.

"I'm going to tell you something, knowing it won't make a lick of difference to you," I said. "Once you accept that certain people's lives don't count, you can be as right-thinking about everything else, and all you'll bring about is misery and ruin."

"You just don't understand history," Susan said.

"No one does. Like understanding time or death. You felt hurt and you chose to hurt others. Social accountability, the state, housing rights—it's all just a nice way to dress up your little grudge. It means jack shit."

Down Alma, past the Yacht Club, closing in on Jericho Beach.

"All we ever wanted was to heal people," Susan said.

I doubted even she believed that, but there wasn't time to quibble. The Colville property loomed ahead.

SEVENTY-TWO

BENEATH THE UNDERDOGS

You couldn't miss the house. Even unfinished, it had a lordly air to it, towering over its neighbours. Solar panels were set in the roof, black eyes turned toward heaven. The entire block, however many homes, had been scraped away to leave a smooth brown canvas for the mansion's construction. A forty-million-dollar beachfront home, that dollar amount not including the cost Colville incurred for clearing the land of whatever had stood there before.

Once this had been a communal spot of the Coast Salish people for fishing and trading. Then the homes of dozens of white families, working class then middle class then rich, everyone else disinvited. And now all of it owned by one man—one dead man.

A perfect hideout, I thought. Double strands of cyclone fencing on the perimeter. Windows covered in black plastic, and the front double doors boarded up. Assuming you could get inside, from the top floors you'd have an unimpeded view of English Bay. No shrubbery or machinery on the property to hide behind. And with the beach right out the front door, that left only three angles of approach. What was the joke about buying waterfront property? The advantage was assholes on only three sides.

I instructed Susan to drive past the house and circle back. From the alley it looked less fully formed. The upper two tiers were covered in sheets of white Tyvek. There was a cement foundation laid for a porch, and beside that a wide walkway leading to the back entrance, where the patio doors would go. I could see through the house from here, all the way to the faint glowing grey of the light coming through the front windows.

"In there?" I asked Susan.

"Think so, yeah." The millionaire's niece stared at the building-in-progress, magnetized by hatred. "It's already worth more."

"What do you mean?"

"My uncle told me when he bought the land that it would be worth a lot more. 'In five years, I'll make back what I put into the building,' he told me. That was only two years ago, and it's already worth more."

Her left wrist was bleeding. She'd been unconsciously pulling away from the wheel. I jammed a napkin into where the cable met the skin.

"What am I going to find in there?" I asked.

"I don't know." Lying, or at least holding something back.

"How does Moody transport the hostages?"

"We had a little cage for my uncle, one of those beige plastic things for big dogs. But he broke it."

I curbed my feeling of revulsion, only nodded. "Mona and the old man will be in something similar?"

"Stronger, like a road case or a barrel or something. Sky said that's what he'd do next time."

Human beings, so much freight to them. "Weapons?"

"He has a pistol," Susan said. "I could phone and maybe ask him to give up, if you let me."

"Get real," I said.

A palm slapped the side door in my blind spot. I lifted the revolver, pushing Susan back into the headrest. The side door opened and Jeff Chen climbed in.

"I come in peace," he said. "Jeez, Dave, point that thing away."

His tone was light and reminded me we weren't soldiers. Neither of us made a habit of mounting rescue operations. Or killing people. A first time for everything.

"According to Susan, the Tsais are in there," I said. "My guess is the second floor, in some sort of reinforced container. Moody has a gun and might be inside already. If not, he's en route."

"What about the construction crew?" Jeff asked.

We looked at Susan. "My uncle had his crew work mornings here and afternoons at one of his developments, so he could charge it all to the other project."

"An underdog needs every advantage he can get," I said. "What about security?"

"There's a guy in a yellow jacket who walks around the outside at night."

"Colville got cheap and hired the wrong people," Jeff said.

Susan's information was more thorough than she could have picked up casually. That meant she and Moody had been watching the place, or they'd grilled Colville on the details, or both. The building was significant to them. I could guess why.

"I'll go in," I said.

"Not alone."

"Has to be. Someone needs to tell me if anyone shows up. If Moody isn't there, I'll let you know and we can get them out quick."

"And if he is?"

My body could still feel the battering it had taken the last time I'd fought with Dagan Moody.

"Well, Sundance, I don't want to sound like a sore loser, but if I'm dead, kill him for me."

Jeff nodded solemnly. From the folds of his jacket, he slid out something metallic and passed it to me. My father's Maglite.

"Probably useful in the dark," he said. "Maybe you can hit him with it before he knows you're there."

From one of our boxes, Jeff dug out an earpiece with a battery transmitter and mic. He could hear me from inside the van and vice versa. I helped him bind Susan's hands behind her, and lower her to the floor, out of sight.

"I want to see," she said.

Knowing her interest in the building, and guessing at her reasons, I bet she did.

I saluted Jeff and sprinted out of the van, down the alley. The rain peppered my shoulders and neck. If anyone saw me, I'd look like an under-dressed man hustling out of the downpour.

The chain holding the two ends of the fence together had been snapped and slung loosely back into place. I worked my way through and replaced it as close as I could. Stomping across the muddy edge of the property, eyes on the upstairs for movement. If Moody was inside, I'd be a difficult target to miss.

Across the mud, onto the cement. Then I was inside.

SEVENTY-THREE

DREAM HOUSE

Like stepping into an anatomy model—skeleton in places, flesh in others, still others fully skinned. The framing had been completed, the walls roughed in and some rooms even insulated and wired. But Adam Colville had made additions and substitutions to the blueprint, extending the property another hundred yards back. This required more concrete, additional lumber, extra spools of cable. The result, no two rooms seemed in the same stage of completion.

I walked through a doorway into a high-ceilinged room that looked ready for paint, up a staircase with a newel post but no bannister. The second story was only partially floored. From deeper in the structure came an insistent *dut-dut-dut* that cut through the crackle of water off the tarps.

Strands of corncob lights had been clipped along the ceiling of the second floor. Supplies were stacked in the wide central corridor, skids of wire and insulation. A pair of large drums near a support beam stood out by virtue of ugliness and age. Rust dappled their lids.

"Anything yet?" Jeff's voice was louder in my ear than I'd expected.

"Not sure," I whispered. "Maybe."

The beam of the Maglite showed part of a label slapped onto the side of the closer drum. Y'S PIZZA AND STE. It continued around the side but I didn't bother turning it. Grease barrels from a restaurant. Large enough in diameter to hold a crouching human being.

The thudding was louder, coming from one of the rooms near the front of the structure. The barrels first. Balancing the Maglite on one lid, I gripped the other and wrested it off. The stench of its contents made my eyes water. Diesel and excrement. The contents murky and scummed with a rainbow of oil.

"No hostages," I whispered. "Two drums of what could be a homemade explosive. Fertilizer bomb of some sort."

"You should get out, Dave."

Good advice, and if Jeff had told me the opposite, I might have dropped things and walked out. Contrarian to the end.

"Few more rooms to check," I said.

A hallway with hunks of insulation stuffed in the walls led to a make-shift office holding industrial fans and heaters, a table and a diamond-plated gearbox. The walls and ceiling had been completed, making this the darkest of the rooms. The *dut* sound originated from here.

Blue and pink Port-A-Johns took up a corner of the room. They'd been padlocked shut, turned to face each other so the doors couldn't open. Knuckles beat on the hard plastic.

I followed the knock, returning it on the side of the blue john. "Mona?"

A small voice from inside, "*getusoutofheremyfatherplease—*"

"You're okay now," I said, putting my shoulder to the side and spinning the john.

"*Myfathersnotbreathingplease—*"

She was begging. Thinking I was Moody.

"It's Wakeland," I said, turning to the pink john. "Jeff is outside. You'll be free in a jiff, okay? I'll get your father out first."

The padlocks were recessed, above and beneath the handle. It was easier to club the entire handle off. Easier but still loud and repetitive work. After every six strikes I'd pause to listen, but I could only hear Mona rapping on the door, that and the rain outside.

Finally the hard molded plastic pulled away from the top hinge. The bigger the gap, the easier to bend and break it further. With a splinter and snap, the door and a chunk of the hinge broke off. The force of the strikes had rotated the john a quarter turn.

Edward Tsai was inside, dressed for bed, slumped on the closed toilet seat. His pose resembled that of a dozing heroin addict I'd once seen in a train station toilet stall. The old man's face was turning an arctic blue.

"Got the father, but he doesn't seem to be breathing," I said for Jeff's benefit. Mona gasped and beat on the door with redoubled effort. Her father's oxygen tube was by his feet. I laid him down on a stretch of foam underlay and checked his airway for obstructions. I reattached the tank.

I didn't want to say the word "dead," knowing it would take the heart out of all three of us, and we still had a ways to go. Then the old man coughed and his chest fluttered.

"Alive," I said. "Bring your car to the gate." To Mona I said, "I'm gonna get your father to Jeff, who'll speed him to a hospital. I'll be right back for you, okay? Hold on."

She didn't answer. I didn't know if she could see it, but I left the flashlight lit and aimed toward her door. Then hefted the old man and his tank and moved for the stairway.

There were muddy footprints on the bottom stairs and I halted, wheeled, looking for Dagan Moody, worried I'd have to drop my burden to clear my gun. No enemies in sight. The prints were mine, I realized. I followed my own path out.

The mud and clay of the yard proved the most difficult obstacle. I ran it like a grunt on a tire course, high-stepping, making it to the fence. Jeff had the chain off and the door of his Prelude open and ready. He accepted Edward's shoulders. Together we placed him in the reclined passenger seat.

"I'll be back quick," Jeff said. "Should I call Gill?"

"Let him know there's a bomb," I said. "I'll get Mona and meet you back at the van."

"Right now she's in there alone," Jeff said. He meant Susan Colville. No doubt with time and whatever sharp edges were in the van,

Susan could worm her way free. But I couldn't leave Mona Tsai alone with gallons of explosive material any longer than necessary.

Slamming the passenger door, I told Jeff I'd deal with it, and for him to rush. I did the same, dashing back across the yard, over the concrete and patches of linoleum, up the stairs, only processing near the top that I was walking over two sets of prints.

Something was on fire on the upper floors.

SEVENTY-FOUR

BLACK TAILS

"Hello, Dave," Dagan Moody called down from above.

The words threw me. I halted and stumbled on the stairs, my elbow clipping wood. Easier to scramble up and keep going, dashing up the last steps and into the unfinished supply room.

Moody knew where I'd head. I headed there anyway. Gun extended in the dark. Smoke seeping down through the ceiling. I heard the groan of a board above me. Moody was on the third floor, setting fire to the mansion.

Planning and replanning on the fly, trying to anticipate what a fanatic would do next. There was a staircase leading up somewhere. Probably two of them. I could wait at the bottom of one and try to snipe Moody as he came down. Or rush for Mona Tsai and flee. Or flee now.

"With you in a moment, mate," Moody called.

Mona was beating on the plastic with both fists. I sprinted to her, thinking I could use the john as cover in a firefight. No good, I decided. Undignified, for one thing, not bulletproof for another. And its occupant was likely to be hurt.

I didn't want to holster the gun so I transferred it to my left and took up the light from where I'd propped it, turned it off, used it to strike the handle of the john in the same place as the other, only without the benefit of the steadying second hand. Mona screaming from inside for me to hurry the fuck up.

What was burning upstairs smelled of wet plastic and insulation and treated wood. It filled the room with a chemical muzz. I worked faster, no result, then slower and more deliberately with still nothing to show. If I could have shot the lock open, if there was a clear angle to hit—but no. I had to smash right through the plastic again.

Upstairs, Moody was singing. I couldn't make out the tune.

Desperate, I slid the gun away and struck the john two-handed with the butt of the flashlight, denting it, crumpling it, but the blue plastic chipped, the latch holding, bending and with a snap breaking open, and Mona all but spilling out.

The two of us recovered, breathing the worsening air, listening as Moody's song grew louder. I caught the melody and something about crossing over Jordan. "Wayfaring Stranger."

"He's up there," I whispered to Mona. "His staircase is somewhere between us and our way out. Can you move?"

Mona nodded. She was in socks and grimy sweats, her hands bloodied, but she seemed fit to travel. Travel was what Moody wanted, what he was waiting for. I looked at the hall, tracing pipes along a ceiling that was only complete in stages. Joists visible in places, sections missing. Moody could track us as soon as we fled the office.

Coughing, I ripped out one of the windows and glanced down. A two-storey drop onto the new concrete. Not ideal. Better than a bullet, if it came to that.

"Going over Jordan," Moody sang. "Going home."

Harder to breathe now, though the open window helped. If we stayed—if he reached those drums—

"No way out for the likes of us sinners, mate. I am a pilgrim, yeah, a poor lonesome stranger."

Something loud. Light. A hiding spot. Slowly a plan coalesced. The torn plastic let in a large square of grey sunlight that fell directly in line with the doorway. Noise and light. A plan.

"You're going to have to hide in here," I told Mona, pushing her toward the pink john where her father had been held. "He's already looked inside."

"I can't go back in there," Mona whispered.

"Only for a minute. Quiet as you can."

I helped her inside, replacing the door at the diagonal it had hung from. Tucked her feet out of sight.

Now for something loud. Taking up the table and flipping it sideways, I collapsed the legs and swung the thing above my head, ran it at the window and threw. As it fell, I rocked the blue Port-A-John onto its side. The falling, crashing table and the thud of the plastic made a decent enough clatter. I moved to the darker side of the doorway, flush with the wall, and held my breath.

Moody stopped singing. He called my name and paused. I slid out the gun, over the vest, raised my left arm with the bulb pointing in the same direction as the gun barrel.

Hit him over the head, Jeff had suggested. One good crack and he'd be out. A nice plan.

Thinking we'd gone out the window, Dagan Moody ran down the stairs and, expecting a trap, entered the room with his pistol drawn. The large figure squinted coming through the dark hall to the bright open window. Approached cautiously, noting the tipped-over john where his remaining captive had been.

Once, on a camping trip in Pemberton, I'd seen my father nearly start a fistfight with a pair of young hunters in a Jeep. They'd almost driven over our tent, stopping close by on a gravel trail. Pacific Coast deer aren't like white tails, skittish and leery of humans. Black tails come right up to your campsite here, and in the morning, you'll see their track, wet black pebbles in the grass. The hunters had a pair of high-powered fog lights mounted on the roof of their Jeep. They were lamping, a term for sitting in the dark, waiting for game to come near and then throwing the lights on, stunning an animal in its tracks so it could be shot unaware, helpless in its confusion. *Could walk right up and plug them,* my father said. That's what angered him, more than the men disrupting our site. The cowardice of lamping, the tilting of odds so far in your favour you lost even the pretense of fairness. Their tactics disgusted him.

Moody squinted coming through the door, and as he looked around, I clicked on the Maglite, aiming at his face, and shot him.

SEVENTY-FIVE
THE NOTHING PLACE

I'd pulled the trigger three times and knew I'd hit Moody at least once, knew from the way he fell and the smoking rent in his leather jacket. He'd dropped his gun, so I crouched and took it, then helped Mona out of the pink Port-A-John.

"Is he dead?" she asked, with no timidity, only a tired hope.

If he wasn't, he was dying. It was better not to waste time. What I'd done made me feel nothing. Not even relief. Certainly not remorse. Dagan Moody was dead and outside, the rain was letting up a little. Maybe it would be nice in the late afternoon. Patio weather. Find a bar with a view that made a good pisco sour and round up a few friends I hadn't seen in a while. Why not.

As we left the office, Mona spat on Moody and cursed him to rot in hell.

I paused at the drums of explosive material only to make sure they hadn't been rigged or wired with anything. They were as I'd left them, no primer or ignition attached. The fire above seemed to be burning itself out.

"This was going to be our forever home," Mona said.

"Yeah? Where was the rock-climbing wall going to go?"

Her mouth formed a smile and she made a slow turn with her index finger out, pinpointing it on the east side. I wanted to keep moving but she was momentarily lost in what the structure could have been, the life, literal and figurative, that had been taken from her.

Mona would never come back here, I was almost certain of it. Assuming she inherited the monstrosity, she'd either sell it or make it into something else. A place with no memory. There were points in favour of forgetting.

People had been coming west for centuries looking for that. For places with no memory. Fresh starts. I imagined Naima Halliday before she'd met Kyle, coming out of the airport knowing nothing of the city and how it could twist people. Of course it was a lie, there were no fresh starts, no blank spaces on the map. But people kept coming here, still looking. Maybe it was time someone left for the same reason.

We were at the staircase when I heard gunshots from outside, two distinct shots, echoing out of the alley. I thought of the van. Had Susan escaped and somehow gotten hold of a gun? Had Jeff driven back already, finding himself in a trap? And where were Gill and the police?

We could be walking out into a barrage, Susan lying in wait. I stopped Mona from taking the stairs and moved to the nearest window, ripping staples and teasing up the plastic. I could see the end of the alley, the back tire of the van. No movement, only the waves beyond the empty beach.

Behind me Mona made an utterance that wasn't a word but an exclamation of danger. I turned from the window in time to face Dagan Moody's charge. A tackle that compressed my body between his and the frame. I felt myself tip over into space, grabbed the outside of the window to keep us from spilling.

We swayed and the ground elevated up to greet us, mud below us here at the building's edge. The frame cut into my hip. My hands were pinned to my sides. Suddenly the vest was a hindrance to drawing breath. Moody was using his size to cut off my air, his wound bleeding onto me, warm. Willing to throw away the last of his life to bring an end to mine.

"*Kill you,*" he was screaming.

I heard a snap in the wood and the frame gave, the entire wall shifting to accommodate our bulk on this one particular point.

Stripped of poise and pretense, in his injured state Moody was rage. As thoughtless and oncoming as the tide. The force hit and the window frame moved farther out, Moody relenting only to gather himself and charge again. All I could do was brace myself and, as the charge came, pivot and turn with it to diminish its brunt and prevent being carried away with it. Almost, but not quite.

Momentum carried him into the frame and through it. He took me with him. We were falling through the bright eye of the house.

Mid-air.

Cold air.

Sunshine.

And then impact.

Slapping the earth, displacing mud, I landed on my left side, hard enough my body went numb. The rain had formed a natural sluice and my arm had landed in it. Stunned, I looked up and saw diamonds of blue between the clouds. I could taste one of my teeth.

I wasn't out. I was cognizant that there were factors I should be cognizant of. Fire. Something about a gunshot. A person named Mona who was in a house nearby. What looked like a bison in the mud next to me, heaving up and gasping into life.

A muddy gauntlet reached out, swiping my shoulder. I wanted to swat it away. *Quit that, you.* I couldn't. The hand thumped on my stomach and my left breast, feeling its way up to my face. Grabbing my chin, seeking my mouth.

I struggled, feebly trying to chop the hand away from my airway. I tried to steal a breath but there wasn't any. The blue diamonds gave way to Moody, a mass of earth tones and blood, compressing my face into the ground. Water filled my ears.

The pressure got worse before it let up. I heard no gunshots over my pounding blood but I felt him shudder, writhe, teeter and collapse onto me. Cosmic surprise on his face.

Moody's jaw hit my collarbone. The force ebbed to dead weight. I moved my neck away from the slack fingers, leaning into his head, like lovers, resting my cheek against the gristle that had once been his.

"Holy crap, Dave, are you okay?"

Kay stood above us, hands clasped prayer-like, a pistol in her hands.

Doing just fine, sis, I wanted to say. Give me a minute or two to collect myself, maybe change my shirt, and I'll be ready to grab that pisco sour. The night is young and everyone that matters to me is alive. Enough of us to celebrate, at least.

"Jeff texted me," Kay was saying. "He's okay. The police...the others are...I should've been here sooner, Dave, I'm so, so sorry."

I wanted to say, Don't worry about it, you got here in plenty of time. I wanted to say all sorts of witty things. Thank you, and do you know how to mix a pisco sour? But I wasn't up to saying much of anything. Vocalizing took effort I didn't have. I barely had enough to raise my head.

Kay was kneeling in the mud, telling me something about the others. The hood of her slicker was up, standard issue Wakeland & Chen sentry wear. The pistol large in her hands, the barrel actually smoking. Behind her slices of blue sky beamed down like an uncorrupted, uncomplicated future.

I was glad to see my sister. More glad than I'd ever been to see anyone. I was glad to see the pistol, too. I'd been looking for it for a while.

SEVENTY-SIX
A WORD BEFORE YOU GO

"A truly miraculous fall," Dr. Ahluwalia said. "You couldn't have planned one better."

"I didn't."

"Aside from your tooth, and a rather disgusting series of bruises, you're free of serious injury. How do you feel?"

"Good question."

Two days after the fall, after Kay had shot and killed an escaping Susan Colville, then rescued me from Dagan Moody. After news stories, civic commendations, stitches and dental surgery. I felt purged of guilt and anger, and pretty much everything else. I felt tired.

The doctor made a note on her tablet. "You should consider yourself incredibly fortunate, David. If I hadn't seen the X-rays of your lower intestine, I would swear you had a horseshoe lodged up there."

I could tell it was a line she'd used before. Professional humour. One of the joys of being a professional.

"So I'm fit to travel?" I asked as I buttoned my shirt.

"You'll survive the ride home, I imagine. Why? Are you planning a vacation?"

"Keeping my options open."

The doctor smiled. "As long as those options preclude brawling and diving out windows."

"I was pushed."

Dr. Ahluwalia nodded in mock understanding. "A hazard of the job, of course. Have you given any thought to choosing a different one?"

In answer I passed her the present I'd brought her, wrapped in a square of butcher's paper. Dr. Ahluwalia tore a corner, teased out the record and chuckled. George Jones, *I Am What I Am.*

"I don't have a turntable," she said.

"Worth finding one for."

"Doubtful, David, but I appreciate the gift."

We shook hands. On my way out of the hospital I thought of looking for Naima Halliday, but decided we'd both had all the goodbyes we could endure. Maybe in a way we'd been good for each other. She deserved to move on to better.

In the hospital parking lot, I found Ray Dudgeon smoking a cigarette, resting against the side of my Cadillac.

"Clean bill of health?" Dudgeon asked.

"A bill, anyway."

"What a hell of a year." The sergeant tossed his cigarette. Ash stained his dark overcoat. He crushed the filter with the heel of his brogan.

"Everyone on the task force got a nice commendation. Letter from our grateful mayor as well. Meantime I can't think of another three-month stretch where I screwed up so goddamn consistently."

"I know that feeling," I said.

"In the end we got 'em all, or enough of 'em that everyone's happy. Deputy Chief calls this a 'new era of cooperation 'tween the department and City Hall.' Cooperation or coordination, I forget which. A new era, anyway."

I unlocked the car. Dudgeon climbed in the passenger seat. He noticed the boxes in the back. "Going some place?"

"Haven't decided," I said.

"But you packed."

"Part of the decision-making."

He nodded. "Montreal?"

"My office, for the time being. I have a present for you there."

"Guess it's still the Season of Giving," Dudgeon said.

It was a short jaunt down Burrard to Hastings. Quicker to walk if the traffic was bad. This morning it was thicker than usual. Dudgeon used the time to smoke another cigarette.

"That student you asked about?" Dudgeon said. "Kevin Novak. Lab pulled prints from the window in his place. Dagan Moody's. Angle of the hammer blows to his skull indicate a taller than average perp. Similar marks to the one on Jeremy Fell's head. So that one's down, too."

"Congratulations."

"Honest to goodness forensic evidence came through. First time for everything, I guess. Like a *Law and Order* or something. But the funny thing, Dave?"

"Yeah?"

I opened the parking garage, slid down the ramp for what might be the final time. A blotch of Peng Liu's blood still visible on one wall.

"We got a close on the artist killing, too. Alex Knowlson. A confession."

I tapped the brakes a few feet from my spot. "You're saying it wasn't the Death of Kings?"

"Exactly what I'm saying." Dudgeon shook a few cigarettes out, leaving them in the ashtray. "For the trip. One present deserves another, yeah?"

"So who killed the artist?" I asked in the elevator.

"Former tenant in the building, evicted a few months before Knowlson's mural went up. Get this: Me and Gill spend half the night with the guy, let him know we got all this evidence, it's over for him, all we don't got is the why. Was this the work of an evil man, that what you want your family to think? Laying it on with a brush. You know the routine."

"I do."

"So he tells us, this fifty-something-year-old man, he got the idea to strike back at the rich oppressors from what happened to Jeremy Fell. You believe it? He's inspired by the Death of Kings."

"I don't believe it," I said.

Down the hallway. I held the door for the sergeant, who paused to finish the story.

"We let this guy run on, putting himself in the frame, explaining how he got up there alone with Knowlson. Then Gill finds out this morning as he's debriefing the wife, your husband has admitted to *blah blah blah*. And the wife, she says, 'You mean he *knew* Alex and I were seeing each other?'"

Dudgeon laughed.

"Turns out Knowlson's been deep-dicking her on the side for years. The art was just the final straw. Imagine driving to the gas station where you work every morning, seeing this ugly mural painted by the guy fucking your significant other. Guy's ego couldn't take it."

"That I do believe," I said.

The office party was in full swing, celebrating Tim Blatchford's first day back. Ryan Martz and Kay had festooned the reception area with Easter decorations, purple and gold balloons. Wine and beer and cookies and punch, some chocolate for the kids.

"Where's my present?" Dudgeon asked.

"Give me a few minutes. I have a couple last errands first."

Dudgeon helped himself to a bottle of Molson.

The office was packed. Ryan and Nikki Fraser, Jeff and Marie and their children, Tim and Paul Royce, Kay, and as many of the part-time staff as could be spared from the various security jobs around the city. Tim had lost muscle and looked ten years older, skin and hair both greyer, but he was grinning. With a wrestler's flair for the grotesque, he showed the children the plate in his skull, the pins inserted into his legs. The kids treated him like a loveable Frankenstein's monster, and he seemed in the highest of spirits.

His thunder was stolen minutes later when Valerie Fell appeared. The mayor and her entourage shook hands with everyone, stood for photos with Jeff and the rest of the team. A hug and handshake for Kay.

When the moment presented itself, the mayor motioned me aside. We went into my office. Ryan Martz had moved a few of his things in. A picture of him and Nikki stood on the desk.

"Evelyn sends her best," Valerie Fell said.

"Mine to her."

"She's recuperating at our house in Maui, about as good a place to get healthy as you could find. Sonny's with her. If you ever want the use of the place and we're not there."

"Thanks," I said.

"How's everything with you?"

A question too large to waste a civil servant's time on the answer. I looked at the pinholes on the wall, left from my commendations and the photo of my father. Packed in the Cadillac's trunk, next to my Rega and the albums I couldn't part with.

The mayor touched my shoulder and held my gaze.

"Obviously there's only so much I can say publicly, given the times we live in. But thank you, Dave. Thank you for finding Jeremy's killers, and thank you for putting them down."

"I didn't," I said.

"Right, of course." The mayor didn't wink or tap the side of her nose, but her mouth curled in a just-between-us smile.

We rejoined the party and she made her exit soon after.

When she'd gone and some of the excitement had been dispelled, I told Jeff it was time. He nodded and pointed to his office. As I followed I passed Kay, chasing one of Jeff's kids, who ducked behind Ryan, then clambered over his lap when my sister spied him.

Ryan smiled at me as I passed him. At home.

In his private office, Jeff had the documents prepared. "You're not totally sure about this, are you?" he said.

"Not a hundred percent. Say ninety-eight."

"How about we just call it an indefinite leave of absence."

"Call it whatever you think best."

"My bet," Jeff said, easing back in his chair, "knowing you like I do? You won't get past the Rockies."

"Always possible," I said.

Years before, when a mistake of mine had caused the company some negative publicity, we'd drawn up papers to give Jeff sole control of Wakeland & Chen. Things had righted themselves, so we'd never filed them. Now we amended the date to today's, and both wrote our signatures.

"I'll get Ryan to witness this," Jeff said. "Good call on him, I have to admit. You gonna stay around for the party?"

"I don't have a schedule, but I want to get started before rush hour."

"Five hundred," Jeff said. "Shit, let's go a thousand. Not one klick past Revelstoke."

I smiled. One last moment together, before everything sundered. If I wasn't driving I would have celebrated with a toast.

There was a knock on the glass. Kay opened the door and said, "We're going to cut the cake. Everyone's wondering where you guys went." Noticing the papers, she asked, "Am I disturbing you?"

"No," I said, "we need to talk anyway. I've only told Jeff so far. I'm quitting."

"Leave of absence," Jeff corrected.

"No way," Kay said. The look on her face made me regret how I'd chosen to leave.

"I already gave up my apartment," I said.

"You're leaving," she said, processing things. "You can't."

"I can't stay."

"Can we talk about this?"

"We are talking about it," I said. "If you need to borrow money, I'll cosign for you, up to a hundred grand. That should cover a proper defence."

"You're actually fucking serious," my sister said. "When did you decide?"

I put the Polaroid from Susan Colville's apartment on the desk.

"When I worked out that you killed Kyle Halliday," I said.

SEVENTY-SEVEN

TRIUMPH AND DEFEAT

"That's total craziness," Kay said.

Without realizing, I'd slipped down into the client's chair across from Jeff. Looking across at my sister, hoping she could convince me of anything other than the truth.

"Jeff told you what was happening at Colville's house. You brought the gun with you. Shot Susan in the van, untied her so it would look like she escaped. Then shot Dagan Moody."

"I was saving you," my sister said.

"When I asked you to look into Kyle Halliday's school, *your* school, you told me you found nothing. At the time I figured it was just because you were sick. School is where you met Moody and the others, wasn't it? Where Boss and Sky recruited Rio."

"Dave, this isn't funny."

"The warning message written on my office window. You knew enough to take out the camera in the electrical room. Then the night the others attacked Tim and I, you let them inside."

"No."

"Was Tim part of it? I know he covered for you on the security job. Filled in your timesheets for you."

"I covered for him," Kay insisted.

"Jeff showed me the sheets. Most nights both of your forms were filled out in the same writing."

"It's just paperwork," she said. "You don't take paperwork seriously."

"How about this," Jeff said.

He turned the screen of his computer around so she could see the footage from the office camera. Kay in the early hours, standing over the reception desk. Arguing with someone on the phone. Hanging up, casting her eyes around the desk. Seeming to debate with herself.

The three of us watched as Kay sat down and typed something into the computer.

"My guess, that was Moody on the phone," Jeff said. "You used your brother's email account to write to the guards I posted at Mona's home, sending them away before Moody got there. Did he threaten you if you didn't help him?"

My sister had backed up to the wall, arms crossed, leaning into the wood panel. Hugging herself. She nodded.

"None of this was supposed to happen," she said.

"Let's go back to the start of it. You went to the meetings at Kyle's place? Hung out with the others? Did you talk about the kidnapping before it happened?"

"Only later, after Jazz left, and there were just the five of us. And then just as an, I dunno, a thing. An idea. Like what if this happened, but instead of taking the money for ourselves we used it to fund all the stuff that should be funded already. Sky said we'd need a gun to pull it off. Then Boss said she had a plan to get one."

"You didn't stop them."

"I couldn't," my sister said. "We never used our real names, but Sky knew. He recruited me. We talked about you, and if I didn't help them, I swear, he'd have killed both of us."

"What happened that night with Kyle?"

Kay was on the verge of tears. A small, frightened young woman. And then some inner force reeled her back, and she looked up, aimed her words toward Jeff. As if I wasn't there.

"Kyle talked about the kidnapping the most, how necessary it was to shake up the city. This great thing we'd be doing. He pointed out examples from history where ordinary people brought about real change. He made it seem necessary. Even cool."

"And then what changed?"

"*He* changed. Soon as Boss started planning to get that gun, Kyle got nervous. He said maybe he could get hold of one a lot easier. And Boss said okay, but it had to be the exact same one. A cop's gun. Like challenging him. And every step he kept dragging his feet, putting it off."

"When did you decide to kill him?"

"I didn't," Kay said. "That was Boss. She and Driver had done the SkyTrain cop. When they couldn't get money from the mayor, Sky said he was gonna do Jeremy. I was the only one left, so I had to, as a test."

"What happened that night?" Jeff asked.

"Driver and I met Kyle in the park. He thought we were gonna go with him to the cops. Tell about what Sky and Boss were planning. I didn't want to be the one, but I had no choice. Driver pointed at something in the water, said something about maybe spotting a killer whale, and when Kyle turned to look, I, you know."

"You shot him," I said.

"Yeah," she answered, in a small, cold voice I'd never heard before.

"It never occurred to you to talk with me, get my help?"

"You were the problem," the voice said. "When you started looking into Kyle and the gun, Boss got real suspicious of me. I said not to hurt you, that you weren't a threat and would maybe even understand."

"So instead you warned me off. Watched them beat me and Tim within an inch of our lives."

"You'd rather I let them kill you?" the voice asked. "If I didn't help with Kyle, they'd've killed both of us. I just wanted it all to stop. But then Boss kept talking about her uncle, this ginormous house he has, all this money and how we could use him to get funding instead. Hold him just until his wife paid. But I knew she wasn't serious about letting him go."

"Between pretending to be sick and no-showing a security job, you had a solid alibi," I said. "Very cleverly done."

I stood up and moved past her to the door. Called for Ray Dudgeon to join us.

"You don't have to talk to the police," I told my sister. "Jeff and I have to give them the evidence, though. For business reasons. This is the new era of cooperation."

"You don't," Kay said. "I didn't have a choice, I told you."

"I don't think you meant it to happen," I said. "It was probably a fun group to be part of at first. Give each other little nicknames. Rio should have tipped me. River, Rio. That's cute."

"You want to know why?" she said.

"Not particularly. One alias is as good as—"

"Why I joined them," my sister said.

Any feeling of hurt or betrayal was radiated back at me a hundred-fold. Kay was struggling to keep her eyes clear, her voice steady. Meeting my gaze was easier for her than me. She knew I owed it to her to listen.

"I think I know why," I said. "But say it for Jeff's sake."

"Because of you. Because remember that time we were driving and you kept pointing out new developments, all the old places you grew up with that were being torn down? And you said to me you wished sometimes you could take a match to them, burn them all right to the fucking ground. Remember?"

I nodded, I did.

"People here say that all the time. They're so hurt by what's happening to this city and they do nothing. They just take it. *You* just take it. Watch your friends leave, people die outside your door. Your own mom can't even keep her house. And rich shits like Colville and Fell, all we wanted to do was make them *feel* that, you know? Feel what the rest of us feel. It was the only way to hold them accountable for what they've done to us. To you."

Do you think, in the end, they understood that? I wanted to ask. But Dudgeon entered. Jeff handed him the Polaroid and a memory stick with the footage. My partner told the cop they had something to discuss.

I carried Kay's words with me out of the office. *Because of you.* I carried them with me through the party, past Ryan, Nikki and Marie in rapt conversation about cunnilingus, past Jeff's kids squaring off in a game of soldiers. Past Tim and Paul kissing over the cake.

I didn't look back to see if my sister had stayed with Dudgeon and Jeff. I wanted to tell her I was sorry. For failing her, for letting this place defeat me, and now for running. But instead, I carried my burden to the elevator. One last downward ride.

SEVENTY-EIGHT
A GOOD RUN

The conditions of our bet didn't cover acts of God. At a garage in New West that shared an office with a hair salon, I had the Cadillac's oil changed and the tires rotated. The mechanic said he found a slow leak in the front left. He could patch it good as new in an hour if I could wait.

In the meantime, I called Sonia.

"Are you having second thoughts about maybe coming out here?" she said.

Second and third, and a hesitation that went beyond thought. Call it a psychic tug of conscience. It anchored me to this place. It told me I was here forever, and Jeff's thousand dollars was smart money.

"Last time we talked, you were cut off," I said.

"That's right, I was."

"You were saying if I came out, you didn't have a couch for me, but you might have something else. What was the something?"

"What would you like it to be?" Sonia asked.

"A bed. I'd like that very much."

"Interesting."

"You won't tell me?"

"No promises, Wakeland. You want an answer badly enough, you'll have to ask in person."

"That's a long way to travel on faith," I said.

"Is it?"

Forty-nine hours of driving. Forty-four if I swung through Washington State. Or I could be home in forty minutes. Unpacked by tonight. Write Jeff a cheque and explain it was a momentary fancy. Nothing serious. Let him laugh and say he knew I couldn't leave.

From here to the highway, east or west. Vancouver to Hope, to Merritt, to Revelstoke, in six hours if I punched it. The Rocky Mountains after that.

Think I can't leave?

Just fucking watch me.

ACKNOWLEDGEMENTS

The impetus for this book started years ago when a development company in Vancouver started using "You don't need a million!" as its slogan. As in, you too can own a home if you have a meagre eight or nine hundred grand kicking around. A number of great Vancouver journalists have done important work on the housing crisis and its fallout, adding nuance and fervor to the discussion of who gets to live here, and who has to leave.

To the readers who've supported Dave over the years, many thanks.

To agent extraordinaire Chris Casuccio, and to the folks at Harbour and Blackstone, especially but not limited to Anna Comfort O'Keefe, Annie Boyar, Berglind Kristinsdottir, and Lynne Melcombe, and to editor Derek Fairbridge for catching a ton of Vancouver details, much thanks for your hard work. To the Cineflix team, Lisa Baylin and Jeff Vanderwal, thanks for believing in the series.

Thanks to Derrick Harder, who answered questions about the inner workings of City Hall.

Thanks to Carleigh Baker, Kris Bertin, E.R. Brown, Chris Brayshaw and the staff at Pulp Fiction, Clint Burnham, Paul Budra, Janie Chang, Sean Cranbury and Real Vancouver Writers Series, Eric D'Souza, Charles Demers, AJ Devlin, Dennis Heaton, Andrew Hood, Dietrich Kalteis, Gorrman Lee, Tara Moss, Nathan R. and Criss at the Bustard Island Writers Compound, Naben Ruthnum, Kelly Senecal,

Brian Thornton, Iona Whishaw, Mel Yap, Mary-Ann Yazedjian and the staff at Book Warehouse, and the owners and staff at all the great independent bookstores in Vancouver and beyond. Your support means a great deal to me.

To my mother, Linda, brothers Dan and Josh, and in-laws Kim, Mark, and John. And Ennio.

Above all I need to thank Carly, my love, for supporting me, enduring a few visits from "Pekoe Sam" while I worked on this. I couldn't ask for a better person to share my life with.

And to those who left the city and those who hold out, this book is dedicated to you.

—S.W.

ABOUT THE AUTHOR

Sam Wiebe is the award-winning author of the Wakeland novels, one of the most authentic and acclaimed detective series in Canada, including *Invisible Dead* ("the definitive Vancouver crime novel"), *Cut You Down* ("successfully brings Raymond Chandler into the 21st century") and *Hell and Gone* ("the best crime writer in Canada"). Wiebe's other books include *Never Going Back*, *Last of the Independents* and the *Vancouver Noir* anthology, which he edited. His work has won a Crime Writers of Canada award and a Kobo Emerging Writer Prize and has been shortlisted for the Edgar, Hammett, Shamus and City of Vancouver awards. He is a former Vancouver Public Library Writer in Residence.

samwiebe.com